BLOOD
AND
BONE

BLOOD
AND
BONE

DON HOESEL

BETHANYHOUSE

a division of Baker Publishing Group
Minneapolis, Minnesota

© 2013 by Don Hoesel

Published by Bethany House Publishers
11400 Hampshire Avenue South
Bloomington, Minnesota 55438
www.bethanyhouse.com

Bethany House Publishers is a division of
Baker Publishing Group, Grand Rapids, Michigan

Printed in the United States of America

Library of Congress Cataloging-in-Publication Data
Hoesel, Don.
    Blood and bone / Don Hoesel.
        pages cm
    Summary: "When Elisha's bones resurface, archaeologist Jack Hawthorne knows what has to be done. But can he destroy the only thing that could heal his son?"—Provided by publisher.
    ISBN 978-0-7642-0926-0 (pbk.)
    1. Archaeology teachers—Fiction. 2. Elisha (Biblical prophet)—Relics—Fiction. 3. Christian antiquities—Fiction. I. Title.
PS3608.O4765B56 2013
813'.6—dc23   2013007738

Cover design by Lookout Design, Inc.

Author is represented by Leslie H. Stobbe

13 14 15 16 17 18 19   7 6 5 4 3 2 1

For Dawn

1

JACK HESITATED FOR A MOMENT, calculating the risk of distracting Romero before reaching over and swatting the tarantula from his friend's shoulder. The huge spider tumbled out of the jeep. To Jack's relief, Romero kept his eyes aimed ahead for as long as it took to make sure the jeep avoided the cecropia that appeared in their path, only turning to raise an eyebrow in Jack's direction once the tree was behind them.

"Believe me, you don't want to know," Jack said.

Romero held the look for a while longer, then turned his attention back to the road ahead.

That road was the 156, the only even marginally serviceable route for those traversing the northernmost three hundred kilometers of Amapá. Most of the 156 had disappeared behind them as they neared Oiapoque, the jeep churning up red clay, bouncing over terrain that, back home, Jack would have described as prime off-roading territory. As if to punctuate that thought, the jeep's right front tire dropped down into a hole, sending a shower of moist red clay into the air. He barely grimaced as some of that shower landed on him; after almost five hundred kilometers he'd given up trying to preserve the integrity of his clothes.

As the jeep navigated a sharp curve, the first sign he had seen in more than a hundred kilometers came into view, the faded wood placing Oiapoque less than twenty kilometers ahead. Then the sign was gone, leaving nothing to prove that anything existed beyond the rain forest, save the road the jungle was ever working to reclaim.

The branches of mammoth kapoks hung over the road, their pods dangling in patches like ripe fruit amid the leaves. Intertwined with the kapoks were other lesser trees, many so snuggly placed against their larger cousins as to provide as solid a wall as any a man could make with brick and mortar. And among this tangle of limbs and leaves that wove a cover over the rain forest, insects and animals in types and numbers Jack could hardly fathom made their homes.

The tenuousness of humankind's foothold in this formidable place was enough to humble even a seasoned traveler, but rather than continue to ponder the question, Jack reached for the travel bag between his feet, fishing around until he found a cigar, a Dona Flor he'd picked up in Macapá.

Romero watched as Jack cut and lit the cigar, not saying anything until he'd released the first puff of smoke to the jungle. "Since when do you smoke cigars?"

"Since the day Jim and I pulled that fifteen-hundred-year-old Mochica headdress out of that royal tomb in Peru," Jack said.

At the time, it was the most valuable artifact ever discovered in the country, and Dr. James Winfield, who was lead archaeologist for the dig, had pulled two cigars from his breast pocket the moment the headdress was packed safely for travel. Considering the magnitude of the find, Jack couldn't refuse the celebratory token.

"As I recall, that artifact was worth 1.5 million," Romero said.

"Closer to two," Jack said.

Romero grunted.

"An occasion worthy of a fine cigar, indeed."

Jack took another puff as the jungle passed by on either side. He glanced over at the Venezuelan.

"How does Espy feel about men who smoke cigars?" he asked, trying to keep a smile from touching his lips.

Romero didn't say anything right away. In fact, the only evidence that he'd heard the question manifested itself in a reddening of his ears. It was a reaction that reminded Jack that while Romero was a friend, his temper was often unpredictable. And he was very protective of his younger sister.

"I think the more accurate question is how she feels about men who are forced to eat their cigars for even entertaining ideas about another man's sister," Romero said.

Jack chuckled, yet he knew enough to let the matter drop, a decision that coincided with the jeep rounding one last corner to reveal their destination—opening up before them, the whole of it, in a single instant.

———

They drove in above Oiapoque, a border town where the streets and buildings lay clustered closely together along the river that shared its name. At first glance, the place looked as if it had been ravaged by a natural disaster, a flood pushing through long ago and leaving behind red silt to mark its passing, filling the streets, staining everything the water touched. Just when Jack figured the town to be dead or abandoned, he saw movement. As Romero gave the gas pedal a nudge to send the jeep in the direction of the river, Jack could see the people who gave the place life.

As the 156 widened, the results of the wet season became visible. Deep ruts had been cut into the slope, sending the jeep bouncing and dipping until finally they reached a spot where the road leveled out. Heading deeper into town, Jack took a long draw from the cigar and watched as people stopped to view the jeep and to size up the visitors. Oiapoque was remote enough to make every visitor an opportunity, and the locals seemed to be experts at assessing the nature of one's need. Because outsiders wouldn't go through the hassle of traveling all the way here if they didn't need something.

Before long, most observers dismissed Jack and Romero, and of those whose gazes lingered, all were men who looked like the kind it would be wise to avoid. It gave Jack a moment's pause to consider that these were just the sort of men he and Romero had come to see.

When they reached Oiapoque's version of Main Street, it seemed to him that everything worth doing in the place had been crammed into a few square blocks. Shops of various sorts sat almost atop each other, a curious mix of modern-looking establishments with a European flair, along with other store-fronts and vendor stalls that had a more local flavor. But the shops were secondary to the people who began swarming the jeep, a great many of them calling out to Romero and Jack, offering a variety of services, their French and Portuguese forming a carnival-like cacophony.

Romero maneuvered the jeep to the side of the road, spurring a more intense movement of entrepreneurs toward the vehicle, but the Venezuelan's glower quickly dispersed them. Thus freed, Jack and Romero stood on the road for a few moments, taking the place in, Jack's eyes seeking out someone who might convey them to Saint George, which was located across the expanse of water separating two nations.

There was something of the Wild West to Oiapoque. Its people, left to their own devices, had created something wholly unique—and maybe even a little dangerous. Jack decided he liked it. Save for the ubiquitous red clay his boots kicked up, which coated everything and everyone.

He took Romero's grunt as agreement.

"I'd say we have as good a chance of finding a ferryman there as any," Romero said, nodding toward a tavern that also had caught Jack's eye, mainly for the group of men gathered beneath its overhang.

As Jack and Romero drew nearer, the odors of fried food, stale beer, and cigarettes wafted through the tavern's open door, along with the hum of conversation and the occasional clink of glass. He saw the look on Romero's face, understanding that Taberna da Esquina was the kind of place to which he could lose his friend if they lingered. So he quickly made use of his rusty French to see if he could find someone willing to take them across the river.

Less than a minute later, he had secured the services of one of the locals, who immediately started off in the direction of the jeep. But when Jack moved to follow, he noticed that his friend seemed rooted to the spot.

Romero's eyes were fixed on the tavern entrance.

"Our meeting is more than an hour off," Romero said. "A

ten-minute river transit should allow time to enjoy some of the fruits of this lovely town."

Jack didn't answer right away because, in principle, he couldn't fault the argument, but pragmatism eventually reared its head. "We can either stay here for a drink and let Paulo get there first, allow him to set things up how he wants them, or we can delay gratification, beat him there, and maybe have time for a nice Malte Barrilete."

Romero turned that around for a time, wearing a frown that told Jack he was without a rebuttal. He grunted again, then turned away from the door. "Fine. Even if I think you're being overly optimistic if you expect to find bourbon of that quality this far from Macapá."

With Romero in tow, Jack started after their Brazilian Charon, who had stopped to wait for them. Soon they reached the marina, where they navigated a cursory customs checkpoint.

It was his first good look at the Oiapoque River, a waterway that wound like a ghost through trees that stood like sentinels along its banks—except where towns like Oiapoque had staked claims along its length, the trees pulling away before converging again downstream. They boarded a small boat and pushed away from the dock. And it wasn't long before Jack could make out their destination on the far bank, watercraft landing and departing at a series of piers that seemed much more orderly than the ones they'd left behind.

When they reached the other side, the ferryman tied off and then led the way up the pier. He stopped before reaching the border checkpoint, where Jack parted with some of the meager funds he had left before heading with Romero into French Guiana.

According to Paulo, the name of the place was Chez Modestine, though the sign hanging above the door was weathered enough that Jack had to identify it by a scant few discernible letters. Like the rest of Saint George, Chez Modestine had a lethargic look to it, with no sounds coming through the tall, narrow open doorway, and a handful of locals lounging on the wooden deck that wrapped around the two-story building.

Inside, it was a different story. The place was packed with nearly every seat occupied, both at the bar and around the scattered tables. About half of the patrons wore the uniform of the largest employer in town, the French Foreign Legion, and hardly any of them so much as glanced at the newcomers.

Jack and Romero shared a look and then started toward one of the back corners of the large room, toward an empty table. They hadn't quite reached it when Jack saw that their attempt to arrive early hadn't worked out.

Paulo Azevedo was a small, slight man whose body seemed like some taut wire. Jack had only met him once before, yet Romero's successful business dealings with the man had convinced Jack to come along, to engage in one of the less seemly sides of archaeological fieldwork. Outside the classroom, the line between legitimate archaeology and treasure hunting could get blurry. Most archaeologists, however, were able to intuit the position of that line and keep themselves on the proper side of it. It wasn't until Jack met Romero—a man who made his living procuring rare items for people with the means to pay handsomely for them—that Jack ever considered engaging in a meeting of this sort.

Paulo sat at a table in the corner opposite the one Jack and Romero had been aiming for. The two men with him—both much larger than Paulo—had similar enough facial features for

Jack to deduce a familial relationship. Fraternal hired muscle. Paulo's eyes were on the foreigners. He was smiling, a cat-that-caught-the-canary smile, and Jack couldn't help feeling irritated that he'd beaten them there.

He changed direction, catching Romero off guard, and slipped into one of the two empty seats at the table, directly across from Paulo. He offered a disarming wink to one of Paulo's men, whose only response was to regard Jack as one might a bug. But when Romero slid into the other seat, Jack felt a bit better about the playing field. While both of the men the Brazilian had with him were imposing, there was something about the Venezuelan that suggested danger beneath a refined exterior. Paulo's guys seemed to sense it immediately. Both shifted in their seats, eyes moving to Romero.

No one spoke right away, and Jack found himself starting to hunt around for what Paulo was to have brought, seeking out something the right size and shape. Meanwhile, Romero flagged down a serving girl and ordered for both of them—the Malte Barrilete for which he'd held out little hope. Not seeing a conspicuous bundle, Jack returned his attention to Paulo. The Brazilian had eyes like a lizard; Jack didn't think he'd blinked since the moment he and Romero had sat down.

"I trust the trip was uneventful," Paulo said in English, with only a hint of an accent.

"We made it here in one piece," Jack answered.

"Where's the dagger?" Romero asked, getting right to the point.

Paulo smiled again, showing a prominent gap between his front teeth. Instead of answering the question, he took a drink of whatever local brew he was working on. Jack responded in kind, sampling the Malte Barrilete. Then Paulo set his drink down and reached a hand beneath his jacket. Jack tensed, but when Paulo pulled his hand out, he was holding the dagger.

Jack's eyes locked on the dagger to the exclusion of all else. It was double-edged, a bone hilt beset with emeralds and rubies. Jack found it stunning. He extended a hand, but Paulo pulled the knife back.

"If I'm going to spend the kind of money we're talking about, I need to see it," Jack said.

After a moment, Paulo extended the dagger. Jack took it from him, trying to keep his excitement in check, concentrating on giving the thing a clinical review. A line of jewels ran along the hilt, which scintillated even in the dim light of the tavern. The gems alone were worth twice Paulo's asking price. He turned the dagger, letting the light play off the stones. The bone hilt had been dulled by time. As Jack ran a thumbnail along it, he saw the markings. He brought the dagger closer. They were near the base of the weapon, a series of lines running along the bottom edge, hieroglyphic in their design. He frowned. He couldn't remember anything from his research that mentioned text on the dagger.

From across the table came the sound of a throat clearing. Jack glanced up, caught Paulo's impatient eye. He looked back at the weapon, studying the mysterious etchings on the hilt. Then, with a sigh, he looked at Romero and nodded.

The Venezuelan leaned over and retrieved the bag. He placed it on the table.

"Fifty thousand, as we agreed."

Jack felt the tension increase, even as the patrons around them remained oblivious to what was transpiring in their midst.

"Unfortunately," Paulo said, "I think we're going to have to renegotiate." He smiled that gap-toothed smile again.

A second later, Jack saw the first gun come out, then another immediately after. He glanced at Romero. This was generally the point when Romero lost his temper and tried to throw a punch or two. Invariably they would walk out without the dagger *or* the money. But what he saw on his friend's face caused him to do a double take. Instead of anger, he saw complete calm—nothing to indicate he was at all bothered by what was happening.

And then he glanced down, saw white knuckles gripping the table. "Great," he muttered, right before Romero flipped the table over.

The next few moments consisted of shouting, glass shattering, and cursing in both Spanish and Portuguese. At one point, one of Paulo's men raised his gun, aiming it at Romero's chest. Jack leaped into action and tackled the man from behind, taking him to the floor and kicking away the gun. Then he heard more glass breaking, after which he saw the first flames.

The bar went up quickly, the flames moving with incredible speed, shooting up the wall, making inroads across the ceiling.

"Romero," Jack yelled over the sounds of the fleeing crowd.

Romero turned toward Jack, who was pointing to the fire. Romero's eyes went wide—right before he took a right hook to the cheekbone. Jack winced for him, but Romero made short work of his assailant and started to follow Jack toward the door. He was halfway across the room when Jack saw him stop and look back.

"Romero," he yelled again. Even Paulo's men had given up the fight in favor of flight. Romero and Jack were the only ones left in the building, which was coming down around them. Jack called out again, but Romero either didn't hear him or he was ignoring him. Jack saw him staring at something across the room.

It was the dagger, lying on the floor, with flames dancing around it. It was beautiful. But it wasn't worth dying for.

"Romero," Jack shouted, louder this time.

Finally Romero's head turned and his eyes found Jack. Wild, feverish eyes. Then a beam crashed down between them, flames rising like a solid wall. Jack lost sight of his friend, but when he rushed forward to where he'd been, Jack found himself struggling to breathe. Still, he lingered for a little while longer, hoping to see Romero emerge from the fire and smoke. But when his lungs could no longer take it, he had no choice but to head for the exit.

As soon as he ran outside, he was grabbed by several pairs of hands and led away. Someone put a cup of water in his hand. Yet his attention remained focused on the building, completely engulfed now. It took a moment for him to realize that shock was threatening to overtake him. The cup tumbled from his hand.

Then something caught Jack's eye. At first he couldn't quite make it out, only that it was something inside the smoke, moving alongside the building. He watched, transfixed, until the figure broke away from the wall, then took on a shape of its own. It was Romero. Several people hurried toward him, giving him aid as they had Jack.

Jack rushed over to join them. He grabbed his friend by the shoulders. "What happened to you?" he shouted.

Romero coughed and said, "I went out the window."

Jack pulled him away from the crowd, made him sit. "Are you okay?"

Romero nodded and waved off Jack's concern. Then he

beckoned him to come closer. He pulled his coat open, just enough for Jack to see the dagger. Romero grinned, eyes shining.

Amazed, Jack returned the smile, but even as he did, he recalled the image of Romero inside the tavern, and the look in his eyes was an expression Jack had never seen before. For some reason, despite the heat, he shuddered.

2

AS JACK TOOK THE LAST FEW STEPS down to one of the sidewalks of Evanston University, leaving the venerable ivy-covered edifice of Whittenborough Hall behind, it occurred to him that he might be getting old. And that estimation had nothing to do with his physical state, which was better than average, despite a knee that had given him trouble for the better part of twenty years. Rather, it was the fact that the last ten minutes of the Archaeology Ethics class he'd just finished teaching were some of the most intellectually stimulating he'd spent in the classroom in a long while—and yet he could already feel the subject matter slipping away in favor of the cigar and porch that awaited him at home.

It hadn't been too long ago when a question like the one raised by one of his students—about the disposition of plundered artifacts during wartime—would have kept him in the lecture hall for an after-hours debate. Such a question might even have spurred him to hours of research later, toiling away, a half-eaten bowl of cornflakes at his elbow. But Jack knew that was unlikely to happen today. Instead he would file the topic away somewhere in his brain, in a nice secluded spot from where it would occasionally raise its hand in an attempt to get his attention. And at some point, maybe years down the road, he would pull it out, dust it off, and start a new book.

He released a sigh just as a student walked past, heading toward the building he'd just left.

"Hey, Dr. Hawthorne," the young man said.

The Evanston University campus wasn't large, and the student body barely topped four thousand, which meant just about every face was familiar, even if the names were not. That was the case here, so instead of saying anything, Jack nodded and gave him a little wave.

Once the student was gone, Jack slowed his steps, finding himself taking deep draws of the spring air, picking out the strong scent of Bradford pear blooms on the breeze. There was something about Evanston that made him appreciate the spring in a way he might not have in some other place. The perfectly manicured grass, the obsessively cultivated flower beds, the way Evanston was nestled within the confines of picturesque Ellen, North Carolina—the season seemed to grant the university and its faculty and students a unique energy that sent ripples across the beautiful campus.

Even though Jack had to cross the entirety of the campus, it took him less than ten minutes to reach his home. The Colonial Revival–style structure, which was much too large for his tastes, sat amid a handful of similar gambrel-roofed faculty homes around the perimeter of the university. During his first teaching stint at Evanston, he lived in a small third-floor apartment closer to downtown—an apartment with spotty hot water and carpet that smelled of old cheese. The only times Jack would venture this way were those occasions when Duckey invited him to dinner. Looking back on those years, he was reminded of how often his friend, and dean of his department, would extend that invitation. In retrospect, it was just possible Duckey was worried about Jack's diet, which at the time consisted mostly of pancakes and breakfast cereal.

Today, after years of living in the house, Jack still found it strange that he and Espy and the boys lived barely a stone's throw from Duckey's place, even though his friend's house was located well back from the road with mature trees surrounding it, allowing him at least the illusion of isolation.

The street was quiet as he reached the driveway. He could hear the barest strains of music floating through an open window, something with a Spanish flavor, he thought. He stooped to pick up a small plastic bag next to the mailbox, a rock and a piece of paper inside—a solicitation for baby-sitting, or pressure-washing, or lawn care. As he straightened, his knee let him know that it was going to be one of those nights when the dull pain that normally made an appearance during his walk home would linger longer than usual. What cheered him, though, was the thought that the knee gave him a good excuse to spend the evening relaxing on the porch.

When he entered the house, the music he could only just make out from the driveway assailed him with renewed vigor, and although he'd suffered through countless iterations of South American pop bands during nearly ten years of marriage to his Venezuelan bride, he never seemed to develop an appreciation for the music of her homeland.

He could hear Esperanza in the kitchen, a series of sounds

that told him she was able to shed her classroom responsibilities early. Heavy class loads, as well as late classes for both of them, made those times when one of them could get into the kitchen to prepare a proper meal relatively rare.

He proceeded down the hallway, glancing into the family room on his way to the kitchen. The former was unoccupied, and when he reached the latter, he found something that made him smile. Espy was making arepas. It wasn't specifically the menu, though, that amused him. It was that she was dancing to a Franco DeVita number, dancing a salsa between the kitchen's island and the stove, where she dropped spoonfuls of cornmeal batter into a frying pan. The batter sizzled in the pan, and Espy used a spoon to corral it into a perfect circle before turning back to the island. It was at that moment that she saw Jack. After adopting an embarrassed look for the briefest of moments, she winked at him and then turned off the music.

"You didn't have to turn off Franco," he said, only half joking.

She answered with an insincere scowl as Jack crossed to the island, where she'd already arranged steak, feta cheese, tomato slices, and avocado.

"*Arepa llanera,*" he said with appreciation. "What's the occasion?"

Jack was familiar with all the ways one could make arepas, most of them having to do with the items that were ultimately stuffed into the cooked dough. For the sake of convenience, their family usually opted for ham and cheese. The fact that Espy had taken the time to marinate steak and pick up avocado suggested at least a minor celebration. But as soon as he asked the question, he remembered Jim's appointment earlier that day.

Espy could see that he'd made the connection, and she offered the same sad yet hopeful smile that was seldom far from her.

"His lungs look okay," she said. She lifted a cutting board from the island and dropped it into the sink. "But his weight is still low."

Hence the arepas, Jack said to himself. Steak arepas were Jim's favorite, and the boy could usually be counted on to eat more than one.

"Clear lungs, that's good news," he said, though he realized she already knew that. So instead of saying anything else, he made his way around the island and wrapped her in an embrace. When he let her go, his wife's eyes were moist.

"He's in his room," Espy said, anticipating the question. Then she turned away to tend to the frying dough. Jack lingered for just a moment, pondering how strange all of it still seemed, but then he turned to go find his son.

He took the creaky wooden stairs to the second floor, a hand on the curved railing. He paused at the door to Jim's room, his mind forming a picture of what he was doing inside. And when he gave a single knock and opened the door, he found the image an accurate one. His son was at the desk that Duckey had bought for his last birthday. It was an antique, large, made of walnut, and more than three hundred years old. Jack had resisted doing the research to find out how much the thing cost, but he knew it was an extravagant purchase, and he suspected that Duckey had bought it for the same reason all of them did many of the things they did for Jim. That thought was one he didn't want to consider at the moment, so he pushed it away and entered the room.

Jack paused after taking a single step, studying his son's

profile. It had always amused him that Jim looked more like Espy's brother than he did Jim Duckett, the man in whose honor he was named. Of his two sons, Jim was the one with the more pronounced Latin features, and he could see hints of Romero in him, especially as he grew older. Even so, there were bits of Duckey he could see in his younger son too—most notably his sense of humor, which was more ribald for an eight-year-old than Jack was often comfortable with. Yet it was a character trait that had served Jim well, considering the lot he'd been dealt.

Over the last few years, Jack had learned more than he ever thought possible about cystic fibrosis, and about all the progress doctors had made in the treatment and management of the disease. Early on, he'd been encouraged by the knowledge that many CF patients lived reasonably healthy lives into their forties. That initial encouragement, though, was what had made Jim's situation harder for Jack to handle—the fact that the disease was progressing with unusual speed through the boy's body. And so the doctors who'd examined him had tried to prepare Jack and Espy for the strong possibility of losing him before he reached his eighteenth birthday.

Jim hadn't yet looked up from whatever he was reading. Jack supposed he was used to his father wordlessly watching him, as if he were some phantom that would disappear if Jack looked away. It was something Jack tried to keep to a minimum; a father should do his best to avoid passing his own fears on to his children.

As if in silent agreement with that thought, Jim finally looked up and flashed Jack a smile.

"Hey, Dad," he said, and as always, Jack found himself listening for anything in the sound of the boy's voice that would signify fluid gathering in his lungs. But the fact that he wasn't coughing, that Jack couldn't hear him wheezing even when silent, told him that Jim was still riding the relatively healthy wave he'd been on for the last few months.

"Hey, pal." Jack crossed to the desk to see what he was reading, and Jim turned it so his father could see the cover of a Batman comic.

"Nice," Jack said. "'Arkham Asylum' is a good one." Then he frowned, considering that he was supposed to do something parental here. "Aren't you a little young for that?"

Jim's answer was a shrug and a crooked grin, as if he knew he'd been caught doing something he shouldn't, yet also understanding that the one who'd caught him was a co-conspirator.

"I got it from Alex's room," Jim said. "And he's only ten."

While Jack wasn't sure the logic worked, he decided not to press the issue, recalling his own stash of comic books when he was his son's age. Admittedly they were a bit campier than the current darker fare, but he was well acquainted with the one Jim was reading and couldn't think of anything that might give the boy nightmares.

"Does Alex know you borrowed it?"

Jim returned the same shrug and smile, a twinkle in his eye, and Jack couldn't help but smirk in return. While he and Espy had kept much of their past from the kids, both boys knew some of the broad strokes. And since Jim was his son, Jack could imagine the path the boy took to rationalize taking the comic book from his brother's room. Something about it not being stealing if he planned on putting it back, eventually. Jack thought that, of his two sons, Jim—the more intuitive—could see a glimpse of the treasure-hunting mentality behind the practice of archaeology.

When Jack left Jim's room, he felt better than he had when he'd gone in. And the smell of steak cooking downstairs ensured that his mood would see no further decline that evening.

Although it was the sort of quiet that made a man think he could hear his own heartbeat if he listened attentively enough, Jack almost didn't hear his phone ringing. But at some point the intrusive chirp made its way through his defenses, pulling him back from a thousand miles away. When the ring came again, he found that he had a choice to make—either answer it and lose the atmosphere he'd conjured over the last few minutes, or ignore it and hope whoever was on the other end would content himself with leaving a message. He was leaning toward the latter as the last ring died off. He waited to see if another would follow it, but as the seconds ticked by, it seemed the caller had opted for voice mail.

He resettled in the chair and took a puff from his cigar, only now noticing the built-up ash that told him he'd been lost in thought for a while. Through the screen door, Jack could hear Espy moving about in the kitchen. He smiled and adjusted his feet on the rail.

He was just about to lose himself back into relaxed mode when his phone started ringing again. Jack sighed and, shifting the cigar to his other hand, fished around in his pocket until he found the phone. He didn't recognize the number, except that it had a local area code.

"Hello?"

"Jack, I need you to listen and not ask any questions. Got it?"

It was the tone of Duckey's voice, more than what he was saying, that brought Jack's feet off the porch rail.

"Ducks?"

"That counts as a question," Duckey said. "And we don't have time for many more of those, so just shut up and listen."

He waited a second, perhaps to make sure the admonition stuck, before speaking again.

"Alright. I need you to go inside, grab your family, and get them out to your car."

Jack was on his feet and heading toward the door, his friend's words still ringing in his ear, which was a testament to their shared experience. Jack also thought it said something about Duckey's ability to infuse urgency into what was otherwise a calm, measured statement.

"What's going on?" Jack asked as he opened the screen door.

"That's question number two," Duckey said. "And I promise I'll answer it, and any others you might have, but later. Right now the only thing you should be concentrating on is getting that family of yours out of the house. Understood?"

A great deal of history existed between the two of them, a history that included Duckey saving Jack's life more than once. He knew he owed Jim Duckett more than he could possibly repay. And he trusted him completely.

"Understood."

"Good," Duckey said. "You don't have time to grab anything but yourselves. Cash if you have any handy. Passports if you don't have to go hunting for them. You may not be able to use them anyway, but they're good to have just in case."

Jack had entered the house, the screen door swinging shut behind him, when Esperanza looked up from the book she was reading, a cup of tea on the breakfast-nook table. Whatever she saw on Jack's face provoked an immediate response. She closed the book and stood, staring at him.

"Once you're out of the house, you need to pick up a new phone," Duckey said. "And make sure you pay cash for it."

"Got it," Jack answered, even as he tried to think of any cash they had in the house. He looked at Espy, who was clearly waiting for an explanation, one he couldn't give her. "I need you to find any cash we have handy," he told her. "And our passports."

"Only if they're handy," he heard Duckey say.

"Only if they're handy," Jack repeated to Espy.

Jack could see Espy processing the information. He suspected there were a number of ways this could go, most of which would cut into the time that Duckey seemed to think was so precious. One of the things he knew about his wife, though, was that she had shared in most of those experiences that had necessitated Duckey's help in years past. It was that history that caused her to nod and begin the task of gathering their meager funds.

"How much time do we have, Ducks?"

"My guess is no more than ten minutes. When you get your new phone, find a way to get the number to that person you used to work with—the one who lived in your old apartment building."

Jack was on the verge of saying Angie's name when it occurred to him that Duckey never forgot anything. If his friend hadn't said the name, there was a reason he didn't want it said out loud. That told Jack that Duckey thought the call was compromised, and that suggested his friend had willingly put himself at risk.

"Understood," Jack said.

"All we can hope for right now is that we stay ahead of them. It can take a while for them to get a track in place. So if we forward phones enough times, we can probably end up with a secure connection."

Jack knew that Duckey wouldn't have him do this unless there was real danger. Yet he couldn't end the call without asking the question. It was a question he'd hoped he would never have to ask, and one that the passage of time had convinced him he wouldn't have to—so much so that he and Espy had gotten rid of the tactical ready bags years ago.

"It's about the bones, isn't it?"

Even as the question left his lips, he knew it was the only answer. There were few episodes in his past that would warrant a flight from his home, and only one with enough open ends to make it a good candidate. When one was hired by a billionaire to locate the bones of a biblical prophet, and when locating those relics meant stealing them from an ancient society organized to keep them safe, and instead of giving them to the man who hired you, you buried them in the desert and let the billionaire die rather than allowing him to play God, you spent a long while afterward looking over your shoulder.

Jack knew that Duckey would be anticipating the question. Still, the silence that greeted him was weighty. He could almost see his friend running a hand through his hair.

"Yes," Duckey said after what seemed a long time. "Now get your family out of there. I'll call you as soon as I can."

The phone in Jack's hand went dead. He kept it at his ear for a few seconds, as if that could help him absorb how drastically his life had changed in such a short span of time. When he pulled the phone away, he started to put it in his pocket but then hesitated. Instead he set it on the kitchen island and headed toward the family room, where Jim and Alex, oblivious to what had just happened, were engaged in electronic sibling rivalry.

He met Espy in the hallway. She had a decent collection of cash in her hand, but Jack's eyes were drawn to the other thing she held. Without a word she extended the handgun toward him. He paused for only a second before reaching for the Glock and tucking it into his waistband. He then took Espy's hand and gave it a squeeze.

Less than three minutes later, the family was gathered at the front door, the boys in light jackets and clutching the few items they couldn't leave without. As Jack looked at them, the one thing that really struck him was that none of them appeared to be frightened, even with him running around like a lunatic. That alone told him there was a lot of Espy in both of the boys, a realization that made him smile.

"Let's go for a ride, boys," he said.

Espy opened the door and the boys started after her, but then Jack remembered something.

"Give me a minute," he said to Espy before turning and bounding up the stairs. In Jim's room he found the boy's nebulizer and medications, and he suffered a pang of guilt that he and Espy had almost walked out the door without them. Wherever they ended up, Jim was going to need his medical supplies.

When he rejoined the family, he saw Espy eyeing what he'd gathered up, and Jack could almost read her thoughts. It wasn't the first time the two of them had been forced to run; it was just the first time they'd had to do so with so many other considerations.

Soon they were all in the car and pulling out of the driveway.

Jack deliberately avoided wondering if it was the last time he would see this house that he'd grown so used to. He glanced over at Espy, who more than anyone in the world could understand what he was thinking, but her face was a blank slate.

It wasn't until they were a few hundred yards down the street that he saw the black SUV behind them, running without lights. He wouldn't have noticed it had he not been looking. It stopped in front of Jack's house, and then the distance made it impossible to see anything more. But he knew that people dressed in black would exit the vehicle and take the house apart, looking for something he hadn't seen in a very long time, something he never wanted to see again.

He looked at the clock on the dash: 9:30. Duckey was wrong. It was seven minutes.

It was because he was looking at the clock that he didn't see the other SUV slip in behind them. It wasn't until he glanced at the rearview mirror that he noticed he could no longer see the road. Then something hit them from behind.

There was a crunch of metal. The impact threw Jack back against his seat and then his body came forward, his head coming down hard on the steering wheel. When he straightened, he couldn't see the road for the stars swimming in front of him. What cut through the confusion, though, were the cries coming from the back seat. Jim and Alex were buckled in; they shouldn't have been hurt. But they were scared now.

Jack willed his vision to clear and looked over at Espy, who was holding her head. His wife gave him a pained nod to tell him she was okay. Only then did he look back, just in time to see the SUV closing in for another strike.

"Hold on, boys," he said. He shifted gears and punched the accelerator, allowing the V8 of their aged-but-still-dependable

BMW to do its work. They took off like a shot, right before the SUV would have hit them a second time. Jack shifted again, and in short order put some distance between them.

They were racing down a narrow residential street. Jack knew that if they were going to get away on speed alone, he would have to find a wider, open road. As if to validate that thought, he saw the SUV begin to close the distance again. It occurred to him that if this was some organized team, then they probably had rides with a bit more power than normal.

The faculty homes were behind them now, the university campus receding. And then they were in Ellen proper, entering an area with more traffic, with businesses to attract college students popping up on either side of the street. He had to downshift as the BMW came up fast behind a pickup. After a glance past the truck, he swerved into the oncoming lane and accelerated. Yet the SUV followed suit and seconds later was close behind them again. Until Jack could get through town and out onto the state highway, he doubted he would be able to lose the SUV.

It didn't help that he was operating blind. He didn't know anything about the people who were trying to run him off the road, or what their objectives were—not beyond what Duckey had already confirmed. The only solid piece of information he had was that Duckey considered them dangerous enough to instruct him to leave his house on a moment's notice. And for now, that was all he needed to know.

They were heading deeper into Ellen, and Jack thought he was driving too fast for the increasing number of people on the streets and sidewalks, many of them Evanston students patronizing the restaurants, movie theater, and coffee shops.

There were cars parked along each side of the road, and

as Jack approached an intersection, the signal light flipped to yellow while he was still a good ways off. He didn't even look to Espy before depressing the clutch and shifting to fourth, praying to God that someone didn't step out from between the parked cars. The signal went to red well before the BMW shot through the intersection. Behind him, Jack heard a screech of tires but no sound of impact. He looked in the rearview and saw that the SUV had been forced to slow down to avoid cross traffic, but the driver had proceeded through the intersection, ignoring the red light.

"It may be safer to stop," he said to Espy. "We're in the middle of town. I don't think whoever it is can just load us into their truck and drive off."

His wife seemed to consider that, her eyes moving to the side mirror. She turned back to him. "Can we take that chance?" Jack knew she was referring to Jim and Alex. When he didn't answer right away, she added, "It's Duckey. We both know he wouldn't tell us to run if there was any other option."

Jack knew she was right. Duckey's counsel had never once led him astray. He nodded silent thanks to Espy, whose own counsel had saved his life a time or two.

"Check their seat belts," he said. He looked in the rearview. The SUV was less than fifty yards back. Without asking why, Espy swiveled to view the boys' belts, reaching back to make sure they were fastened.

They were now nearing the center of Ellen, the SUV almost on top of them. They hit another intersection, the light green this time, and shot through it, weathered brick buildings speeding by on either side. Jack's hands were tight on the wheel, and his pulse raced as he imagined any one of the people on the sidewalks darting in front of the car.

"Jack," Espy yelled.

He saw it a second later. A minivan, parked in front of a line of restaurants sharing a single façade, had started to pull out. The BMW was much too close, and moving too fast, to avoid hitting it. Jack slammed on the brakes and heard the tires shriek in protest. He spun the wheel to the left, trying to will the car into the oncoming lane, praying there was no one coming. The next few seconds were a blur, the clearest thing about them the moment of impact. It was a blow that nearly took him from his seat, throwing him in Espy's direction, but the seat belt held, momentarily pinning him between the two front seats. Somewhere along the way he'd lost the wheel, but it didn't matter. The car was now in the hands of greater forces.

It seemed like an eternity, those two seconds of violence, the rear passenger quarter panel crumpling. But then it was over and, somehow, they were on the other side of it. The steering wheel was spinning back to the right, and by instinct, Jack grabbed for it. The BMW was still moving, though the engine was threatening to stall. It was instinct again that depressed the clutch, downshifted, and corrected the car's momentum, bringing the BMW back to the proper lane.

Jack's heart was racing again as he picked up speed, and he couldn't help but glance in the rearview mirror to see how the minivan fared. Which was when he witnessed the black SUV run headlong into the stalled minivan. Wide-eyed, Jack watched the minivan driven forward, going sideways under the bull rush of the other vehicle. There was a metal-on-metal scream, and then the minivan completed its turn, its back end snapping into the line of parked cars on the other side of the road. The driver of the SUV, with the way now clear, tried to stop his counterclockwise spin but overcorrected. The front tires broke to the right at a sickening angle and the truck began rolling, its windshield shattering.

Jack kept the BMW moving forward, his eyes scanning the wreckage behind them, watching as the mangled SUV disappeared from sight. The sudden silence that settled over them felt strange. He shifted his eyes down to find Jim and Alex, both of them frightened but holding it together. Next to Jack, Espy turned to make sure the boys were okay—giving them a good once-over, taking their hands, forcing eye contact. Jack heard words of motherly assurance. It was only after she'd satisfied herself the boys were fine that she turned back to him.

He spared her a short look, his adrenaline keeping him focused on the road ahead. But in that brief exchange, Jack saw a hundred questions, hardly any of them he had answers for. This was a place he and Espy had been before, which was why she swallowed every one of those questions for the time being. And that left him free to do what was necessary, to concentrate on staying one step ahead of whoever was after them.

For that, though, Jack knew he needed help. And there was no one better positioned to provide that than Duckey. With that thought in mind, Jack set off in search of somewhere to purchase a few cheap disposable phones.

3

AT SOME POINT IT HAD STARTED TO RAIN. Jack wasn't sure when it had happened; he couldn't remember even turning on the wipers. But as he pulled off SR74 and onto the gravel road of the small airfield, the light rain created rivulets tracing their way down the windshield. The road had been absent any other vehicles for almost thirty minutes, and as the headlights of the much-abused car arced out over the airfield, there wasn't even a hint of movement.

The boys were asleep in the back, having lost the fight with adrenaline and fear about an hour out of Ellen. It hadn't taken them long to start asking questions, but they'd only done so after the first stop to pick up the disposable phones, after Jack thought they were far enough away from the carnage behind them.

The problem Jack faced was that he had no idea what to say to the boys. How did one explain a pursuit by ghosts from his past?

He'd checked in with Duckey a few times, but their conversations had been brief, only long enough to create some communication moats between them and anyone who might have been listening. And to arrange a flight.

The airfield had a single runway, designed for small aircraft. The tower was dark, as were the field's two hangars. The gravel crunching beneath the car's tires sounded louder than normal as they neared the buildings. There wasn't another vehicle in sight, no sign that another human being had been there in a long time. Jack looked at the dashboard clock. It was approaching midnight. He and his family were late in getting there, and he started to wonder if Duckey's friend had already left, thinking they weren't going to show.

Next to him, Espy scanned the flatland. In the darkness, Jack couldn't read her evaluation, and she didn't comment. He took her silence as tacit agreement that they needed to continue on, even if she was beginning to get the feeling, as he was, that there was danger lurking in this quiet place.

Not long after leaving the outskirts of Ellen, Jack had filled Espy in on the call from Duckey that had sent them running. She'd absorbed the scant information and then, after a nod, settled back to see how things played out. She had a different set of priorities now than she did years ago in Australia, where the two of them buried the bones of Elisha rather than turn them over to Jack's employer, and those priorities were sleeping in the seat behind them.

They were almost at the hangars before Jack saw the cracked door, a gap of no more than three inches through which he could see the faintest of lights inside. He stopped the car and cut the engine, and the silence that followed was just about total, save for a hint of labored breathing from Jim, a slight rasp. Jack didn't move for several seconds but just sat and studied the hangar, more a weathered shed with large swinging doors. Then, without asking Espy to remain in the car with the boys, he opened the door and stepped out into the night air, leaving the keys in the ignition.

The rain was cold on his neck as he took his time walking to the hangar door. Once there, he peeked through the crack. He couldn't see much of anything, not even an undefined shape. Understanding that whoever might be inside saw the headlights as they drove up, not to mention heard the sound of tires on gravel, he put a hand on the door and gave it a shove. It slid more readily than he'd expected, moving as if on a well-oiled track, revealing the source of the dim illumination—a single utility work light hanging from a hook in the ceiling. Beneath the glow of the light, a man was leaning into the cockpit of an airplane. Once Jack had stepped inside the hangar, escaping the rain, it took the man several seconds to acknowledge him. Even then it took almost a full minute before the man pulled back from the plane and turned toward Jack.

"You must be Jack," he said.

"Which makes you Russell," Jack answered.

Russell Hodges stepped forward, giving Jack a better view of a man around his own age, maybe a few years older. He wore worn jeans, a rumpled shirt, and cowboy boots. Hodges smiled and offered Jack a hand, and even if the man hadn't been a friend of Duckey's, it was the kind of smile that would have won Jack over anyway.

"Jim tells me you're in a bit of trouble," Hodges said.

Jack smirked and shook his head. "Duckey's always had a talent for understatement."

At that, Russell's smile took on a different aspect, almost conspiratorial. "They don't make many like him." Then Hodges looked past Jack, to the open door and to the car where Espy and the boys waited. Jack turned around and saw that the younger one, Jim, was awake now, his face pressed to the window.

"Precious cargo," Russell said.

"That they are," Jack agreed. "And tired cargo."

Russell chuckled and gestured to the plane. "She's just about set. And once we're up in the air, she flies pretty smooth, so you folks should be able to catch a nap while we're getting you someplace safe."

"I don't suppose Duckey's suggested a destination?"

Russell shook his head. "My impression is that he's going to work that out with you."

Until Russell said it, Jack hadn't given much thought to where they would ultimately end up. It was enough to keep moving and let Duckey direct him. Now, though, he realized that he and Espy had some serious decisions to make.

"All that's important right now is that we get this bird in the air," Russell said. "We can figure out the rest of it after that."

The "bird" was a twin-engine plane, a sleek-bodied six-seater, its tail adorned with the Piper logo.

"It's a Seneca V," Russell said, noticing that Jack was looking the plane over. "Had her about a month." He ran a hand over the wing. "Just about have the kinks worked out of her."

In the past, Jack had taken more than his share of flights in planes that were little better than flying tubs—planes that flouted the laws of physics every time they got airborne. So he knew the plane in front of him was not for the faint of wallet.

"I don't know how Duckey talked you into this but I can't thank you enough," Jack said.

Russell waved him off. "Jim and I go back a ways and I couldn't remember if I owed him a favor or if he owed me one. So I figured I'd err on the side of caution and build some equity."

"Do you mind if I ask how you know him?"

"The Company" was Russell's simple response, and Jack knew right away not to expect elaboration. Even Duckey rarely talked about his CIA days, despite his and Jack's long friendship.

"Give me a minute or so and then I can taxi the plane out of here. Then you can pull your car in. That'll keep it out of sight for a while." Hodges grabbed a rag and began wiping his hands. After a few moments he looked up, a grim expression on his face. "They'll find it eventually, though."

In that moment it occurred to Jack that Russell knew more about the people who were after him than he did himself. Which meant that Hodges and Duckey had talked over a few things while Jack was in transit.

"Any chance you can let me in on the secret?" Jack asked, half expecting the man to tell him to take it up with Duckey. So he was a little surprised when Hodges answered.

"The Company," he said again, the corner of his mouth taking a rueful turn.

Jack's initial response was silence, and it took a while before he realized that was because, of all the entities Russell might have mentioned, the CIA was far from being on the list. It was also a revelation that sent a shiver up his back, and explained Duckey's almost frantic phone call. He opened his mouth, but Duckey's former associate cut him off.

"Before you ask, I have no idea why they're after you. And, frankly, it's none of my business."

A statement like that left little else to say, and so Jack nodded and started to head back to the car. Then something occurred to him. "You said they'd find my car. Won't that mean they'll know it was you who helped us escape?"

Russell chuckled, shook his head. "I wouldn't worry about that. This hangar belongs to them. And one of the things my former employers taught me was how to use available resources without leaving a trace."

He laughed then, and Jack couldn't help but smile as he walked back to the car.

When he slipped back in, Espy communicated everything she needed to with a single raised eyebrow.

So Jack responded with a gesture that did about the same thing: a shrug. It took less than a second before he understood his mistake.

Although the passing years had tempered a bit of Esperanza's legendary fire, there were times when Jack caught a glimpse of the woman who'd once traipsed around the globe with him, and who wasn't afraid to dole out a punch or two along the way. In fact, there were times he was amazed that he'd survived those early years reasonably intact. Now he could tell that his response had awakened that younger, nonmaternal version of his wife, if only in the fierceness he saw in her eyes.

"Uh-oh, Mom's mad," Jim said.

"I'm not really sure how this is my fault," Jack tried.

Espy didn't say anything right away. Instead she just looked at him, with the same steely, unflinching gaze that had often brought the boys to obedience without her having to say a word. And under that gaze, Jack felt like a ten-year-old. He was just about to speak when she beat him to it.

"I know it's not your fault," she said, "but I have to hold someone responsible for the situation we're in, and you're the only one handy."

"Okay, I can see how this is at least partially my fault," Jack said, trying to head off her anger. "If I hadn't gone looking for the bones, then this wouldn't be happening. But in my defense, I haven't done anything recently to cause the CIA to come after us." He paused to weigh the validity of that statement. "Okay, maybe the occasional box of Cubans Duckey gets me every so often, but beyond that—"

A voice from the back seat interrupted him.

"What bones?" Alex asked, his voice heavy with sleep.

Jack turned toward the boys. "I promise I'll explain, guys. Someday. But right now we have to get ready to take a little trip."

Alex pointed at the plane. "Where are we going?"

"Yeah, where are we going?" Jim repeated.

"It's a surprise," Jack said, and the boys seemed to accept his response. When he turned back to Espy, to see if the side-bar with the boys had allowed sufficient time for her anger to disperse, he was greeted by a wholly different expression—one that prompted a raised eyebrow. "What?"

"What's this about the CIA?" Espy asked.

"Oh, that." Jack took in a long breath, releasing it as he considered how things had changed even since they'd arrived at the airfield. He was just about to tell her what he'd learned from Russell when he remembered the other two members of their party. He glanced in their direction, then back at Espy. "How about we talk about it once we're in the air?"

He could see that she was reluctant to let the matter go, her eyes promising him that the conversation wasn't over. Jack was saved from pondering that, though, because Russell emerged from the hangar and slid both doors open wide.

"Why don't you take the boys and get them buckled in,"

Jack said to Espy. "I'm going to touch base with Duckey and see if he has any thoughts about our destination."

As Espy exited the car with the boys, Jack pulled out one of the disposable phones, punching in Duckey's number.

"Okay, how about we figure out how to get you out of this mess?" Duckey said before Jack could get a word out.

"Hey, Ducks."

"Hey back," his department head returned. He sounded tired. "I assume you're in the air?"

"Not yet. Espy's getting the boys loaded up now."

"Good. So now we just need to figure out where you're going."

"I have an idea or two along those lines, but first can we back up a bit?"

"You're right," Duckey said. "There probably *are* a few things we need to get out of the way first."

"Maybe a few," Jack agreed. "For starters, why is the CIA interested in the bones?"

"Did Russell tell you that? Because he's only partially right. The man who's after you is Marcus McKeller. He's an agent, but this isn't a CIA project." Duckey paused. "He's a rogue agent, Jack. He doesn't report to anyone."

Jack absorbed that, wondering if that was a better or worse state of affairs. "Why is he after the bones?"

"I did some digging when I started to hear things," Duckey said. "It seems his wife has cancer. Bad prognosis, maybe two months."

"I guess that's as good a reason as any," Jack said. "But how did he find out about them?"

"To put it in the simplest terms—the diversified business interests of the late Gordon Reese."

Jack considered that, and it didn't take long before he understood. When ailing billionaire Gordon Reese hired him to find Elisha's bones some thirteen years ago, the world knew him primarily as a technology magnate, and yet someone with his kind of money had his hands in many pots. "Reese did some work for the government," Jack posited.

"Not just *some* work," Duckey said. "Reese Industries has contracts with just about every government agency. And from what I've been told, some of those contracts involve top-shelf projects—the kind that require pretty high security protocols."

Jack nodded, his eyes moving to the plane. Espy was getting herself and the boys situated inside the aircraft. "Okay, I get that. Because Reese's company does some hush-hush work for Washington, the government keeps an eye on them. But Reese has been dead for more than a decade. Why is your agency friend only coming after me now?"

"Listen, Jack, just because he's Langley doesn't mean he's a friend of mine. I've been out of that line of work for a long time. I hardly even know anyone over there anymore."

Jack decided not to remind him that, apparently, he still had contacts enough to give him advance warning that someone was coming to Jack's home.

"As to why nothing's happened sooner, my guess is that it's just simple bureaucracy. When Reese died, someone in Washington probably got nervous about the state of Reese Industries, even though he'd essentially ceded control to his son almost a year before he kicked it."

"They were worried that a man who knows he's dying might be a security risk," Jack said.

"So they went through his files," Duckey added. "And not just his business files, his personal ones too."

"I'm not going to get into how I feel about their ability to do that."

"You have no idea, believe me. When you're talking a company the size of Reese Industries, you're getting into a volume of data that would rival the Library of Congress. My guess is they did a keyword scan on everything, and anything that didn't get a hit would have been set aside."

"So Reese kept information about the bones in his personal files, which were then copied over to a government server."

"Where it sat unnoticed until, as best as I can tell, about two months ago," Duckey said.

"When Marcus McKeller discovered it," Jack said.

"I started to hear some things a while back. Someone asking questions. I still have a few friends over there, and they let me know."

"And now McKeller's looking for me because Reese's notes told him I'm the last link in the chain of possession." Jack said it more to himself than to Duckey, working things out in his head. "I guess what I'm having a problem with, Ducks, is why he wouldn't just come and ask me. I mean, if you send a few CIA agents to someone's house, they're usually pretty forthcoming. Why the heavy-handed approach?"

"A threat to one's loved ones can make a man do crazy things," Duckey said. "Also, since this is an off-the-books op, McKeller couldn't rely on his CIA status to get you to cooperate."

"I guess that makes sense," Jack said.

"There's something else, Jack," Duckey said. "I told you that McKeller's gone rogue, which means he's not using CIA personnel for this. He's paying outsiders. Some of them will be ex-Langley, others probably retired cops."

"Mercenaries," Jack said.

"Something like that."

Jack released a sigh. "Well, tell me about this guy. What am I facing here?"

"He's NCS."

"NCS?"

"National Clandestine Service," Duckey answered. "Under normal conditions, he would know where you are even before you know that's where you're going."

Jack knew he was tired because that almost made sense to him.

"And he's good at his job. A real technical wizard. Meaning he'll be managing this thing by himself, using only the resources he knows he can trust." Duckey paused. "You couldn't have done much worse than tangle with this guy, Jack."

"Thanks for the pep talk," Jack said.

"Don't mention it."

"But at least if he's working solo, he can't use the entire array of CIA tricks he'd normally have at his disposal."

"Probably not," Duckey said. "Don't fool yourself, though. Even if all he has are the people who were in and out of your house in less than five minutes, you're still in serious trouble."

Jack raised an eyebrow. "How do you know how long they were in my house?"

"Because you live about a hundred yards away from me, and I did used to do this sort of thing for a living, remember?"

"Something I've been thankful for, and more than once," Jack said. A wave from Russell caught his eye, prompting Jack to hurry. "So tell me about your friend Russell."

"About as decent a guy as you'll find," Duckey said. "And a good pilot. Don't let the hand fool you."

Jack frowned. "The hand?"

"He lost it to an IED in Iraq," Duckey explained.

Jack found his eyes moving to the plane again. Espy was descending its stairs. She caught Jack's eye and then headed back toward the car. As his wife drew closer, Jack looked past her, finding Russell Hodges doing something at the back of the plane. He couldn't see the man's hands at the moment, but then he hadn't noticed anything out of the ordinary about them when they were talking together earlier. For some reason, he felt something dark and cold settle in his stomach. "Ducks, does he use a prosthetic?"

"Sometimes" came the reply. "He has one of those hard plastic ones. Nothing fancy. Why?"

Espy had almost reached the car, and Jack shifted his focus until he caught her looking back at him. Then he directed his attention back to Hodges, who'd emerged from behind the plane. He went up the aircraft's stairs. Jack thought he saw two perfectly normal looking hands. Just before Hodges climbed into the plane, he turned and looked toward the car. Jack saw a hint of something in his expression, maybe a smile.

Espy had a hand on the door handle when Jack dropped the phone. She'd slipped the gun into the console between them, and Jack reached for it. He opened the door just as Espy opened hers. He didn't pause to answer her puzzled query before starting for the plane.

He heard the engines rumble to life, the twin propellers spinning.

It had been years since he'd held a gun with the willingness to use it, years since the events of his life had conspired to make him welcome the feel of the cold metal in his hand. There had also never been an occasion in which a man who Jack knew was not named Russell Hodges stood between him and his boys.

This other man must have seen him coming because, before

Jack reached the plane, he appeared again at the aircraft door. He raised a gun toward Jack.

Jack raised his own gun and almost squeezed off a shot, and it took everything in him to keep from doing it, knowing the boys were in the plane.

"Jack?" Espy called from behind, but her husband didn't answer, his attention wholly on the man who stood between him and his children. Whoever he was, he didn't shoot, although he had as clear a shot at Jack as he could want.

Jack took a step closer. The man calling himself Russell Hodges extended his gun, and Jack stopped moving. Behind him, Espy had gone silent, likely having put the pieces together.

"So, what now?" Jack asked.

"You put your gun down and climb aboard and I take you to meet someone who has some questions for you," the man said.

Jack was shaking his head before the man—apparently some kind of mercenary—had finished. "I have a better idea. You let the boys go and you can take me wherever you want."

The man shook his head. "You don't have the high ground, Dr. Hawthorne. Your only option at this point is to do exactly as you're told."

As much as Jack hated to admit it, he couldn't argue the point. "Who are you?" he asked, since it was clear the man was not Duckey's friend. Jack stopped himself from considering what that meant for the missing Russell Hodges.

"Someone doing a job" was the response. The man gestured again with his weapon. "Now drop the gun."

Jack took a deep breath, coming to the realization that he didn't have much of a choice. He was just about to lower the gun when his eye caught movement from the plane, from behind the mercenary. He caught a glimpse of brown hair, a black jacket—Alex's jacket. His heart jumped into his throat, but he clamped down on the shout that wanted to escape. He moved his eyes back to the enemy, locked them there. "I need some assurances. I need to speak to your boss. He has to convince me there can be some end to this that my family and I can walk away from before I get on that plane."

He felt, more than saw, Espy step up next to him. She had to have seen Alex. Jack's son was slipping up behind his captor. Jack saw his face for just a second, a mix of fear and resolve.

It took a moment before the man responded to Jack's request, and he did so by putting a hand in his pocket and withdrawing a phone. He flipped it open, glanced down.

There was a flurry of movement behind him—Alex rushing. Jack's son hit the mercenary hard. The man pitched forward, Alex's weight taking him halfway out of the open door. But before he fell from the plane, the man reached out and grabbed the doorframe. His phone clattered to the tarmac.

For just an instant, Jack had a full view of his older son, the boy clearly framed in the doorway. He was breathing hard, a look on his face that seemed to express surprise over what he'd done. He was looking at the man he'd hit, but his eyes soon moved to his father. Jack stepped forward.

Before he could close the distance, the mercenary regained his balance. Jack saw the man's arm swing back, saw it catch Alex under his chin. The blow sent the boy flying back into the recesses of the plane. Jack heard Espy scream.

Jack shut the sound out. The mercenary filled the doorway, his attention pulled in another direction. Jack had a clear shot. He brought the gun up, steadied it. And hesitated. He couldn't pull the trigger. If he missed . . .

The moment was gone, and before Jack could take another

step forward, the man had brought his own gun level. Jack could hear Espy choking back a sob, yet he couldn't look away from the man and from the plane that held his injured son.

Then the nameless man did something unexpected. Keeping his attention on Jack, he crouched and reached for the stair pull. He had the stairs retracted before Jack could register what was happening. The aircraft's door was closing, and only then did Jack's legs begin to move. He rushed toward the plane, but the door was shut and locked before he could make it there. Seconds later the plane began to roll.

A wave of panic came over Jack. He ran alongside the plane, pounding on the door as it taxied away from the hangar. He was shouting, but his words were lost to the increasing sound of the engines. He backed away, thought to circle around to the cockpit window, to try to get a shot off. But as he moved to get around the wing, to avoid the deadly propellers, the plane's pilot executed a sharp turn and began accelerating toward the runway.

Jack's panic had turned into real fear—a fear unlike any he'd ever known. As the plane picked up speed, he tried to keep up, running alongside it like a madman. He held the gun helplessly in one hand while with the other he banged on the cold metal of the aircraft. It didn't take long for the plane to leave him behind, to leave him watching the gap that widened between him and his sons. By the time the plane reached the runway, it was too far ahead for Jack to do anything but stare as its pilot opened the throttle and lowered the flaps.

Before long, the plane was in the air.

Jack stood frozen on the tarmac, watching the plane become a vanishing point in the dark sky. From behind him came the sound of Esperanza's unchecked sobs.

4

✝

DUCKEY WAS SILENT FOR A LONG WHILE. When he did speak again, the voice coming through the phone held a weight Jack hadn't heard before. "Jack, I'm sorry."

Jack had no answer to that. He knew it wasn't Duckey's fault, that his friend had only done what he had so many times before—used his connections to try to dig Jack out of a bad situation. But there was much more to it this time, and Jack had to apply all his energy and skill to the task of getting his sons back. If he paused to deal with anything else, to consider anything other than Jim and Alex, he knew that fear would immobilize him.

Esperanza sat in the car beside Jack. The crying had ended and she had gone silent. Her eyes seemed fixed on something outside, perhaps the point in the night sky where her children had disappeared.

"Any idea who he was?" Jack asked.

"No," Duckey answered, and Jack heard a tightness in his voice that bespoke concern for the real Russell Hodges. While his thoughts and emotions were tied up in his children, he couldn't forget that Duckey might have killed a friend by asking for a favor. Jack could only imagine the weight he bore.

"Where will he take them?"

"I don't know," Duckey said. "It'll be a safe house that McKeller feels comfortable in, but the Agency has more of those than I can count, even Stateside."

The ex-CIA agent fell silent, and Jack followed suit. He looked over at Espy. She seemed to be somewhere else. The blackness that had settled over the airfield made Jack feel as if there wasn't another soul around for miles.

"I don't get it, Ducks," Jack said, breaking the silence. "You told me McKeller couldn't use his resources to track me down. So how does he take out Hodges and get someone else in place on such short notice?"

Duckey sighed. "Because the man did his research. I told you he was NCS. He studied his target, catalogued any hindrances, then planned for them."

"You mean he knew I'd go to you?"

"It's what I would do," Duckey said. "He would have looked at everyone you work with, and my name would have raised a red flag. After that, well, I've probably asked for a few too many favors on your behalf for there not to be some record of it in their system. All it would have taken is for McKeller to develop a list of my old Company contacts, determine which ones I'd be most likely to call on, and then have his people in place if I did."

Duckey's words sobered Jack even more. Their earlier conversation had almost convinced him that the man who was after him would only have a small handful of people in whom he could confide the details of the project. But when he started tallying—when he considered the people in both SUVs back in Ellen, along with the people necessary to counterbalance help from Duckey—Jack found the potential threats growing to what seemed unmanageable proportions. That thought also sparked serious concern for his friend's safety.

"I'm worried about you, Ducks."

"You have more important things to worry about right now," Duckey said. "Besides, I've survived bigger threats than McKeller."

Jack couldn't help but smile at his friend's confidence, remembering there were few he knew with the track record to back up that sort of bravado. "So, what do you suggest we do?"

"I have a few ideas, but ultimately I don't think you're going to like my answer." Duckey paused and Jack had a mental picture of the man running a hand through his hair. "Look, you can go to the police, or the media, or pretty much anyone else you can think of, but McKeller's among the best in the world at making people disappear. All McKeller has to do is say he has no idea what you're talking about, that the Company doesn't have any domestic operation targeting a university professor, and that they certainly don't abduct children. And believe me, he'll have a wall of plausible deniability so thick you'll never be able to break through it."

It took Jack only a moment to accept the truth of what Duckey had said, despite that the very idea of it—the government-sanctioned disappearance of U.S. citizens—seemed like something relegated to third-world countries.

"What about McKeller's boss?" Jack asked. "Who does he report to?"

"The deputy director. The problem, Jack, is at this point I'm not even sure trying to bend the director's ear is the best way to go. For one thing, I've been out of the Company long enough for my word not to mean a whole lot."

"And doing something like that is a good way to get yourself killed," Jack added. Even as he said it, though, he knew it wouldn't be a consideration as far as Duckey was concerned. Jack had no doubt that his friend would take a bullet for the boys if it came down to it.

"I'm more worried about what would happen to Alex and Jim if the director decided to open up some kind of investigation. If we spook McKeller . . ." He went silent.

"If we spook McKeller, he might cut his losses," Jack finished.

There was a pause. When Duckey spoke again, his voice was quiet. "He'd get rid of any evidence, Jack."

The cold feeling in Jack's stomach was returning. He looked over at his silent wife, thankful she couldn't hear their entire conversation. "Which means I have to go back," Jack said. "I have to trade myself for the boys."

It was the first thing he'd said that provoked any response from Espy. She turned her head, her eyes finding his. He reached over and took her hand for a moment, gave it a squeeze.

"I think it may come to that," Duckey said. "But I'd sure like to turn over all the other stones before we settle on that one."

"Except the longer I wait—"

"The longer the boys will be held someplace nice, given regular meals, and probably a Nintendo to keep them busy," Duckey said. "Look, Jack, McKeller doesn't gain anything by hurting the kids." When Jack didn't answer, Duckey added, "Believe me, whoever he has holding your boys is probably ex-Company. They'll treat them right, keep them safe, while we figure this out." Jack started to answer, but Duckey cut him off. "They'll know about Jim's medical condition. Wherever they're taking him, they'll have everything he needs—medicine, nebulizer, the works."

Jack tried to raise another objection, but try as he might, he found it difficult to come up with anything beyond the requisite parental fight reflex, the one that wanted to send him running directly into the enemy camp to save his family. What tempered that impulse, though, was Duckey's counsel—a history of sage advice that had guided him through other difficult episodes.

"Well, if I'm not going to turn myself in, where do we go?" Jack asked.

"You need a safe house of your own," Duckey said. "Just for a little while."

Jack shook his head. "If you're right, they'll have eyes on anyone we'd go to. And while we have enough cash for a hotel, my guess is that it wouldn't take them long to find us."

"Which is why I'm thinking somewhere exotic," Duckey said.

Once Jack realized what Duckey meant, he turned to Espy. "Is your brother in Caracas?"

"He should be," she said, the first time she'd spoken since the boys were taken. "He was in Paris last week, but I think he got back a few days ago."

Jack turned his attention back to the phone. "With our bird leaving without us, we'll have to fly commercial. And if we do that, our friends will know where we're going."

"Eventually," Duckey agreed. "McKeller will have placed something in the system to flag your credit cards, along with commercial flight manifests. So you wait as long as you can, buy at the gate, and hope to God I'm right about McKeller not having the manpower available to have someone waiting for you in Caracas."

"That's not as encouraging as you might think," Jack said.

"Hey, it's all I have at the moment."

That pulled another smile from Jack, but it also tugged at something in Jack's mind—something he'd forgotten but that seemed important. Something he had . . . When it came to him, he jerked up in his seat. He glanced down, sending his eyes to the center console where he'd placed it.

"He dropped a phone, Ducks," Jack said. He grabbed the cell phone and brought it closer, peered at it—as if the thing would act as some compass pointing him to his sons. It was powered off.

"Who dropped a phone?"

"Whoever took Jim and Alex dropped a phone when Alex hit him. I've got it here."

Duckey responded with a grunt. "Okay, so that makes it easier for you if you decide you have to turn yourself in, but I'm not sure it changes anything at this point."

Jack mulled that over, feeling his excitement ebb. "Because if I turn this on and make a call, we're beholden to whoever answers. We'll be playing their game, not ours."

"Exactly."

"It's not a game," Espy said. Her voice was quiet, but the words came with a conviction that immediately made Jack regret the remark.

"You're right," Jack said, giving her an apologetic smile.

"For the time being, I think you should keep the phone in your back pocket," Duckey said. "But I wouldn't turn it on. In fact, you should probably remove the battery and SIM card. If it's a Company phone, McKeller might be able to track it even with the power off."

"Noted," Jack said.

"Along those same lines, you folks have been at that airfield way too long," Duckey said. "Whoever it was that took the boys probably checked in as soon as the plane was in the air."

The same thought had been circling in Jack's mind for the last few minutes, but he'd ignored it. With Duckey bringing it out into the open, Jack was forced to acknowledge the reason he and Espy were still sitting in the car at a deserted airport when in all likelihood mercenaries attached to a rogue CIA agent were closing in on them. Was it because leaving meant conceding that the boys were really gone, and driving away would make it real?

As he sat in the darkened car, silently holding the phone to his ear, Jack felt a hand take his. When he looked over at Espy, he found he could read her eyes, knew that his thoughts were hers as well.

"We're not doing anyone any good sitting here," she said.

Jack took in a deep breath. When he released it, he felt as if something else went with it. He squeezed Espy's hand. "We're on our way, Ducks. I'll call you from Caracas."

After he ended the call, he took one last look into the dark sky before starting the car and leaving the airfield behind.

5

✝

EVERY CITY CAME WITH ITS OWN SMELL, a blended aroma influenced by region, infrastructure, and the culinary sensibilities of its residents. And so, while it had been years since Jack had walked the streets of Caracas, the smell of it, enhanced by a recent rain, made him feel as if barely a week had passed. Espy felt the same way; he could tell just by looking at her. Despite what had happened over the last twenty-four hours, she was smiling. It was a sad smile, but it was also one that only coming home could evoke.

An enormous city, Caracas lay sprawled along a valley floor like a grand spill, its size and din at the center slowly giving way to smaller, poorer sections that spread out past the city's outskirts. Yet in the affluent neighborhood of Chacao, where Espy's brother kept his place of business, there might as well have been a curtain veiling the undesirable periphery from view.

Jack and Espy walked along Avenida Libertador, the street congested with traffic, the city around them filled with a level of noise and spectacle unique to this part of the world. They were heading uphill, the angle of ascent bothering Jack's bad knee, but Romero's shop was close by, its dark doorway a sliver toward the end of a long, nondescript white wall.

When they reached it and Espy stepped through, Jack couldn't shake the impression that he'd just watched his wife jump down a rabbit hole. At the top of a narrow, dimly lit flight of stairs stood a large, brown metal door that Espy pushed open, flooding the corridor with light.

Romero didn't know they were in the country. Jack had thought about calling while in transit, but considering the resources McKeller had at his disposal, Jack had decided against it. And while the flight from North Carolina to Caracas meant they probably knew where he was, he had no desire to assist them by engaging his brother-in-law via a technology susceptible to prying ears.

He closed the door behind them and then turned to survey a place where he'd spent a good deal of time during his younger days, taking it in with a glance that told him little had changed in the passing years. Not long after retiring from a more adventurous—and dangerous—life and opening a place where he could sell things that others took the risks to procure, Romero had discovered the necessary elements to a successful high-end retail establishment: refinement and austerity. It was a combination that had served him well, making him more comfortable than Jack suspected he ever thought possible when a younger man.

The retail floor was empty. Jack looked toward Romero's office, the glass wall revealing his absence. He frowned. He knew the place almost as well as he knew his office back at the university. There were few places to hide, and Romero would never leave without locking the door. It was a mystery that immediately set him on edge, even as his physical self seemed to decide on its own course of action. Before he even realized he'd moved, he was halfway across the room, standing in front of a display of ancient weapons, a pair of impressive stone axes framing several smaller knives that, if his guess was correct, were copper alloy. As his hand reached for one of the axes, his mind continuing to puzzle over Romero's absence, it occurred to him that his attraction to aged things was a force he couldn't control, something that compelled him regardless of external influences. Yet it was one such external influence that stayed his hand—a good-natured oath coming from behind him.

Jack turned to see Espy's brother, a hand on the top of his head, absently rubbing it as he processed the sight of his sister and closest friend unexpectedly standing in his store. Then the Venezuelan's mouth split into a grin and he was moving forward. In the hugs that followed, most of them reserved for his sister, Jack allowed himself a respite from the cares that had forced them to take this trip.

The reprieve proved to be short-lived. Before long, even as he wrapped his sister in another embrace, Romero's eyes moved past her, taking in Jack with a look that suggested an understanding that something beyond a simple visit had brought them to Caracas.

Before Jack could say anything, he saw Romero glance around, his face assuming a puzzled expression. "Where are my nephews?" he asked in his deep baritone voice.

Jack reached over and took Espy's hand, then refocused his attention on his brother-in-law. "We need your help."

In the span of a few seconds, Romero's face darkened, concern leaching away the joy of the unexpected visit. He locked eyes with Jack, then moved his gaze to take in his sister. "What has happened?"

Jack released a heavy sigh, wondering where to begin. "Let's go to your office."

Romero nodded and started to lead the way, Espy following. Jack started after them, but then he paused to return to its case the beautifully wrought pre-Columbian ax that had somehow managed to appear in his hand. When he looked up, he found Romero staring back at him, wearing a frown.

"Old habit," Jack said with a shrug.

Romero sat at his desk, his hands entwined on its wooden surface, a thoughtful look on his face. He hadn't said anything for several moments, although the longer the tale went, the more he leaned his large frame toward Espy's chair, as if in some unconscious protective gesture.

While he considered what Jack had told him, it struck Jack how silent it was in the store. Knowing his boys, he knew they would be out on the sales floor, two thousand square feet of near-priceless objects their playground. Romero would have been a nervous wreck. At the moment, though, he imagined Romero wouldn't have had it any other way.

Jack shook that thought away and returned his attention to Romero, who had been silent for some time. Jack had watched a range of emotions play out across his brother-in-law's face, notably fear and a growing anger at the fate that had befallen his nephews.

"So you must do everything in your power to get your sons back," Romero concluded.

"The problem is figuring out the best way to do that," Jack said.

"Duckey says the boys will be safe for now," Espy added.

"And do you believe that?" Romero asked.

"I believe Duckey," Jack was quick to say. "Besides, McKeller needs something from me. It wouldn't make sense for him to hurt the boys."

Romero looked less than sure, but he let the matter drop. He leaned back, his large frame eliciting a groan from the chair. "Let me make certain I understand. Gordon Reese, the man you were afraid would have you killed while he still lived, decided to wait until he was dead before trying to accomplish the deed."

"In a nutshell," Jack said. He looked over at Espy and saw the beginnings of a frown.

"For the record," she said, "no one's said anything about wanting us dead."

Despite the circumstances, a smirk curled Romero's lip. Jack knew what he was thinking. Over the years, there had been a number of people who would have paid to see Jack dead. Reese was simply the one best positioned to make that happen. Except, even as he thought that, he knew it wasn't entirely true. There was another entity with the resources to see to his demise, and unlike Reese, they had the benefit of a shroud of secrecy. When Jack and Espy buried the bones of the prophet Elisha, they weren't just keeping them out of Reese's hands, they were removing them from the care of an ancient organization that had safeguarded them for millennia. Ever since that day, he'd wondered when they would come looking.

Espy, who'd lived through those events with him, was the one who could best understand his train of thought. "They're not involved," she said. "If they were going to come after us, they would have done so a long time ago."

Jack nodded in agreement, suspecting that if the original guardians of the bones were to ever come looking for them, he doubted they would go through the trouble of infiltrating the CIA.

"So now that you're in something of a holding pattern, what will you do?" Romero asked.

The question hung in the room, and the absence of an immediate answer told all three of them how few options they seemed to have.

"The one thing that keeps rolling around in my head is that this is a government agent we're dealing with," Jack finally said. "I mean, this isn't Reese. Even if it's an off-the-books operation, like Duckey says, McKeller will follow Company protocol."

Romero grunted. "From what you've told me, it would appear he is operating under a single directive: acquire the bones through whatever means necessary. And the very fact that it's an 'off-the-books operation,' as you say, means there are no rules. You're also speaking of a man driven by grief and fear."

"Which brings us back to me calling McKeller and making a trade—myself for Jim and Alex," Jack said.

Romero's head was shaking before Jack had finished. "You said Duckey considers this to be a rogue agent within your CIA. To me, that suggests a person who would leave no witnesses once he gets what he wants."

Jack had always appreciated Romero's ability to frame any situation within the confines of dispassionate truth. In this case, though, the potential collateral damage was too much to consider without it sending a shiver up his back. He saw those words have a similar effect on Espy.

"It's a risk I'm going to have to take," Jack said.

"If there is a rogue element within the CIA, then maybe there are factions that would like to know what this rogue element is doing?" Espy ventured.

Romero nodded. "Right. Have one set of dogs call off another."

"Or get this so out in the open that they can't do anything to us, regardless of whether or not they get the bones," Espy said.

Both of them turned to Jack.

"If doing something like that would help, Duckey would have suggested it," Jack said. "But he said the exact opposite. He thinks putting this out in the open is more dangerous for the boys. What it comes down to is that Ducks told us to run, to get as far away as we could. And I can't believe he would have done that if he thought there was any chance of us talking our way out of this mess."

Jack saw that both of them—especially Espy—would have liked to argue the point, but he knew neither of them would. When it came to dealing with the CIA, all of them knew only one man who qualified as an expert, and that man was Duckey.

Espy, who had again lapsed into silence, rose from the leather chair next to her husband and began to walk around her brother's office, reaching out a hand to run it along the smooth wood of his desk. After a few moments, she turned to the others.

"We had a chance to destroy them years ago and we didn't," she said. "I mean, we certainly should have for all the trouble they've brought us."

"Are you suggesting this man will believe you if you tell him the bones are gone?" Romero asked.

Espy shook her head. "What I'm saying is that instead of destroying them, we buried them in the desert. There was no reason to do that. Too many people died so that we could find them. We should have ground them to dust. But we didn't." She looked to Jack. "I think, maybe even subconsciously, we knew we'd have to find them again. We kept them around just in case. And the way I see it, this is the *just in case*."

What Espy was suggesting was obvious enough that Jack mentally kicked himself for not thinking of it. "You want to go and dig them up?" he asked her.

"I don't see any other way around it."

Though it was her idea, Espy's face was inscrutable. Jack traded a look with her that seemed to last a long while. What it came down to was that, ultimately, everything now happening to them was his fault. All of it stemmed from his decision to take a job more than a decade ago, a simple yes that had altered the course of many lives. To return to Australia was to revisit events and remember the people they were before having children, before getting married, and to become those people again, if only for a short time.

"Okay," he said.

She gave him a half smile. "As much as the idea of flying to Australia so that we can dig for bones in the desert doesn't appeal to me, what it comes down to is that if this man is as dangerous as Duckey says he is, our only chance of getting through this is if we have something to trade."

"So our next trick," Jack said, "is to figure out how to get me to Australia without buying a ticket on a commercial airline or showing my passport to anyone."

"If there's one person I'd trust to figure out how to travel a few thousand miles without spending a dime, and sneaking into a place you don't belong, I'd put all my money on you. Except there's just one thing wrong."

Jack raised an eyebrow.

"There's no way I'm staying behind," she said.

She delivered the message in a tone Jack knew well—one he'd never successfully argued against in the almost two decades of their relationship. So he didn't even bother trying. Instead he turned to Romero. "Think you can help facilitate travel arrangements?"

Even before he finished the question, he could tell something was wrong. Romero was sitting more upright in his chair than normal, his hands in front of him on the desk, one with a strong grip on the other. In all the time Jack had known Romero, he'd never seen him nervous, excepting those occasions in their younger days when Jack may or may not have gotten him into a sticky situation or two. What Jack was witnessing now, though, was a different sort of nervousness, one he couldn't decipher.

Espy frowned, which told Jack he wasn't imagining things.

"What's wrong?" Jack asked. He could feel his stomach tightening, almost as if he knew what his friend was going to say.

The Venezuelan shopkeeper didn't answer right away. It was all he could do to meet Jack's eyes.

"I don't think you'll find them," Romero said, the words coming grudgingly.

"Won't find what?" Jack asked, despite already knowing the answer.

Romero released a heavy sigh, after which he stilled his hands and leveled his gaze. "I went looking for them. A few months after you returned from Australia."

"You did what?" Espy asked.

The steel in her voice made her brother wince. "I didn't find them," he said. He was speaking to Jack rather than to his sister, perhaps assuming a more sympathetic ear.

Espy stood, placed both her hands on the desk, and leaned in closer to her brother, looking him in the eyes. "Why would you go looking for them?"

"Because they're worth a fortune," Jack answered for him. And then he did the only thing that seemed appropriate: he started to laugh. It was a thin, sardonic laugh.

To his credit, Romero didn't flinch beneath his sister's glare. "Because they're worth a fortune," he affirmed. "I thought I would recover the bones and market them to a select list of my former clients."

Espy's shoulders tensed and her back went rigid. Her small fist came down hard on the wood of her brother's desk, causing both men to nearly jump from their chairs.

"What were you thinking?" she asked. "After what we went through to find them, do you think anyone had a stronger claim?" She paused, as if waiting for an answer—one that didn't come. "But we decided no one should ever use them again. Then you come along and think to dig them up and sell them?" Her fist came down a second time, causing Romero's phone to rattle.

As Jack watched the scene play out, he found it odd that he wasn't angrier than he was, even as he suspected the reasons for his calm. The first was that Espy was doing a better job of verbally eviscerating her brother than Jack could ever have hoped to. The second was that, if he was going to be honest with himself, what Romero had done wasn't a complete surprise.

In some ways, Romero and Jack were cut from the same cloth. Jack could picture himself in his brother-in-law's shoes. If he knew that something priceless was out there, something not just valuable but also vested with the very power of God, he doubted he could avoid seeking it out. He knew Romero well enough to understand the battle he'd fought—and ultimately lost.

"As I said, I didn't find them," Romero said.

Jack's eyes narrowed. "It's a big desert. So if you didn't find them, what makes you think they're gone?"

"Because before I made the attempt, I chanced a few inquiries to gauge the interest of some of my wealthier clients," Romero explained. "At the time, none of them seemed willing to part with the sort of money I thought the find warranted."

"But you went anyway," Jack said.

"I just had to," he said with a sigh. "But while I'm convinced I was in the right area, I couldn't locate them. After a week had passed, and after missing a few sales here, I gave up the search."

"But someone else didn't," Jack guessed.

"Perhaps a week after I returned, I received an inquiry from a man who had never purchased anything from me but whose name I knew from the London circle."

"So the feelers you put out spread a bit further than you'd intended," Jack chided.

"As I expected they would. Yet I considered the story fantastic enough to discourage anyone who heard it secondhand from believing it to be anything other than fiction."

Jack granted him that with a nod.

"But someone believed it," Espy said.

Jack straightened in his chair, an ominous idea forming. But before he could put voice to it, Romero responded to his sister.

"His name is Quinn Chambers," Romero said. "He's a member of the House of Lords, and a major player in the aerospace industry. He comes from some of the oldest money in Britain."

Espy looked between Jack and Romero, as if suspecting that

something had passed between them. She adopted a puzzled look.

"It's them," Jack said. "This Quinn Chambers is one of them."

The *them* was the nameless, faceless organization that had watched over Elisha's bones for thousands of years. Jack had met one of them in Australia: George Manheim, a man he'd watched die at the hand of Manheim's own son. A member of a secret fraternity charged with protecting the prophet's remains. Jack had always known they were the ones who got him and Espy sprung from an Australian holding cell, and who had all records of what happened there either sealed or erased. He'd never known why; he still didn't.

"That was my thought as well, though not immediately," Romero said. "At first, I thought he was simply a very wealthy man with a desire to own something extraordinary. Only later did I begin to suspect something else, and then only after some surreptitious research."

"But you couldn't find the bones," Jack said. "What good, then, could you have been to this guy?"

"That was what I told him. But he still promised half of my original asking price simply for telling him the general location of my search area." Romero looked up, and while there was no pleading in his eyes, there was something close to it. "Half of what I was asking just to point to a spot on the map. For items I'd given up on finding."

Jack was forced to admit that it would be a difficult deal to pass up. He was tempted to ask how much Romero got for the information but let the urge pass.

"What makes you think he would have been any more successful than you were?" Espy asked. She pushed away from the desk, and her body language showed she wasn't yet ready to release her anger, although she didn't look as driven to hit her brother.

Jack was the one who answered. "Because if the man belongs to this organization, he has all the resources he needs to comb every square inch of that desert until he finds them."

"So they got the bones," Espy said slowly. "Alex . . . Jim . . ."

A heaviness settled over the room as all of them considered the implications of Espy's words.

Having established that their only chance of getting out of their predicament involved retrieving the bones and trading them to McKeller for the boys, and then discovering the bones had likely been reclaimed by their caretakers—thus putting them out of reach—left Jack feeling more weary than he had in a long while. "Right now, we can only act on what we know for sure," he said. "Thirteen years ago, we buried the bones in the Australian desert. Until we find out otherwise, we have to assume they're still there."

He looked for a glimmer of hope in Espy's eyes but didn't see any. What he did see was the strength that Espy had carried through all of their past trials.

Jack turned to Romero. "Now, about those travel arrangements. I'm thinking you'll want to cover the cost of that?" He gave his brother-in-law a shrewd smile.

6

JACK THOUGHT IT INCONGRUOUS THAT, as the desert stretched out before them, he felt a chill. He knew the reason for it: the last time he was here, it was to fashion an end to one of the most defining episodes in his life—a span of weeks that wrought personal, vocational, and emotional change in violent fashion. Now they had come to undo an interment they'd thought permanent—if someone else hadn't already accomplished that task.

When they'd chosen to remove the relics' influence from the world, he and Espy had wanted to place them beyond even accidental discovery. So, despite their reluctance to once again venture into such a forbidding environment after having survived in the desert for several days with no shelter, no food, and little water, they chose to see the task through as best they could. Which was why this return trip saw them sitting in a Toyota Land Cruiser almost 150 miles from the nearest thing resembling a road, the ticking of the truck's engine the only thing breaking the complete silence.

After the passing of so many years, Jack was worried they wouldn't be able to find the spot, no matter the GPS coordinates he'd jotted down. The sameness of the landscape, the shattered rock and sand of the gibber plain, continued into a point on the horizon with only a few hardy plants and small rock formations to provide any sense of depth. Around them, the Great Victoria Desert spread out in every direction, the road they'd left hours ago—National Highway 1, running along Australia's southern coast—well behind them. To the north was the Plumridge Lakes Nature Preserve, seen from their position as only a faint line marking a change in elevation.

Jack sent his eyes out over the terrain, trying to find the spot without reverting to the GPS, but he couldn't see anything that made any one spot different from any other. He thought he possessed a decent mental picture of the place where they'd buried the bones, but now that he was there, he was discovering the image he'd carried with him could have been reproduced a hundred times within a single square mile of the place.

"Romero could have dug holes for a hundred years and never found the bones," Espy remarked.

"Even with the GPS coordinates, I have my doubts *we're* going to find them," Jack said.

Espy's lip curled as she reached for the door handle. Jack followed suit, and moments later they were standing beneath a sun heating the air around them to almost ninety degrees, with no cloud cover to offer respite. The GPS tracker in Jack's hand told him he should have been almost on top of the burial site, within ten meters. So after exchanging a look with his wife, he stepped away from the truck and headed north.

Under his feet, the rock-covered ground appeared untouched, as if no human had ever set foot or wheel on it. It gave him hope that in spite of the wealth of resources someone like Quinn Chambers commanded, even he might have come away from his quest empty-handed.

As he crossed the forbidding landscape, he wondered again why he and Espy had not destroyed the bones. In the clear light cast by more than a decade of distance, the only real answer seemed to be that preserving the bones was a self-serving act. By not destroying them when he had a chance, he'd ensured that he could use them again in the future.

Except that he wasn't certain that was the entirety of it. He wondered if there was another reason, a more primal one—one rooted in fear, in the power of stories told to children.

"It's a serious thing to destroy something touched by the hand of God," he said quietly, the desert wind seeming to carry the words away.

When they came to the spot—at least according to the GPS tracker—they found a nondescript plot of land that looked identical to every other like-sized plot of land around it. There were no obvious signs that anyone had been there in the intervening years, but after more than a decade, the weathering of desert forces would have removed any such traces.

"Does this look right to you?" Jack asked.

Espy frowned. "We buried them thirteen years ago, after running for our lives across three continents, seeing I don't know how many people killed, and then spending almost a week in a foreign prison, and I'm supposed to remember which rocks might have been where?"

"Good point," Jack said.

With the absence of any certainty beyond the GPS tracker, Jack returned to the Land Cruiser, opened the back, and took out a shovel. He returned to where Espy waited and began digging. The sun was hot on Jack's back as he drove the shovel into ground harder than he remembered it being, and it wasn't long before he was sweating. After a while he took a break, and Espy handed him a bottle of water. He drained half the bottle, then got back to work.

Jack remembered that he'd buried the relics deep, a good three to four feet down. So he worked for a long while, widening the hole, cutting down a few more inches, then widening the hole again. After an hour he had opened a crater some six feet in diameter and a little more than two feet deep. His shirt was soaked through. Breathing heavily, he tossed the shovel down and sat on the rim of the hole, where he drained a second bottle of water.

Espy, who had been watching in silence since her husband started, causing Jack to lament the fact that they'd brought just the one shovel, took a seat next to him.

"I'm beginning to think we're not in the right spot," he said.

She didn't answer right away. Her eyes were focused on the landscape past the dig site. After a time, she reached over and put a hand on his knee. "We're in the right place," she said.

Jack looked over and saw that she was still looking off into the distance, as if she could see something he couldn't.

"What happened to not remembering which rocks were where thirteen years ago?" he asked.

"I still don't. But somehow I just know. Almost like I can feel them under our feet." She chuckled and shook her head. "It's ridiculous, I know."

"Absolutely absurd," he said.

Espy's practice of the faith they both shared had always differed from his. Her faith was more intuitive; she felt God's influence on a much more personal level than did he. Jack knew himself well enough to realize that his faith was a decidedly more empirical thing. Unless he could see it, touch it, and turn it into something he could understand on a logical or philosophical level, he had a hard time buying into it. It was a makeup that had kept him away from the religion of his parents for so long, that had kept him from giving God more than a passing thought. In fact, if he owed anything to the ordeal that had ended in this desert years ago, it was that its culmination gave him the chance to witness the very real power of God on a level too grand for him to deny.

Espy, on the other hand, would have still believed even if she'd never witnessed the bones raise someone from the dead.

Espy patted his leg and stood. Crossing to where he'd dropped the shovel, she retrieved it and, picking a spot within the crater, started to dig. And Jack unashamedly leaned back and let her.

Espy drove the shovel into the hard ground, using her foot to push the implement deeper. As she did, Jack began to wonder if the fact that the ground was so packed was proof this wasn't the right place. Even after so long, and even if no one came after them to remove what they'd hidden, the ground under which the relics were buried shouldn't have been as densely packed as the ground around it. It was a discouraging thought, and so Jack decided to ignore it for the time being, choosing instead to watch his wife dig with holy purpose.

Fifteen minutes passed and Espy had cut through another six inches, but her diameter was smaller, maybe two feet. Jack took another sip of water and then stood, ready to take over. He stretched his legs, giving extra attention to the bad knee, then started toward Espy. He'd almost reached her when the shovel came down again. Espy gasped.

By the time Jack reached her, she'd pulled the shovel away

and her eyes were on the hole, on the piece of rotted fabric in which the bones of the prophet Elisha had been wrapped. The wrappings were old. While not the original burial cloth, Jack had once dated them to the ninth century. The portion he saw peeking up from beneath the earth looked every bit of those intervening centuries. He shared a celebratory grin with Espy before going to his knees and using his hand to brush away the dirt from around the cloth.

It took only a minute before he recognized that something was wrong. As he worked to expose more of the cloth, irritated that he didn't have any of the tools he would have normally used in the field, the portion of fabric already exposed moved, although he hadn't touched it. Rather, it moved as the dirt around it moved, as if the cloth he saw wasn't anchored to anything below. It was worrisome enough to cause Jack to go against every archaeological instinct he had. With his finger and thumb he took the corner of the cloth and tugged. It came up too easily, a small portion of fabric about two inches by three inches. He stifled a curse, but the sick feeling in the pit of his stomach returned.

He looked at Espy and saw a mirror of his own thoughts. Then, casting protocol aside, he took the shovel back from Espy and started to dig. He drove the point of the shovel well beneath the spot that had yielded the scrap of fabric, and the first thing that struck him was that the dirt felt looser there, a telltale sign that someone or something had filled in a hole. Twenty frantic minutes later, Jack had removed another foot of dirt, widening the area where Espy was working until he found the edges, the place where the dirt was again packed solid. There was nothing there, yet he kept digging another few inches downward, until the shovel felt the same resistance from beneath. Only then did he straighten. The red dust of the place had caked his clothes. Lines of rust-colored sweat ran down his face and arms. Jack stood and looked down in the empty hole, feeling something like violation that the secrets they'd deposited there were once again loosed to the world.

Jack stood there for just a short while until, without a word, he turned and headed back to the truck, Espy at his side. They didn't bother filling in the hole.

———

It was full dark as Jack guided the Land Cruiser toward the Adelaide airport. He'd never been to the city prior to touching down that morning, and in their rush to get to the desert, he'd had no chance to take in any of it. Coming back at night deprived him of any view beyond the city lights, which were impressive in their own right. Espy, though, was in no position to enjoy them. She'd been out most of the last two hours, the flat sameness of the desert lulling her to a sleep Jack knew she needed. She didn't even stir when their steady speed slowed as they entered Adelaide's evening traffic flow.

Alone with his thoughts, Jack considered the silver lining to Romero's betrayal. As recompense, it was easy to talk him into floating them the money for their flights and expenses. Jack had no doubt he would have done so anyway, but there would have been a lot more grumbling—and less enjoyment for Jack.

In his previous life, Jack had been adept at traveling under the radar. After all, in addition to the important, well-connected people and organizations he'd ticked off over the years, there were a number of other people, spread across the globe, who wouldn't have passed up the opportunity to do him harm.

Most of those people, ironically enough, had developed those feelings over loans—advances he might have neglected to repay for one reason or another. He knew that Romero, who'd been with him when some of those loans were made, suspected he might join the ranks of Jack's creditors, but in this instance, Jack doubted he would complain too strongly.

What Romero's money had enabled him to do was to take advantage of the one thing that most countries had in common, the thing designed to keep people like Jack and Espy out: paperwork.

In this case, Romero used actual paper, in the form of a great deal of money, to facilitate the procurement of two clean passports. The deal was made possible because of the nature of Romero's business, which while about as clean as an antiquities reseller could be, was nonetheless helped on occasion by the cultivation of friends with some influence in the area of foreign commerce. Sometimes it could be difficult to get a questionably procured artifact through customs.

Romero had gone local, finding new identities for them in the form of Venezuelan passports. With Espy, it had been a simple matter to find an existing Venezuelan passport featuring a woman with enough physical similarities to pass for her. Even finding a doppelganger for Jack hadn't been that difficult, with the mix of ethnicities in Venezuela. In Jack's opinion, the only thing that could trip them up was if he was forced into a lengthy conversation. While his Spanish was passable, there was no hope of him fooling someone into thinking he was a native. Fortunately, though, the duplicate passport in his possession listed him as one Julien Mendoza, Doctor of Psychiatry, which gave him an excuse to seem distant, even odd, as he passed through security checkpoints.

The fact that Romero went for Venezuelan passports instead of American ones was a stroke of genius, and one that Jack hoped would give them an edge on their adversaries. If Duckey was correct, if McKeller had only a small handful of people he could count on, then he wouldn't be able to use any Company resources in either Venezuela or Australia. But if the man had the foresight to place a team in Venezuela early in the operation, they would almost certainly be watching for American-issue travel documents.

Jack pulled the Land Cruiser off the A13 and onto the A6, then onto Sir Richard Williams Avenue, the wide treelined road still busy with traffic despite the hour. Not long after that, he pulled into the parking lot of an Avis rental location. They had almost two hours before their flight departed, which would take them to Sydney for the first of three layovers before reaching Caracas.

Before booking the flight, he'd debated the merits of returning to Venezuela. With the dead end in the desert, the inactive Company phone in his pocket nearly begged for use, telling Jack that with his hope of procuring the bones now dashed, he had to barter with the only asset he had: himself.

While he trusted Duckey's assessment of the boys' safety, he couldn't allow them to remain in government custody indefinitely—if for no other reason than because of how frightened he knew they had to be. And it wasn't just his sons who concerned him; when he and Espy had discovered the bones missing, his wife's demeanor had changed, almost as if someone had flipped a switch. She looked tired, defeated.

Still, there was some indefinable something that caused him to rebel against the idea of replacing the phone's battery and SIM card. He knew what that something was. It was the part of him that refused to admit that some things were out of his control. Once he made the call, it would be tantamount to admitting defeat, and while he didn't have a clear course of action, he couldn't bring himself to take the phone out of his pocket.

Espy resisted his first attempts to wake her, but soon she was wiping sleep from her eyes and looking through the window at the lines of parked cars.

"I guess we're here," she said.

"Indeed we are, Ms. Muñoz."

Espy, or Valentina Muñoz, according to her new passport, curled her lip in distaste at her new moniker and reached for the door handle. Minutes later, they were on the airport shuttle. In transit, Jack slipped one of the disposable phones from his pocket to see if either Romero or Duckey had called, only to find that the battery had died during the trip back from the Australian version of God's country.

"They don't make these things to last, do they?" he remarked before sliding the useless thing back in his pocket. Both Romero and Duckey had the numbers to the other phones, as well as the order of use for each, so if they felt an urgent need to reach Jack, they would have left messages on the next phone, which happened to be in the travel bag racked at the front of the shuttle.

Before long they reached the airport, where Jack and Espy grabbed their bags, exited the shuttle along with about a dozen other people, and followed the lines on the pavement meant to herd them into the terminal. Once inside, Jack stopped to get his bearings, looking for the e-ticket area. Once he located it, he used a preloaded American Express card to secure their boarding passes. That accomplished, he set his mind to what he considered the most pressing task of the last several hours:

finding someplace to eat. The airport offered a wide range of eateries, and it wasn't long before Jack and Espy were comfortably seated in one of the nicer establishments, scanning the menu.

Since it was running into the later hours, the restaurant was only half full, with most travelers having caught their outgoing flights already. Jack leaned back in his seat and did his best to lose himself to the experience, it suddenly occurring to him how much he'd missed this sort of thing. Since returning to Evanston almost eight years ago, he hadn't done much traveling, save the occasional trip to Caracas to see Espy's family. As a younger man, he seldom felt as alive as he did when hopping from country to country, even on those occasions when he was doing so under duress.

He glanced over at Espy, surprised to see what looked like a similar sentiment in her expression. At that moment, Jack was struck by how familiar all of it was. The place was different, but the players were the same, and the circumstances similar enough to others in which they'd been. Over the years, with Jack returning to Evanston and Espy leaving the University of Caracas to accept a position there, then becoming parents, and having to deal with Jim's condition, much of what they'd experienced earlier in their relationship had become buried beneath the rest of it. But at its heart, Jack and Espy's relationship had been forged through trial, through frantic flight, through working together to put enough pieces of a puzzle together so they could come out of a tricky situation alive.

He reached over and placed a hand atop his wife's.

"I've missed this," Espy said with a tired smile.

"You've missed false identities, people trying to kill us, and bullets flying?" he asked.

Esperanza pretended to consider that for a while, but the smile never left her face, and the answer she gave was devoid of any reminder that, as yet, no one had tried to kill them.

"Absolutely," she said.

Jack chuckled and released her hand. He looked at his watch. Boarding was still more than an hour away.

They took a few minutes to study the menu and the waiter took their order.

"What now?" Espy asked when he left.

The question caught Jack off guard, butting up against the sense of relaxation he'd just manufactured. Then he remembered that in those lost days, Espy was most often the one resetting their compass.

"I don't know," he admitted. "Now that the bones are gone, probably back in the possession of their guardians, I'm becoming convinced that our only option is for me to turn myself in."

Perhaps it was the setting, the foreign scenery and the sense of distance that allowed him to say something like that without feeling some kind of panic. Whatever the reason, he felt reasonably calm about the prospect.

Espy responded with a thoughtful nod. "What about this Quinn Chambers?"

"What about him?"

"Well, he's in London and we're going to Venezuela." She paused as another traveler walked past, a man who took a seat at a nearby table. "If he's the one who dug up the bones, why are we going in the opposite direction?"

"How about because, if I'm right, he's a member of the organization formed to protect the bones? The ones who for some reason decided to let us live? Who know our address, our kids' names, your shoe size, and the fact that I always properly toast my cigars before I smoke them?"

Jack didn't know where all of it came from, but he knew every word of it was true. A brotherhood more than three thousand years old, that had watched the rise and fall of civilizations, that was old even when Christ was born and prophecy fulfilled, certainly knew the minutiae of the lives of the two people who'd stolen their charge and hidden it away.

Espy listened, sampled her sparkling water, then nodded. She didn't say anything for a while after that, but Jack could see her thinking.

"Do you remember when Jim and Meredith were killed?" she asked.

It was a question she couldn't have asked without eliciting a near visceral response from him. She knew the guilt he'd carried since the Winfields' deaths.

When Jack was first hired to search for Elisha's bones, Dr. Jim Winfield, his friend and mentor, and Jim's wife, Meredith, had been murdered by rogue members of the organization charged with the care of the bones. He and Espy had barely escaped with their lives, and Jack had carried that guilt with him over the intervening years.

"Of course I do," Jack said.

She nodded. She moved her hand to the water glass, but didn't lift it. "Do you remember when we were sitting in the truck, wondering what we were going to do? Jim and Meredith were dead, you'd just killed two people, and their whole house was going up. I'm sitting next to you and I'm ready to lose it. Do you remember what you did?"

Jack did, yet he didn't say anything.

"You drove us into town, got us clothes and food, and then

turned us straight for the people who'd killed Jim and Meredith. Without a second thought, you just pointed the truck in that direction and took us to face the ones who'd chased us halfway across the globe."

"And ended up getting us stranded in the desert," he reminded her.

"Not the point," she said. "What *is* the point is that you made a decision to confront the people who were after us. You didn't wallow in Jim's death; you acted."

And those actions had consequences that were still making themselves manifest. But Jack understood what she was saying. "So you want to go to London and find the guy who had the nerve to dig up the bones we buried?"

"Precisely."

"And if we show up at his doorstep, what then? Tell him that some rogue CIA agent is after us, and would he be so kind as to let us have the bones back so we can turn them over to the American government?" He was trying to keep his voice low, but the restaurant was quiet. He saw the man at the nearest table glance in his direction.

"I don't know what we'd do," Espy said. "The only thing I feel reasonably confident about is that going back to Caracas isn't the right thing."

"What about the boys?"

For that, she had no immediate answer. Jack saw a flash of pain mar her features.

"You don't think I'm scared to death?" she asked. "Not a minute goes by when I don't wonder what's happening to them. But what do you think will happen if you call McKeller and don't have anything to trade but your own skin?"

Jack didn't have a rebuttal. Everything Espy had said made

sense. The proper course of action was to confront the demons head on, to force their hand. The only issue he was running into was that the organization of which Quinn Chambers appeared to be a part did not have a hand that needed forcing. They'd accomplished what they'd set out to do: they'd recovered Elisha's bones. The only other agenda item they might possibly have had an interest in was the elimination of anyone who knew their secrets. And since that group included him and Espy, he didn't see their rushing off to pick a fight with them as wise. Still, Espy was right. If they returned to Venezuela, what good would that do?

"Let me call your brother and let him know we're changing plans." He retrieved the phone from his pocket, forgetting about the dead battery. Setting the phone on the table, he got his bag from the floor and fished around for a new phone, checking the number until he found the next one in line. When he looked up, he caught the eye of the man sitting near Espy. It wasn't the fact that he was looking at Jack that piqued his interest; it was the way he quickly broke eye contact. Jack watched for a few seconds longer, but the man—wearing jeans and an Adelaide United football jersey—didn't look up again. He was nursing a draft beer and looked content to continue nursing it. Even so, Jack kept an eye on him as he dialed Romero's secondary number, the one he gave when he purchased the new disposable phone at the Caracas airport.

The phone didn't get past the first ring before Romero answered.

"Where are you?" Romero asked, the abruptness and urgency of the question putting Jack on the defensive.

"We're at the airport. Our flight leaves in about thirty minutes."

"I tried to call you on the other phone. You need to get out of the airport."

Even before he asked why, Jack was preparing himself to move. Although he hadn't yet motioned for Espy to stand, she was already picking up on the fact that something was wrong.

"Valentina Muñoz was detained by airport security two hours ago," Romero said. "Apparently she had a speaking engagement at Berkeley and they nabbed her for being in two places at the same time."

Jack's mind was going in a hundred different directions. If the computer caught the real Valentina Muñoz, then it wouldn't take long for them to figure out where the fake one went. He looked at Espy, who was silently imploring him to tell her what was going on. He gave her a quick headshake and returned his attention to Romero. "Two hours ago?"

"I have a friend in the Ministry of Interior and Justice. He's the one who gave me the passports. He said they took her from the airport in handcuffs." Romero paused. "It was quite the spectacle."

"I imagine it was," Jack said, even as he wondered what it meant for him. The only certainty was that, with Espy's fake passport flagged, there was no way she could board the plane. Beyond that, he wasn't certain. Australia was a long way away from either the States or Venezuela—much too far for McKeller to send a team that stood any chance of finding Jack and Espy in the airport. He realized he was still operating under the assumption of an off-record mission, but it was all he had at the moment.

Jack's eyes were drawn to the man sitting near them, the one who he now noticed had no luggage, not even a carryon.

The man who seemed to be taking great pains to avoid looking in their direction.

"Thanks, Mom," Jack said, a bit louder than the situation warranted. "I love you too." He ended the call as Romero was still speaking, ignoring the question in Espy's eyes. "We're going to start boarding soon, sweetheart. We should probably get moving."

Taking her cues from Jack, Espy rose and grabbed her bag. Jack tossed some money on the table, and then he and Espy started off. He avoided looking over his shoulder.

Their departure gate was B4, toward the end of the concourse. Jack put a hand to Espy's back and guided her toward it, taking in their surroundings, cataloguing all of it. They passed a number of retail establishments, and he began looking for one they could duck into without drawing attention. He spotted a place to their left that was showing off cakes and chocolates in their storefront display and steered Espy toward it. Once they stepped inside, Jack glanced back the way they'd come. He saw the man immediately, the one from the restaurant. He was walking in the same direction, and as he reached the confection shop, he hesitated for just a second before proceeding. It was enough to let Jack know he was right.

"What's going on?" Espy asked, but Jack didn't have time to tell her. He looked around the shop. There was no way out other than the way they'd entered.

"We're being watched. Just stay close and be ready."

With Espy in tow, he left the shop. Instead of continuing toward their departure gate, he reversed course and headed toward an escalator. The big question, the one he couldn't answer, was whether this guy was alone. If McKeller couldn't have sent anyone to Australia so quickly, the man had to be a local mercenary. But was he the only one?

Jack set the pace, hurrying while trying to look as if he wasn't hurrying. When they reached the escalator, he looked over his shoulder just in time to see their tail disappear behind a trio of travelers standing in front of a newsstand. Jack turned and smiled at Espy, just to let the guy know he wasn't suspecting anything, then took her elbow and directed her onto the escalator. They gave the descending staircase a little help, walking the stairs as they were carried downward. Once they reached the bottom, Jack glanced back and saw him again. This time their eyes locked, and Jack knew the subterfuge was over.

"Let's go," he said, striding fast toward the exit. They passed the security checkpoint, where he scanned the terminal, looking for a potential partner for their pursuer. The more he thought about it, the more convinced he was that this guy had backup.

Jack saw the movement out of the corner of his eye, someone running out from behind the information booth. Jack had just enough time to push Espy out of the way before he was leveled. Breath was forced from his lungs in a rush and he crumpled beneath the mass of his attacker. He heard a scream and the only thing he registered was that it wasn't Espy.

The man on top of him was using his weight to hold Jack to the floor while with his free hand he delivered punches to Jack's side. Jack was at a bad angle, his face to the carpet, left arm pinned beneath him. Somehow he freed his arm and rolled onto his back, taking some of the assailant's weight off him. Then he lashed out with his left hand, a clumsy blow that nonetheless caught the man under his eye. Jack heard a grunt, and the other man pulled back for a moment, giving Jack enough time to hit him again.

Then he saw the gun. It was in a shoulder holster, hidden beneath the attacker's coat. Clamping a hand around Jack's throat, the man reached for the weapon, his weight pressing down. Jack grabbed at his gun hand, but he had no leverage. The man's hand tightened around Jack's windpipe. A moment later the gun was free and swinging toward Jack.

The gun was almost to Jack's head when he saw his attacker jerk upward, felt the hold on his neck loosen. Jack drew a quick breath, the air burning his lungs before the hand tightened again. But the man was jerked up a second time, and Jack heard an accompanying groan. He twisted his head against the tight grip just in time to see Espy's booted foot come up. The third try did the job, sending the attacker rolling off, the gun tumbling to the floor.

Espy offered a hand and helped Jack to his feet. A wave of dizziness nearly took him down again, but he steadied himself, found his bag, and started off after his wife. Looking back, Jack saw their original tail just emerging from the escalator. That told him the fight couldn't have lasted more than five seconds. It just seemed a lot longer.

As Jack and Espy made their escape, Jack saw dozens of heads turned in their direction. He ignored them and hurried toward the exit. There were two men after them now, and Jack doubted either one was saddled with a bad knee. By the time husband and wife hit the baggage claim area, their pursuers were almost on top of them again. As Jack did his best version of a sprint past a moving carousel, he grabbed a suitcase, came to a quick stop, and putting as much force behind it as he could, brought the suitcase into contact with the sternum of the man Espy had kicked in the kidney. The momentum of the suitcase stopped the man cold, sending him backward into his partner. The blow caused the suitcase to burst open, sending a shower of clothes everywhere.

But when Jack pivoted to swing the suitcase, his knee had buckled, nearly sending him to the floor on top of the man he'd felled. Only Espy's hand kept him upright and they started off again, although Jack's knee slowed him.

Jack kept expecting a shot to come from behind, but they made it through the baggage claim area unscathed. Only now, as they neared the exit, they were presented with another obstacle. Airport security had mobilized, and there were two uniforms posted at the exit. They hadn't yet locked eyes on Jack and Espy but were scanning the crowd the way first responders do when assessing a situation. They knew they were supposed to be looking for something, though apparently they didn't have enough of the details to narrow their focus.

Jack stopped, the move catching Espy off guard. He reached for her hand as she flew past, slowing her, pulling her close. She gave him a puzzled look and started to look over his shoulder. "Don't," he said through his teeth.

So far, the security personnel weren't keeping people from walking in or out. So with his carryon slung over his shoulder, Jack walked toward the exit, ignoring the fact that two men with guns were quite possibly closing in from behind. They were less than ten feet from the exit when Jack saw the eyes of the security guys snap in his direction. He almost froze, but then Espy took the lead. She had his hand in hers and, wearing a smile, she kept going as if nothing was happening. Only then did Jack realize the guards were looking past him. Without turning around, he had a good mental picture of what the guards saw.

A few steps later saw them beneath the Adelaide night sky, and only then did Jack look back, just as the sliding doors shut behind them. The security guards had stepped away from the exit, advancing toward the two mercenaries. It was an interval Jack had to take advantage of.

The exit had deposited them in a high-traffic area, with a line of shuttle buses to the right and an area for individual pickups to the left. The setup reminded him that he and Espy had very little money, and now that Espy's identity had been compromised, Jack had to assume that anyone traveling with her had also been flagged. It meant that he was no longer a psychiatrist. It also meant that once they got past the paltry sum in travelers checks they still had, there wasn't much to fall back on. He thought he might have thirty American dollars in his wallet, which wouldn't buy them much of anything.

But they'd lived to fight another day.

He started off toward the far side of the road, toward a line of cabs that were their quickest way to leave the airport behind. In years past, Jack had been forced to melt into a foreign city, to settle back and wait for an opportunity to move. He suspected that would be the case now, but he and Espy couldn't initiate that assimilation until they were out of the fire.

They stepped out into the street, threading their way through two cars sitting in pickup spots. Jack was raising an arm to signal to one of the cabs when a shout came from behind him. He turned and saw a man in a suit emerging from around the corner of the terminal building. A third mercenary, his gun out, pointing in Jack's direction, shouting for them to stop.

Jack grabbed Espy's arm and propelled her toward the cab. He yanked open the back door and guided Espy in. Just before he slid in after her, he looked back, a hasty calculation telling him that they weren't going to make it, that there was no way he could get the cab driver to get them out of there before the gunman stopped them. Still, he was committed and so he jumped in and slammed the door, yelling at the woman behind the wheel to take off.

The woman behind the wheel was sleeping. When the door slammed, she straightened, her body arching forward. She looked in the rearview mirror, eyes wide. "Where to?" she asked once she'd registered the presence of customers. But by then it was too late.

The man ran out from between the same cars Jack and Espy had walked between, his momentum taking him out into the through lanes. Jack didn't know if the man was so focused on his quarry that he didn't see it or if he thought he could outrun it, but the shuttle bus slammed into him with a screech of brakes. Espy, watching the scene play out, gasped. It was over in an instant, the man's body landing somewhere beyond the field of vision of anyone in the cab.

The cab driver's eyes were on the accident, and Jack couldn't tell if she was going to get out of the car or drive off.

He leaned forward to get the driver's attention. "We're in kind of a hurry."

The driver looked at him in the rearview. He couldn't read the expression on her face, but after another moment of hesitation, she pulled away from the curb. Jack settled back in the seat just in time to see the other two men emerge from the terminal. Neither of them seemed to notice the cab. Instead they were focused on one of their own, who was lying motionless on the pavement, a crowd gathering.

Soon Jack and Espy were leaving the scene, pulling out onto Sir Richard Williams Avenue. Only then did Jack allow himself a sigh of relief, even as he considered the trouble they were in.

They were stuck in Australia.

7

✝

FOR MOST OF THE LAST FOUR HUNDRED miles, Jack had been silent, allowing the Australian landscape passing on either side of the truck to put him in a place where he could think. Espy too had remained quiet, lost in her thoughts.

The idea had come to Jack not long after he and Espy had left Adelaide behind. He knew it was the only thing that made sense, and also what had made their trip more somber than an escape from certain capture warranted.

From the second he saw the guy tailing them in the airport, he wondered how McKeller could have gotten someone there so quickly. Jack had no doubt the man had extensive contacts worldwide, but he still clung to the belief that McKeller did not have the luxury of contacting friends in every city on the globe. Yet the evidence seemed to indicate he had the freedom to do just that.

That was when another, more disturbing possibility presented itself. Back at the airport, when Jack spied the third man, the one who'd shouted for Jack and Espy to stop—it wasn't until later that Jack put a finger on something that had been nagging at him. It was the man's voice, the accent decidedly Australian. It didn't take long before Jack had convinced himself that the men at the airport weren't allied with McKeller.

Aside from his own government, there was only one organization Jack knew of that had the resources—and the motivation—to track him across continents. For the last decade, that mysterious entity had stayed its hand, had allowed Jack and Espy to live in peace. But was it possible that they might have viewed Jack's return to this place as a breaking of some unspoken truce?

The more he thought about it, the more it seemed to him that in trying to escape one monster, they had woken another.

Every once in a while their driver—an older woman named Esther, who'd picked them up in a place called Balranald—glanced over at her two passengers, all of them crammed into the front and only seat of the pickup, and seemed to regard them with curiosity. She'd tried to pull them into conversation early on, and Espy had done her best to reciprocate, but the dialogue had a strained quality that saw it end within the first few miles.

With the revelation that they now likely faced two adversaries, Jack and Espy had been forced to reconsider their decision to head to London. But the more they discussed it, the more it seemed to them that little had changed. What Jack kept returning to was that they needed Elisha's bones in order to secure the handing over of their children, and accomplishing that would have angered the guardians of the bones anyway.

The slowing of the truck pulled Jack out of his reverie. He refocused until he saw a sign just ahead. It said *Wallsend*. Esther took the exit and less than a minute later was pulling into a gas station. Jack looked down the road, saw nothing for miles. Soon Jack and Espy were standing in the gas station parking lot, bags in hand, watching the truck disappear, leaving them some seventy miles from Sydney. Once the truck disappeared around a curve in the road, Jack looked over at his wife.

"Do you ever get the feeling you've been someplace before?" he asked.

Espy smirked and started for the building. Esther had told them there were bus runs between Sydney and Newcastle, and as promised, Jack saw a sign marking the place as a stop. He followed Espy in and used some of their dwindling funds to buy sandwiches and water. Borrowing a bus schedule from the clerk, he noted the time of the next Sydney-bound bus, about thirty minutes away, then followed Espy outside, where they sank onto a bench partially shaded by a rusted metal overhang.

Once situated, Jack pulled out his phone and called Duckey.

"I have good news and bad news," Duckey said before Jack could get a word in. "Which one do you want first?"

"It's been a banner week," Jack said. "Surprise me."

"Your target's dead," Duckey said.

"My target?"

"Don't tell me you haven't already decided to go to London and track down this Quinn Chambers."

"He's dead?"

"Car crash, two years ago," Duckey confirmed. "Played chicken with a cement mixer."

"Suicide?"

"No one knows. All we know is there wasn't much left of him to identify. A closed casket deal, if you get my meaning."

Jack sat back heavily, feeling adrift. "What's the good news?"

"I lied. There isn't any," Duckey said.

"Thanks."

"Don't mention it."

"Now what?" Jack asked after a time.

"Beats me," Duckey said. "But since you'll probably end up going to London anyway, I took the liberty of digging up as much as I could about the deceased."

"And I'm guessing you wouldn't mention it if there wasn't something there," Jack said.

"Before you get too excited, I didn't find out a whole lot. Primary address, next of kin, major business concerns—that sort of thing. What I *can* tell you is that he had about as many irons in the fire as Reese did. Industry, politics, high society, there probably weren't too many influential people whose ear he didn't have."

A level of influence cultivated over thousands of years was the first thing that came to Jack's mind, but he kept that to himself. He hadn't told Duckey about his suspicions, that he believed Quinn Chambers was a part of the guardianship of the bones.

"Anyway, there's a lot here. I've gone through it and made some notes, but you probably need to take a look yourself."

"But both my phone and my computer now belong to the government," Jack said.

"We'll do it the old-fashioned way," Duckey said. "Once you get to London, find a copy shop with a fax machine."

"Are those still around?"

"I did notice one thing," Duckey said, ignoring him. "I don't know if this has anything to do with anything, but about every two years Chambers would take a trip to Paris. Always in October."

Jack turned that over but failed to see the significance. "Isn't

London to Paris a pretty common business trip for someone in his position?"

"It is, except that in the month before his death, he made the trip no less than four times." He paused, and there was the sound of pages rustling. "I'm not saying it means anything, but if something doesn't fit the pattern, that's what you should probably focus on."

"So you think those trips have something to do with the recovery of the bones from Australia?"

"I don't think any such thing," Duckey said. "All I'm saying is that our boy did something he doesn't normally do, and then he was dead a month later. You do with that what you will."

As Jack processed what Duckey was telling him, something about the track of the conversation was giving him pause, and it took several seconds before it hit him. When this thing started, it was just a recovery operation, one that took them first to Australia and now to London. But as far as Duckey knew, Chambers was just a rich collector who had something Jack needed. Except that what he was describing—unexplained trips to Paris, a mysterious death that may have been a suicide—spoke to some kind of conspiracy. It made him wonder if Duckey suspected more than he was letting on.

"I'm not an idiot, Jack," Duckey said, and the fact that he was addressing something Jack hadn't vocalized almost made him drop the phone. "Chambers approached your brother-in-law and got the information he needed in order to locate the bones, after which he mobilized sufficient resources to find them in the middle of a desert. Now, I don't know who this guy really is, but I'm guessing he didn't go to all that trouble just to have some trophy to set on his mantel."

"I think he's one of them, Ducks," Jack said.

"It's the only thing that makes sense. But if you're right, that means you're about to tick off a group of very powerful people. And need I remind you that you already have some of those after you?"

"It wouldn't be the first time," Jack said, deciding not to tell his friend that he suspected that horse was already out of the barn.

"But it may well be your last if you're not careful."

The road running in front of the gas station was quiet. Jack hadn't seen a single vehicle pass since he'd sat down. He looked up, squinting against the glare of the early afternoon sun. "I guess that's as good a segue as any. Ducks, I think you need to bow out of this now."

"I appreciate the sentiment, but I don't think that's your call," Duckey said.

"Except that this isn't you doing background research when Reese was after me. This is you putting yourself and Stephanie in danger. McKeller knows you're helping me. And once I make some new people mad, they'll figure that out too. Which means at some point they're going to force you to stop doing that."

"If that happens, I'll take care of it."

Out of all the people he knew, Jack believed Jim Duckett to be the one most capable of coming out on top in an altercation with a rogue CIA agent. But that didn't matter. He was about to say that when Duckey beat him to it.

"Jack, when Steph signed on, she knew what she was getting into. And if you think she'd let me write you off on account of her, then you don't know my wife like I thought you did."

Jack couldn't help but smile at that. He only hoped that Duckey didn't get in too deep.

"Understood, Ducks. And thanks."

"Don't mention it," his friend said.

When he hung up with Duckey, he sat on the bench next to his wife for a long while. He had almost dozed off when Espy reached over and took his hand.

"I think it's time to make the call," she said.

Jack knew the request was coming, and in truth he didn't disagree with her. While he had a strong desire to avoid contacting McKeller—while he agreed with Duckey when he said they stood a better chance of recovering the bones by working alone—he simply couldn't avoid initiating contact with the man who held his children.

He removed the phone from his pocket and reassembled it. After restoring power, he pulled up the list of calls made and received. There were several distinct numbers but one that stood out in frequency.

Someone picked up on the first ring.

"I'm assuming this is Dr. Hawthorne," a man's voice said.

"Which makes you Marcus McKeller," Jack returned.

That was greeted with a chuckle. "You're as resourceful as I expected you to be," McKeller said.

"Resourceful and very, very angry," Jack said.

McKeller didn't answer right away. When he did, Jack thought he heard a note of regret.

"It was not my objective to take your sons. However, one learns to be fluid when one runs into unforeseen snags."

"Did it ever occur to you to just knock on my door and ask me about the bones?"

That elicited another chuckle. "Had I felt certain you would have been forthcoming with the information I need, I would have done so."

"Except that I don't have anything you can use," Jack said. "The bones are gone, lost. I have no idea where they are."

"Then I suggest you find them," McKeller said. "Or you will never see Jim and Alex again."

At the sound of his sons' names, Jack felt anger rising. "Where are they?"

"Safe," McKeller said. "For now."

"Let me speak with them," Jack demanded.

"They're not here."

Jack's heart sank.

"I need you to come in, Dr. Hawthorne. I need you to tell me where you're going now that you've left Adelaide."

"I work alone," Jack said. "I always have."

"That's not how this is going to work," McKeller said.

"That's precisely how it's going to work," Jack countered. "You have my children, and my aim is to get them back. The only way I know how to do that is to find the bones so that you can take care of your wife. And to do that, I need to work alone."

Jack had taken a gamble in mentioning McKeller's wife. The man's pause indicated such. Jack took advantage of the break.

"I'll call you when I have them," he said. "And I promise you, if anything happens to my boys, you will pay dearly." Then Jack ended the call.

Not long after that, he and Espy were on a bus heading into Sydney. The phone, still powered on, lay in the back of a pickup heading the other direction.

8

✝

THERE WAS A CERTAIN SENSE of liberation that came
from having their options stripped away. Left with a single
choice, things became simple. That was what Esperanza's
flagged passport had accomplished. Unable to use the false
travel documents, Jack and Espy had reverted to their real
ones, along with his credit card to pay for the flights. And in
making that choice, Jack had announced their destination to
anyone who wanted to know. It was a matter of pragmatism
and it would either prove innocuous or get them killed.

Jack and Espy exited Heathrow and jostled with other ar-
rivals for a cab. Once they'd secured one, Jack pulled out his
current phone and made a reservation at a hotel near the airport, then settled back and analyzed their situation.

Part of that meant giving at least a passing thought to the
resources McKeller might call upon in London. He had to
have an array of friends. And that, coupled with the incredible breadth of video surveillance in London, suggested their
arrival had not gone unnoticed.

105

Regardless, he couldn't help but feel exhilarated that he was in London. The city had always been one of his favorites, and his present circumstances couldn't change that. He suspected the place reminded him of his old mentor. James Winfield had never stopped being a Londoner, even after years spent living abroad.

Jack had the driver take them a few miles into the city proper, where their first stop was at a bank. While Espy waited in the cab, Jack slid his American Express into an ATM and withdrew five hundred pounds, trying not to think about how he was going to pay for all this if they happened to survive into the next billing cycle. When he returned to the cab, he had the driver take them to the nearest copy shop, which deposited them on Camden High Street. As Jack paid the driver, he slid the phone he'd used to book the hotel room beneath the back seat of the cab. A few minutes later, he had Duckey on a clean phone. Not long after that, the fax machine in a little place called Prontaprint came to life.

It took what seemed an interminable length of time for the forty-page fax to run through, but then the stream of paper finally came to an end. After paying the bill, along with a tip sufficient to coax the clerk into letting them leave via the back door, Jack and Espy walked three blocks until they found a coffee shop. Once they'd ordered drinks, they found an open table farthest from the counter, where Jack handed Espy half the stack of paper.

"What am I looking for?" Espy asked.

"I don't have any idea," he said.

"How come I knew you were going to say that?"

They sat in silence for almost an hour, going page by page through the information Duckey thought important enough to send them. In some places, Duckey had included handwritten notes—comments on itineraries, monetary figures, even Quinn Chambers's personal life. But Jack wasn't seeing anything that jumped out at him, nothing that might tell him how the man was related to an ancient organization whose name Jack didn't even know.

They got through their respective stacks within a few minutes of each other, after which they switched and began again, hoping to catch something the other had missed. But after finishing, they were no closer to finding anything that might tie Quinn Chambers to the guardians. And with the man dead, Jack was starting to fear that any secrets he might have had died with him. He rubbed his eyes, took a sip of cold coffee.

"If nothing else, they're certainly an old family," Espy said.

"I picked up on that too," he said. "In fact, I'd be surprised if they weren't around when the first stone was set for the Tower of London."

"According to this, they've kept the ancestral property for almost eight hundred years."

Duckey's research said that King John made a gift of the property to the Chambers family in 1213 AD. From what Jack could see, the land, in an area now called Highgate, had remained in the family's possession since then, surviving famines, plagues, disease, and wars. The current home, a sixty-eight-room mansion known as Parkhurst, was completed in 1918 and had served as the family's seat of power ever since. It was at a time like this when Jack missed his computer, with which he could have pulled up a picture of the estate.

"Parkhurst is a monster," Espy said, scanning the paper. "Sixty-eight rooms, more than forty thousand square feet." She shook her head. "This is bigger than Reese's place."

Jack recalled his impressions of the Reese estate, when the man had first brought him there to discuss the job that had changed Jack's life. He had a difficult time picturing a structure more ostentatious.

"If you were a part of a family that had spent centuries connected with a secret society, and if that family had lived in the same place for more than eight hundred years, where do you think the likeliest spot to house a record of that relationship is?" Espy asked.

Jack leaned back in his seat, watching the people passing by in front of the coffee shop window. When he looked back at Espy, he released a sigh. "You know we'd be grasping at straws thinking we could walk into an estate that size and find anything at all, right?"

"Absolutely."

"And you're aware that incredibly wealthy people don't usually let nosy poor people walk in off the street and go through their things?"

"That's where you're wrong," Espy said.

"Come again?"

"Parkhurst has been designated as an English Heritage site. The Chambers estate allows tours two days a week."

That was good news, but it still didn't change the fact that a chaperoned walk through a massive place like Parkhurst was unlikely to yield the kind of information they needed. Jack wouldn't expect to find private letters between Chambers and other members of this secret society lying out in the open. Still, if experience had taught him nothing else, he'd learned that getting his hands dirty almost always yielded better results than trying to formulate a theory in a sterile environment.

"When's the next tour?" he asked.

London was the sort of city that seemed designed for someone whose intent was to remain unnoticed. The crush of people, the whole swaths of the city where buildings formed tight scrums, the continual turnover of the tourist population—all of it bred an environment suitable for finding a hole and staying there. So, with two days before the next tour of Parkhurst, Jack and Espy found a spot in which to burrow.

The hotel room Jack had booked from the cab remained unoccupied, Jack choosing another room on the other side of the city and paying with cash. His hope was that the misdirection would occupy the people hunting for them, at least for a while. By using the disposable to book the room in his real name, he also ensured that some of the enemy's resources would be spent tracking a cab around London.

Yet, despite those steps, there was simply no way for them to know if anyone was watching—either McKeller's men or emissaries of the organization that frightened Jack more than did the CIA. So Jack did the only thing that seemed logical: he simply ignored the possibility that there was someone outside their door. Getting Espy to do the same took some work, but the prospect of research aided him in that endeavor.

Over the last forty-eight hours, Jack and Espy had spent most of their time in the hotel's business center, sitting in front of the computer. The time, though, had been productive. Using Duckey's initial research as a jumping-off point, they had learned a great deal about the Chambers family—their rise as one of Britain's oldest and richest families, their politics, economic fortunes, even their scandals. They had also garnered much detail about their seat of power: Parkhurst. Of primary interest was the floor plan, indeed the original architectural drawings. Reviewing those had allowed Jack to get a feel for the whole of the mansion. He could see the layout in his mind, picture the different rooms, the winding staircases, the grand ballroom, the gallery hallway. He wanted to have the details right so that as they walked through it, they would stand a better chance of noticing something amiss: a wall that shouldn't have been there, a door where there was no door in the plans. He knew it was a long shot, but they had scant few other leads.

The tour started in a little more than an hour, and Jack and Espy were in the business center one last time, just to make sure they'd absorbed everything possible. But there came a point when the human mind resisted retaining anything more, and when that moment arrived, Jack closed the browser window.

"I think we're as ready as we'll ever be," he said.

Espy yawned in agreement, and before long they exited the hotel.

The cab ride to Highgate took about fifteen minutes. Even with a stop for coffee and pastries, they reached Parkhurst twenty minutes early for the tour and stood in the designated waiting area for several minutes before other tourists began to arrive. By the time Jack's watch read 9:59 a.m., there was a group of almost thirty people milling at the side gate, but no one had yet arrived to take control. Then, a few seconds before the watch clicked over to 10:00, a man in a tuxedo came into view, making his way toward the side gate via a cobblestone walkway that led from a freestanding smaller building to the gate.

When the man opened the gate, his imperious demeanor had the effect of corralling the tourists into something resembling a straight line. The man collected tickets and then herded the crowd past the gate, which he shut and locked behind them. Ten minutes later, after listening to the man discuss the grounds and the outbuildings, the group was standing in the entryway of the three-story Georgian-style mansion.

Jack couldn't help but feel an appreciation for the place, its history and all its details, the expert workmanship evident in every aspect of the mansion's construction. The styling, the embellishments evinced a knowledgeable aristocratic taste. He was fairly certain the painting he saw behind a red rope—a scene of a woman in black, in repose—was a Manet. He saw the same appreciation on Espy's face, but soon the moment was gone. The two of them had to get down to the serious business of finding their needle in a very large haystack.

Their guide led them through the lower level. The tour route seemed to stay within the center of the mansion, except for a walk through the drawing room in the back—a room with double doors that opened onto the perfectly manicured grounds. As they moved through the place, Jack tried to match what he was seeing with the architectural drawings he'd willed into his head. Of course, there was a good chance that the finished product differed from the original plans at the outset, prior to any secret doors and hidden rooms. Jack knew it wasn't uncommon for the person in charge of seeing an architect's vision brought to life to change things as the realities of constructing a building of this size arose.

Twenty minutes after stepping into the mansion, the group

was ascending one of the winding staircases to the second level. It was as they reached the top of the flight of stairs that Jack saw a woman emerge from a long hallway to his left, a direction in which the guide did not appear inclined to lead them. Jack knew that the woman was a member of the family that called this place home. He knew it from the way she carried herself, with a certainty that everything she touched, everything she saw, belonged to her. She gave off the impression of royalty as only someone from an old and powerful family could. The last clue to her identity came from the reaction of the tour guide. Instead of turning at the second stairway to descend to the first floor, the woman started coming toward the group.

"Ladies and gentlemen, this is a rare privilege indeed," the guide said with a marked change in his manner, an enthusiasm that appeared from nowhere. "This is Mrs. Chambers, Lady of Parkhurst."

The lady was striking, a pale beauty with skin that looked like parchment pulled tight over a frame.

A few of the tourists started to applaud, but it was a sad sound that faded almost immediately. Mrs. Chambers—Olivia, Jack recalled—stopped next to the tour guide and graced the crowd with a wide, insincere smile.

"Thank you for coming," she said. "I trust you're enjoying yourselves."

The group responded with nods of their heads and other acknowledgments and then, responding to the beckoning of the guide, began to move off. As they did, Jack and Espy lingered, allowing everyone else to go ahead. The guide, perhaps flustered by the arrival of Mrs. Chambers, didn't seem to notice he was leaving them behind. One person did, though. Olivia

Chambers observed them with eyes filled with either disinterest or contempt; Jack couldn't tell which.

"You have a lovely home, Mrs. Chambers," Espy said.

Mrs. Chambers didn't reply right away, not before giving Esperanza a once-over. Jack was included in that review, but only at a cursory level. "Thank you," Olivia said. "I enjoy allowing others the chance to experience it, if even for a short while."

"It's very kind of you," Espy said. "I believe I'd find it unnerving to allow strangers to walk through my home, gawking at the Manet or the Cellini sculpture. Perseus, if I'm not mistaken. And of course the Bayeux Tapestry in the drawing room. A reproduction, obviously."

She said the last with a smile as charming and as icy as the one worn by Mrs. Chambers, and Jack watched the words do their work, a flicker of something crossing the Englishwoman's face.

"You know your artwork," Chambers granted her. Her eyes moved to include Jack, as if she were noticing him for the first time. He could see her calculating; she could sense that something was happening here, but she couldn't yet define what it was. "It appears the rest of your tour group has moved on without you. I'd be happy to show you around myself."

"Thank you. We'd like that very much," Espy said.

Olivia offered a polite smile and then gestured for them to follow her. She started off in the direction opposite the one the tour group had taken, leading them toward the hallway from which she'd made her grand entrance minutes ago. When they entered the hall, their hostess stopped.

"This wing was the first completed during the original construction," she said. "Consequently it has remained the primary living quarters for most immediate members of the family, despite that the master bedroom on the first floor is twice as large as any of the rooms on this level."

Jack feigned looking interested as Olivia Chambers led them on, passing a number of rooms, most with their doors closed, until she reached a room toward the end of the hall. The door to this one was open, and Chambers preceded them in. The room was much larger than it appeared from the outside, and Jack could see they'd accomplished that by removing a wall. At first glance it looked like a conference room, although one with a casual feel, plush couches and oak tables. At the far end was an enormous flat-panel television screen. Olivia led Jack and Espy to a cluster of chairs, waiting for them to sit before doing the same.

"Please forgive me for being direct," she said, "but you don't seem like the tourist type. Or am I mistaken?"

"I'd say we're more appreciators of the finer things than we are tourists," Espy replied.

Chambers looked slightly irritated. When in the company of someone like Olivia Chambers, Espy's education and above-average social graces made her seem as if she came from money. She was equally comfortable in run-down taverns at the far corners of the globe, sharing time with colorful locals.

"I'll imagine, then, that you've enjoyed seeing some of these, as you say, finer things throughout my estate," Chambers said.

"I have," Espy said. "You have some exceptional pieces."

"Are you an art dealer?"

Espy laughed. "Not at all. I'm an historian. I'm working on a book about European estates that have remained within the same family for hundreds of years. Parkhurst is one of three around London that I'm visiting."

Although Espy delivered the lie like a pro, Jack doubted Chambers was buying it. Still, she smiled.

"A historian and author. Is that right? I read a great deal of history. What's your name? Perhaps I've heard of you."

"I'd be surprised if you haven't," Espy answered. "My name is Emily Manheim. This is my husband, William."

For just a moment, Jack was frozen in his seat, until the brilliance of what Espy had just done hit him. When he and Espy had traveled to Australia in pursuit of the bones, they'd ultimately found them in the care of a man named George Manheim. Manheim's family had been involved with the mysterious guardians of the bones for generations. By throwing out the name—one unusual enough to be instantly recognizable—Espy was hoping to provoke a reaction from the woman.

That reaction came in the form of eyes that widened a fraction. "I'm not sure I've read anything you've written," Chambers said. "But you're right. Parkhurst was built on land that's been in the family since the thirteenth century. Only three pieces of land have remained with the same family longer than this one has."

"I'm particularly interested in how these families were able to retain their land rights through times of political and social turmoil," Espy said. "In fact, I'm exploring the relationship between long-term land ownership and perceived power."

"*La maison est le siege du pouvoir*," the Lady of Parkhurst said with a smile.

"*Et la cause de plus de guerres que tous les gouvernements*," Espy answered in kind.

Surprise touched Olivia's eyes for just a moment. When it faded, she seemed to have adopted a new wariness toward this strange woman. "Land has always meant power," Chambers said, suddenly appearing flustered. "Which is why it's so often difficult to hold."

"Unless you have the power to hold the land," Espy remarked.

"Well, apparently our ancestors were in possession of sufficient power to keep this land beyond the reach of even kings," Olivia said, ice in her voice. Then she stood, the action abrupt. "I have something to attend to. I think it's about time I return you to your tour group."

"By all means," Espy said, rising to her feet. "We wouldn't want to keep you."

Olivia Chambers didn't speak again as she led them back up the hallway, then across the walkway leading to a second set of stairs. She glanced at her watch. "Your group should be in the library on the third floor at this point." She appeared to have regained her lost decorum. "It's been a pleasure talking with you."

"The pleasure was all mine, Olivia," Espy said. It was a parting shot at a woman who would spend the next few minutes trying to remember if she ever told Espy her first name.

Once they were alone, halfway up the stairs to the third floor, Jack put an arm around Espy and leaned in. "You have no idea how much I love you right now."

"Probably not as much as you should," she said with a wink.

As the Lady of Parkhurst said, the tour group was in the upstairs library, and no one seemed to notice when the stragglers slipped back in among them. For the next half hour they moved with the group through various points of interest, keeping their eyes and ears open, even as Jack became convinced they'd garnered more information from the impromptu interview with Olivia Chambers than if they'd been given free rein to explore every nook and cranny of the estate.

As the end of the tour approached, the guide herded the group through a set of ornate walnut doors and into the largest room they'd seen so far. The grand ballroom was almost entirely empty, with only two serving tables and a single large fireplace breaking up the flow of walnut that covered the floor. The walls were paneled with the same wood, recessed columns evenly spaced along the perimeter. It brought to mind a long-ago era, one marked by formal dances, gentlemen and their ladies arriving in carriages, and strings playing a waltz.

"Beautiful," Espy said.

At intervals along the walls were large, identically framed paintings. The tour group spread out in response to the openness of the room. Jack crossed to the nearest painting. He guessed it to be a portrait of one of the family's patriarchs—a severe-looking, humorless man—but it looked to have the skill of a master in each brushstroke. From the subject's attire, he dated the painting to the mid-seventeenth century. Walking along the wall, he saw a similar theme, the men of the Chambers family captured by exceptional artists. But while the features of each of the subjects seemed to maintain a certain consistency, prominent noses and thick jowls, the styles varied. Some were posed as staid portraits with little background evident, while others were more generous in their use of props and placement. One even featured the subject astride a horse and dressed for the hunt. It was something unique to the well-bred, this capture on canvas of ancestors for veneration by their progeny.

Jack was halfway around the room when the guide, who'd been talking the entire time, raised his voice to gather his straggling flock. With the tour complete, the visitors were being ushered out. Jack sighed, disappointed they hadn't found anything of note. On the other hand, Espy's conversation with the Lady of Parkhurst had come near to confirming his instincts about the Chambers family. What he would do with that information, he wasn't yet certain.

He started in the direction of the rest of the group, walking past the last in the portrait series, when he saw something out of the corner of his eye. An impression. It stopped him. He turned and looked at a painting. It was of a man in a frock coat and top hat. He was posed in what looked like an office—in front of his desk, a hand resting on its wooden top. Jack guessed the picture had been painted sometime in the 1880s.

He stood there for several moments, trying to figure out what it was about the picture that tickled his subconscious as the tour group exited the room. The guide stood at the entrance, calling for Jack, his voice impatient. But Jack was locked into the painting, his mind working overtime. Whatever it was, it wouldn't emerge.

Espy appeared at his side. "What is it?"

"I don't know," Jack said. "There's something here. I just can't see it."

While Espy shifted her attention to the painting, Jack turned and saw the tour guide approaching at a fast clip.

"Excuse me," the man said. "The tour is over. You need to follow the rest of your party to the exit gate."

"Shh," Espy said.

"Excuse me, ma'am?"

"I said *shh*," she repeated. "As in, be quiet."

"Do not tell me to 'be quiet'—I'm the one who tells people to be quiet. Now, I really must insist that you and the gentleman follow me."

Jack stepped forward, made eye contact with the man. "Please, sir, just one minute longer?"

After a pause, the man, looking exasperated, said, "You have one minute."

"Thank you," Jack said, quickly turning back to the painting.

Up to now, he'd been focusing on the nameless Chambers patriarch, the lord of the manor, and coming up empty. Instead he forced his eyes to the desk on which his hand rested. Beyond a ledger with no discernible features, the desktop was empty. Next, Jack's eyes went to the wall behind the subject, which included a mantel with items on it. One was a small painting, its subject difficult to make out. Beside it was a clock, an elaborate affair with three faces. But it was the third item, partially hidden, that caught Jack's attention. It looked like a sculpture of some kind. There was something about it, something almost frightening. It occurred to him then that he'd seen it before, if only he could place where.

He felt a firm tap on his shoulder, and at that very moment, the thing dancing just beyond the edges of his understanding stepped into the light. At first he had a hard time believing, but once he'd convinced himself of the truth of it, he spent several seconds imprinting the image on his brain, lamenting the fact that he didn't have a camera with him. When he finished, he flashed a grin at Espy, grabbed her arm, and turned on his heel, leaving the tour guide tapping on empty air.

9

✝

IT SEEMED A VERY LONG TIME AGO that Jack and Esperanza had stood in a hidden chamber in a proto-Mayan temple in the middle of a rain forest in Venezuela and made a series of discoveries that ended up changing their lives forever. It was thirteen years ago, in fact, and at the time Jack and Espy were barely on speaking terms. He was still dealing with the pain from the injuries she'd inflicted on him for having the nerve to show up and ask for her help five years after leaving her.

But in that temple they'd uncovered pieces of a puzzle that set them on the path of the bones of one of the most famous people in the Bible. Had it not been for that trip into the rain forest, Jack wouldn't be married, he wouldn't have the boys, and he wouldn't be sitting in the faux business office of a cheap hotel trying to identify a symbol he'd spotted in the painting at Parkhurst—the same symbol that appeared as one in a line of such symbols in the Venezuelan temple.

After leaving the mansion, Jack hadn't said anything to Espy until he ran around the corner and down the street, in search of a retail establishment that would part with a piece of paper and a pen. On the paper he transposed the picture he held in his mind as faithfully as he could, despite its fuzzy representation in the painting. When finished, he handed it to Espy for her review and, hopefully, to elicit confirmation that he wasn't crazy.

Now they were once again monopolizing the computer in a hotel that seemed reluctant to allow them to take a room again but whose manager eventually took their money.

Espy, an expert linguist, was looking at the paper again, studying the drawing. It was an obvious serpentine shape, but primitive. A line ran through its coils, and on the paper, Jack had made tentative marks indicating a barb on one end. Those marks were more impression than an accurate accounting of what he saw. Or perhaps they were a memory from his first introduction to the symbol back in Venezuela. If he'd had his laptop, he could have pulled up the detailed photos he took during that time rather than relying on scribbles.

"I'm not positive, but I think this is a Pictish symbol," Espy said. She held the drawing up and looked at it more closely.

"I'm not as up on my Pictish as I'd like to be," he said. "So if you wouldn't mind . . ."

"There's not much to say about it. It's a language that used to be spoken in Scotland sometime around the seventh century. But the records are so limited that some scholars think it may have been just a regional dialect as opposed to a fully developed language. In fact, some of the most compelling evidence that Pictish existed as a spoken language in its own right is a series of symbols they carved into giant stelae." She paused, tapped the paper. "This looks like one of those symbols."

"Do you know the name of it?"

She shook her head. Lacking any other direction, Jack typed *Pictish serpent symbol* into the search engine. Less than a second later he was rewarded with a page full of pictures, some of which matched his hand-drawn version.

"'Serpent and Z-rod,'" he read. He shared a look with Espy.

Back in the temple all those years ago, they made a number of significant discoveries. Among them was the uncovering of an early Coptic inscription amid the ruins, a find that turned everything he knew about ancient cross-Atlantic intermingling on its head. Now, given what Espy had told him, and what an internet search had validated, a seventh-century Scottish language could also be added to the list of things that shouldn't have been at the temple, yet were.

"So we've matched a Pictish symbol from a nineteenth-century oil painting to the same symbol in the temple outside of Rubio," he said. "How far does that get us?"

"It gets us as far as tying the Chambers family to the bones," Espy answered.

"A definite win. But I think you already established that in your conversation with Olivia Chambers."

"Establishing and proving are two different things," Espy said. "And this one provides an obvious next line of inquiry."

"As in, if this symbol is important enough to appear as a sculpture in Granddad's office, then where else does it appear?"

Espy gave him a wink and they set to work. One of the issues they ran into right away was how often the symbol appeared, although most of them seemed to be recent references relegated to mystic websites and blogs. Even filtering through these to find mentions that placed the symbol legitimately at some point in history left a great many choices. But on the third filter, an attempt to tie the symbol to the Chambers family directly, or tangentially via its appearance in or around London, they reached a much more manageable data set. Although, at first blush, Jack saw little that seemed to mean a whole lot. Espy was inclined to agree.

"Unless I'm missing something," she said after they'd spent almost an hour poring over the results, "the only other family connection is that letter Henry Chambers wrote to Longfellow."

"Which brings up a few troubling questions on its own," Jack said.

Espy ignored his implication that the conspiracy—if that description fit—stretched to include even renowned literary figures. Jack couldn't blame her; they'd already bitten off a great deal.

"So we move on," Espy said. "Knowing the Chambers family has had a strong presence in London since the ninth century, my guess is if there's a smoking gun, we're practically sitting right on top of it."

He found it impossible to debate that kind of enthusiasm, and so they started again, going through everything they'd already looked at.

"What's this?" Jack asked more than an hour later. It was something he'd skimmed over during the first go-around, a brief article on a man named John Claudius Loudon, a landscape designer of some small fame. Reading with more care this time, he found something that all but jumped off the page. Halfway through the article, in a section that discussed Loudon's interest in designing cemeteries, Jack saw the name Henry Chambers. It was tucked into a paragraph denoting financial backers for a few of Loudon's projects.

He pointed out the find to Espy, and together they read through the article in its entirety. There was no mention of the Pictish symbol or of a Loudon tie to the Chambers family beyond the one occurrence. According to the writer, Chambers had provided a good portion of the funds for the design and development of a cemetery.

"Bath Abbey Cemetery," Jack read. He looked at Espy, who was wearing a puzzled expression. "What's wrong?"

"What's wrong is that I know where this is going," she said, her accent more pronounced than usual. "You're going to convince me to go to the cemetery. Just to look, you'll say. Then once we're there, somehow you're going to talk me into helping you desecrate somebody's tomb. And I don't want to desecrate a tomb."

"Well, how about I make you a promise? If there's any tomb desecrating to be done, I'll do it all by myself."

She looked unconvinced. "You say that now, but then we get there and it's, Espy, help me move this. Espy, can you read this for me? Espy, do you mind holding the dead body up so I can look underneath it?"

Jack swiveled his chair and regarded his wife, marveling at his ability to anger the woman without saying so much as a word. She looked ready to spit.

One thing Jack knew about her anger, however, was that it seldom clouded her ability to make rational decisions. And he had no doubt that if there was any tomb desecration to be done, he was on his own.

The moment Jack stepped from the rental car onto the grounds of Bath Abbey Cemetery, he was reminded of how everything in that part of the world seemed older than things did back in the States. It was a phenomenon that extended even to things that weren't very old. Completed in 1844, Bath Abbey was relatively new, yet it still held that indefinable quality peculiar to Europe that suggested that if you stood in one place and waited long enough, you'd see a hint of magic.

As they walked through the cemetery, they made an effort to avoid stepping on any graves. Their trip to Bath had left them with an hour of sun left, maybe two. From what Jack could see, they would need every bit of that just to cover a portion of the place. Aside from the lack of available daylight, what bothered him was that they'd arrived there on the barest wisp of a clue, without a clear idea of what it was they were looking for, save something that connected this place to the Chambers family.

"I know they have a family burial plot on their own land, so why would a Chambers put a lot of money into a cemetery unless they were planning to use it?" Espy asked.

"To bury their enemies?" he suggested.

Espy scowled and headed for the nearest gravestone while Jack took a moment to unfold the map he'd purchased from the Bath Abbey bookstore. The cemetery was something of a tourist attraction, as much for the wildlife that had worked to reclaim the land as for the stunning monuments and its mortuary. Yet at the moment, he and Espy were the only ones there—at least that he could see.

With the mortuary behind him as a point of reference, he found the structure on the map and then located a path that looked to meander among the plots. But when he looked up, sending his eyes over the landscape, he saw the overgrowth had done a thorough job of obscuring the path from sight. With a sigh he refolded the map and headed toward Espy, who was conducting her investigation in a more empirical fashion.

He found her crouching in front of a gravestone, which was leaning at a precarious angle. By the time he reached her, she'd pulled away a few vines of ivy, enough to see a name. The letters carved into the stone said *Hotham*. A proper English name. He looked up, taking in the five acres of such plots, wondering what they had gotten themselves into.

Espy seemed to be thinking the same thing. She stood, wiped her hands on her pants, and reached for the map. She did the same thing Jack had, locating the mortuary first, looking over his shoulder to fix its position before looking back at the map. When she finished her perusal, she turned to him.

"Start with the obvious," she said.

The mortuary was exquisite, its white-stone Gothic spire rising at least fifty feet, blind arcading supplementing the few clerestory windows. When John Claudius Loudon designed the cemetery, Jack thought he must have had this building in mind as the focal point, the place where every eye would turn as visitors stepped onto the property.

He and Espy approached the tall, heavy oak door. It looked as if no one had opened the door in centuries. But despite the appearance of age, as well as the impression Jack got that they weren't supposed to be trying to enter the mortuary, the door swung open easily.

Stepping inside, he looked up and saw that the tower rose to its full height just inside the entrance before giving way to a small chapel only half as tall as the spire. The interior was modest, a mix of stone and old wood. His initial impression was that the occasional funeral service was performed here before interment.

"I could curl up with a book in here," Espy said, running her hand along the stone of one of the walls.

"You and all the dead people buried in the walls," he said as he moved deeper into the mortuary.

Along the walls were square sections of stone, most of them inset with a handle, although some of the older ones appeared to lack the feature. Regardless of what he'd told Espy, Jack wasn't inclined either to grave robbery or tomb desecration, even if it seemed he was called to those two activities on an oddly frequent basis. Today, though, he had no plans to open any of the tombs.

He took his time, using the light coming in from the high windows, walking near the wall to his left, looking at names, taking in all the details. When finished, he did the same with the second wall. The name Chambers did not appear once, but then he hadn't expected it to. Like Espy said, they had their own burial plot, a place where they could mourn in private. Jack figured that a member of the family would have had to be an irredeemable black sheep to end up spending eternity in this place.

At the far end of the room, opposite the entrance, was a small altar. It sat on a level that was raised just a few inches off the floor. Jack stepped up onto the raised area and stepped behind the altar, glancing at the smooth, unbroken stone along the back side. The altar consisted of the same stone that made up the floor and walls. When he emerged from behind the altar, Espy raised a questioning eyebrow.

"Nothing," he said.

Espy looked up at the windows. "We're losing our light."

Jack nodded. They were losing the light and had made little progress. He began contemplating a return trip for the next day. "Alright, how about we try finding that path our map shows is out there?"

When they left the mortuary, it was much dimmer outside than was the case when they'd entered. It made Jack wonder if they had spent more time examining the walls than he'd realized.

Taking the map back from Espy, he reviewed the page, seeing the path that, according to the folded paper in his hand, made a giant S through the acreage. He looked up and could find little evidence that such a thing existed. Instead he saw large, unruly bushes, wildflowers, and more of the ubiquitous ivy.

"Nothing ventured," he said with a shrug and started off, with Espy right behind him.

Finally he found the start of the path, about ten yards to the west. Half-obscured by wild bushes, it led off the main walkway, back toward the cemetery entrance. He pushed a few scraggly branches aside so that Espy could pass, and then he followed. Once on it, it didn't look as difficult to navigate as he'd anticipated. He saw that the reason it was hard to spot from the mortuary was because it was little more than a narrow dirt path.

In following the path, Jack and Espy made a wide arc that had them approaching the property line. Then it looped around to send them back in the other direction. Once they'd made the turn, it was difficult to see the part of the path they'd left behind. Farther along, the path made a second loop, and as they approached the end of it, there was a much sharper curve that brought them to the other side of the cemetery, where they were greeted by what looked like a single-person mausoleum.

It was a towering monument, at least ten feet from the base to the top of its dome. Six columns supported the dome, which covered a massive urn carved from stone. Ivy had claimed this monument as well, vines of the invading plant advancing into the urn.

Six stone steps at the front of the mausoleum led to the interment chamber belowground. The door to the chamber appeared to be marble and was sealed shut. Jack didn't try to open it.

Beyond the structure, there didn't appear to be much other than a smattering of smaller plots, all of the gravestones toppled. Whether by age, weather, or vandals, he couldn't tell.

Jack glanced at the sky, saw the sun close to vanishing, and chided himself for not remembering to bring a flashlight. "Ready to head back?" he asked.

Espy seemed as reluctant to leave as he did, but then she nodded and started walking back toward the mortuary. As they took the second curve in the path, Jack pondered how the S shape made the walk seem longer than it really was. Then it hit him. A moment later, flush with excitement, he was fumbling for the map, unfolding it in what was now near darkness.

Espy had walked on ahead, and Jack was so focused on what had just occurred that he didn't call out to her.

He brought the map close to his face, yet the light was essentially gone, and he just couldn't see enough to understand what he was looking at. And even if he was right, he didn't know for sure what it meant.

Suddenly Espy appeared out of the darkness and touched his arm.

Jack wheeled around. "I think I've got something."

"What is it?" she asked.

"First, I need someplace to work. And I need light."

10

✝

"LOUDON WAS A DESIGNER," Jack said to Espy as she nursed a Starbucks latte in Bath. "He planned the cemetery from the ground up. Every detail." He had the map opened up on a table, turned so that it faced the right way for Espy. "Look at the path." His finger traced the path's course through the cemetery. "What does that look like to you?"

Espy took another sip of her latte and looked down at the map, her brow knit into a frown. "Like a winding path through an old cemetery?"

He nodded. "Right, like a winding path through a cemetery. And all winding paths look like . . ."

Espy set her drink down, looked again at the map. "A snake?" she asked, her voice tentative.

"Exactly." He used a pen to mark the line of the path on the map, then drew circles around the cemetery's entrance and exit. "You have the head here." He pointed at the circle he'd drawn at the spot where he and Espy had exited the cemetery—a rounded clearing that was only missing a forked tongue. "And the tail here." He indicated the overgrown opening near the mausoleum.

After a while, Espy looked up. "Okay, you may have something there," she said, though she didn't sound convinced.

"Work with me," he said. He turned the map sideways, so the path he saw as a snake looked to be slithering across the table rather than toward his wife. Then, using the pen, he drew a line through it, making sure the ends came out near the path openings. That done, he sketched a few lines at the end designated as the tail. Finally he turned the map around so that Espy could judge for herself.

Jack knew he was reaching, that he could be seeing something that wasn't there. He watched her face as she reviewed the sketch, as she recognized what he was hinting at.

"You think Loudon designed the cemetery as a replica of the Serpent and Z-rod?" she asked.

"I think it makes sense. The Chambers family has—or at least had at some point—a sculpture in the shape of a Pictish symbol. Then a member of that family gives a renowned architect a sum of money to design a cemetery the family is never going to use. But why would someone whose family has owned prime burial land for hundreds of years donate money to build a cemetery?"

Espy didn't answer, and after a few seconds, Jack supplied the answer.

"It's a repository of some sort."

Espy stayed silent for a long while, and there was nothing on her face to tell Jack what she was thinking. Still, after she reviewed the map for a moment longer, she looked across the table. "Isn't a map sometimes just a map?"

Jack smiled. "Sure. Except on those occasions when it's not."

She looked unconvinced. "Here's what I'm having trouble with. Say I'm Henry Chambers, a member of some secret organization that's been protecting the bones of a biblical prophet for three thousand years. In fact, let's think about that. Not only am I part of a secret society, I'm a member of what might be the oldest priestly, political, and social entity the world has ever seen."

She paused and took a sip of her drink. Jack could see her mind working.

"So, our purpose is to protect the bones. I'm not sure from what exactly. But that's not the important thing right now. What *is* important is that you can't have any organization exist for that long without developing incredible influence over the rest of the world. And I'm betting more money than most countries have."

"Is there a question in there somewhere?" Jack prodded when it seemed she was on the verge of letting her initial thought escape.

"The question is, if I'm a man wielding the kind of influence that comes from being a part of something so powerful, what am I trying to hide in a cemetery?"

"I thought that same thing," Jack agreed. "But don't forget what we found in Quetzl-Quezo," he added, taking Espy back to the ruins they'd unearthed in Venezuela. "We ended up uncovering what turned out to be a road map that took us all the way to Ethiopia. Someone placed those stones to show others where to go. Why shouldn't this be the same sort of thing?"

"Because it shouldn't have been necessary in the nineteenth century," Espy countered. "When Quetzl-Quezo was built, there weren't a plethora of reliable methods for preserving important information. Scrolls disintegrated, and there weren't all that many books in the world. I mean, half of them were probably being lost at Alexandria right about the time they were clearing the land for the temple."

Jack nodded as he listened. He couldn't fault her logic.

"By the time Henry Chambers had anything to do with these people, there shouldn't have been any need to preserve the organization's ideas this way. Simply put, the old methods were no longer necessary."

Jack knew she had a valid point, but he refused to believe that what he hoped to find at Bath Abbey Cemetery didn't exist. It just meant that if what had happened there more than a century and a half ago wasn't for the purpose of preserving their information, then there was another reason for it.

"It was personal," he said. It was the only thing that made sense. At Espy's questioning look, he continued. "If Henry Chambers didn't contract with Loudon to create something at the behest of the guardians, then he did it for himself."

"Which leads us to an obvious question," Espy said. "What was he trying to do?" She pulled the map closer, leaning over the table to get a better look at it. "Okay, so if the cemetery is a giant reproduction of the Chambers family symbol, what does that mean to us? What would our guy have been trying to accomplish?"

Jack shrugged. "I'm not sure, but I think it may be a matter of perspective."

While walking through the cemetery, Jack had noticed only two structures large enough to stand out as exceptional. And both of those stood at the two path openings. He didn't think it inconceivable to believe the mortuary and the mausoleum were meant to serve as points of reference.

Pulling a napkin from the dispenser on the table, Jack unfolded it. With the pen he drew a representation of the Serpent and Z-rod, trying to eyeball the general size of its twin on the cemetery map. When finished, he placed the thin paper over the map. Under the bright lights of the coffee shop he could see through the paper, though not with much clarity.

"I think this was meant as a map," he said. He turned the napkin, the body of the snake riding along the path marked out on the map. Then, moving the napkin in the other direction, he turned it until the head matched the path's exit beneath it. Jack was pleased to see that his amateurish drawing had brought the tail to within a centimeter of the other opening.

In the overlay, the line bisected the graveyard, a spear piercing the serpent path at two points. The line fell across four of the graves. When Jack bought the map at the bookstore, they'd told him it was an accurate representation of the grounds.

"You're kidding," Espy said, once it occurred to her what he was thinking. When he didn't respond, she launched into Spanish. Jack didn't pick up all of it, but he understood enough to realize she would not have said any of it in front of the boys.

He stayed silent, letting it play out. After all, he was asking her to help him with something he'd promised her he wouldn't make her do. He needed her to help him dig up gravesites.

———

It was near midnight, and a thick cloud cover mitigated what moonlight might have revealed the two figures moving among the dead. Twin beams of light played over the ground, guiding them along the path leading to the mortuary.

Before returning to Bath Abbey, Jack and Espy had made a few stops. The first was to a copy shop, where they found a picture of the Serpent and Z-rod symbol and then played with scale until they wound up with something that, when printed, matched the dimensions of the map. Then, lining up the head and the tail, Jack was able to draw a more accurate line between the two. In doing so, he discovered that his initial thought was wrong; the line didn't run through four gravesites. Instead it ran through just two.

The second stop was at a hardware store, where they purchased two good shovels and a pair of flashlights. When Jack handed one of the shovels to Espy, he wondered if she was going to hit him with it.

Once they'd reached the mortuary, Jack was tempted to spend some time going through it again, but with limited hours until sunrise he decided to put the structure at the bottom of the list.

It took some work to find the path again, the opening more difficult to spot using only flashlights. Once on the path, Jack pulled out the map, which now had two gravesites circled, and began heading in that direction. Even with the map as a guide, their objective proved hard to find. Several factors conspired against them, chief among them the damage that years of ne-glect had wrought on many of the gravestones. As Jack moved the beam of light over the graves, he tried to count them, but there were several plots where their stone monuments seemed to have disintegrated. Others had either toppled over or were obscured by overgrowth.

Still, he kept at it, searching for the right spot—the grave that the invisible line passed over. He was beginning to think they should have waited until morning and returned here without the shovels. If necessary, they could have tried their hands at surveying, viewing the cemetery from an elevated position, getting a clearer idea of what they were looking for. But a sense of urgency had told him not to delay, and so he followed his gut, taking himself and Espy out into the dark.

Jack stopped, more irritated than he wanted to admit, shining the light over the same area he'd scanned six times already. It was a cluster of six plots, any of which might fall beneath the line. And that was if he was even close to being right about where he was standing. He thought he was straddling the line connecting the path's two access points, and the main structures attached to each, but there was no way to be sure.

Espy added her light to his, illuminating a section of broken stone and wildflowers.

"Sometimes you just have to get your hands dirty," she said. With that, she stepped from the path and proceeded to the nearest plot that sat within the suspect area. Unlike many of the stones around it, the grave marker identifying the one interred was still standing. Jack joined Espy and studied the stone, his flashlight illuminating the name E. Claudius Finnegan, along with the relevant dates.

He ruled it out right away, the 1917 date of death precluding it as a hiding spot in a cemetery completed in 1843. The adjoining plot fell in the same category, and he started to move on when the irrationality of what he was doing occurred to him. He stopped and turned to look again at the grave he'd all but ruled out.

"Tell me something," he said to his wife. "If you're constructing a cemetery and you've been tasked with building some kind of map or treasure box or clue, or whatever, into it, how would you do that if there won't be any graves until after you're done?"

The expression that appeared on Espy's face told Jack that he wasn't the only one who hadn't thought of that.

"So we're not looking for a grave," she said.

"I don't think so."

She stood in silence for a time, her eyes on the same grave that he was staring at. "That complicates things."

"A bit," Jack agreed.

Despite the revelation, he decided to check all the remaining burial plots in the area. The markers for the two nearest were deteriorated to the point that little remained besides dust and a few loose stones. There was a larger stone, about the size of two fists, but all Jack could read on it was the number eight. Disgusted, he put the stone back where he'd found it.

The last two graves that he believed were close enough to warrant a review also yielded nothing, no further clues, and so he and Espy started off again, heading for the curve that would take them to the next site. Once there, he found a scene similar to the one they'd just left.

As he looked out over the cemetery, he couldn't help but feel disappointment in not finding something more, something that suggested they were heading in the right direction and making some progress. Something that would bring them closer to getting back their precious boys.

He cleared his throat, forcing his thoughts back to the task at hand. There was a possibility that if something of the kind he was after existed in this place more than a hundred years ago, time or neglect or even thievery may have removed all traces of it by now.

He'd come across five older graves, markers of gray slate, marble, and sandstone. These seemed to have survived the passing of time better than the others he'd studied earlier. He crossed to the front of the stones to look at the names. Sure enough, the plots were older, with dates showing deaths in the

1840s and '50s. The first two were common English names, and a third looked French. Jack straightened and glanced at the remaining gravestones, getting the impression of Swedish family names. He was about to walk away when what he'd seen registered. The names were identical on two of the stones: Gerhardsson. More unusual was that the dates they'd lived were the same: 1839–1846. The years marked the passing of children, a brother and sister perhaps, each seven years old at the time of death.

Despite the relentless march of time, Jack was filled with sadness for two children who'd died before his own grandparents were born. Here, though, he was looking at two kids who left the world in the same year. He would have been lying to himself if he denied they made him think of Alex and Jim.

For the past few days he'd been able to function—to survive—by not thinking about Alex and Jim. He had to continue believing what Duckey had told him—that the boys would be safe in the care of their captors. It was a thin deception, but it was one he knew he had to maintain in order to preserve any chance of all of them coming out the other side of this thing.

The one reality he couldn't shake was that aside from their accommodations, the games they had, the food served them, the boys had to be really frightened. They had to be wondering what was happening, who their captors were, and why they had been taken away from their parents. Most difficult for Jack, they had to be wondering why he hadn't come for them. Such thoughts put things in perspective for Jack, also causing him to feel incredibly guilty.

And yet he was well aware of the unique circumstances that had brought him back to active fieldwork, and how it meant he would never again be content with spending years at a single dig site hoping to unearth a cooking pot. After a two-week dash across the globe with Espy, the two of them trying to stay a step ahead of people who wanted to silence them, and the recovery of an item he thought was only legend, how could the practice of legitimate archaeology compare?

Granted, there was a lot he could have done without, namely others shooting at him and otherwise doing him bodily harm. But the truth was he'd never felt as alive as he had during that time. He suspected Espy felt the same way. Occasionally he thought he saw glimmers of the woman he used to know bubbling to the surface.

As Jack mulled things over, standing in a foreign cemetery in the middle of the night, he heard what sounded like laughter. It started out quietly, the sound so low that he doubted whether he'd heard anything at all. It was only when his wife began laughing harder that the sound cut through his reverie.

Turning away from the gravestones, he saw Espy on one knee in front of one of the other graves, the one with the French name. She had a hand on its marble headstone. He ran over to where she was.

"What's so funny?" he asked.

Shaking her head, she stood and faced him. She pointed to the gravestone, inviting him to read its inscription. "Take another look," she said, still chuckling.

When he'd reviewed the stone earlier, he'd noted the French name but little else about it. *Monsieur Ammon Prix* had been expertly carved into the marble. Jack didn't wonder about the deceased's nationality. The proximity of Britain and France made for a wealth of expatriates; he imagined the same had been the case 150 years ago.

Yet now that he was focused on the marker, he had to admit

it looked unusual. The chief thing that struck him was that the headstone was absent the two dates that would indicate when Monsieur Prix had lived and died. Even so, Jack couldn't find anything that would explain Espy's amusement.

"I don't get it," he admitted.

Espy's smile widened. "It's the name."

Jack turned his attention back to the marker. "Ammon Prix," he said aloud. He let it roll around in his brain for several seconds before shrugging. "Still nothing."

"Ammon isn't a French name. It just sounds a little like one—enough so that most people wouldn't notice."

Jack frowned and spoke the name again, realizing he was imparting a French pronunciation to the name Ammon because of its connection with the family name, which he was certain *was* French.

"So if it's not French, what is it? And why does it matter that Mr. Prix's parents were multicultural ahead of their time?"

"It's Greek," Espy said. "But its roots are Egyptian. The name Ammon means *hidden one*. Or just *hidden* in some translations."

The moment her words reached his ears, he felt something familiar run its fingers up his spine. It was the intellectual excitement, the expectant energy that came from discovery.

"It could just be coincidence," he said, trying to keep himself from jumping to conclusions.

"Could be," she agreed. "But it's not."

He gave her a quizzical look.

"*Prix is* French," she said.

"And I'm guessing it means something relevant to why we're here?" he asked.

"It means *prize*."

Jack tried to keep his mouth from falling open, but failed. "What you're telling me is that the literal translation of the name is *Mr. Hidden Prize*?"

Espy nodded, but the gesture was slowed by something. Whatever it was, it had turned her grin into a slight frown. Then it hit him too, and he knew what she was thinking. What she'd discovered was so spot-on that it bordered on the ridiculous. It was almost too convenient. What Espy had to be thinking was that this wasn't a clue at all. Rather, it was either a coincidence, a clever joke played by the dead man's parents, or it was something meant to throw seekers like them off the trail.

What kept him from diving headlong into that pool, though, was the conversation he and Espy had had at Starbucks before coming out. They'd established that if Henry Chambers's intention was to use Bath Abbey Cemetery as a cache of some secret knowledge, it was likely he'd chosen to do so for personal reasons. Perhaps, whatever his motive, he didn't want the other members of his organization in on the secret. It was an intriguing thought.

"If Henry Chambers hid something here, it was because he didn't trust it anywhere else," Jack said, assembling his theory as he spoke. "He wanted it hidden because he didn't trust the people in the organization. Which means he would have wanted whatever's hidden here to be found in case—"

"In case something happened to him," Espy finished.

"That's my guess."

Espy nodded, her eyes on the headstone. "What now?"

"We dig."

When he said it, he saw it dawning on her, the task her triumph had pledged them to.

He reached for a shovel. Espy gave him a dirty look and set

the point of her own shovel on the ground, leaning it against an adjoining gravestone.

"I told you I won't help you desecrate a body," she said, crossing her arms. "I won't."

Her tone was the kind that brooked no argument, and so Jack did the only thing he could do: he started digging, beginning near the headstone. He dug for a long while, guessing at the edges of the original plot. After more than an hour, it appeared that Espy was starting to feel guilty, because she finally let out a sigh and then picked up her shovel and joined him.

The work went much faster with her helping out. In another hour they had pulled up perhaps three feet of the soft ground. Somewhere along the way it occurred to him to wonder if this was even a grave—if there was anyone interred in the plot. He thought it possible that this one marker was here the day the cemetery was consecrated, an addition by Loudon at the request of his benefactor. Or perhaps Chambers had someone else come later and set the marker, with the prize he thought so much of buried in place of flesh and bone.

Jack was also thinking about how much time they had. At sunrise they would lose the opportunity for further exploration. Even as untended as the cemetery was, it wouldn't be long before someone noticed their nocturnal activity. And when that happened, security protocols would likely change to make anything of the sort impossible for them to repeat. Even worse, the work they'd done might get the wrong people to look more closely at the headstone with the peculiar name and no dates. If that happened, if others began to investigate the plot before he and Espy could find and remove whatever was there, they could lose their chance forever.

With that thought hounding him, he dug faster, tossing

dirt out of the deepening hole as quickly as he could, with all pretense of preserving the site forgotten. Yet despite the extra effort, the ground was getting harder, the packed earth more difficult to carve into. He was just about to take a short break, to climb from the hole and get a drink of water, when the point of his shovel struck something that made a decidedly metallic sound.

Espy's head jerked up, her eyes wide. She tossed down her shovel and crossed to Jack's side of the hole. Carefully he used the point of his shovel to prod whatever it was he'd struck. The sound of dull metal came again, and he felt the thing give beneath the pressure of the shovel.

Dropping the shovel, Jack went to his knees. He started to pull away the dirt with his hands, his heart racing. Espy got down beside him and did the same. It didn't take long before he saw it, the sheen of gray metal turned dull and rusted after its long burial.

Jack shared a look with Espy, whose face mirrored the anticipation he was feeling. He pulled away more of the moist earth until he found the edges of the thing. It was a metal box, its dimensions about ten by fourteen inches. There was no handle that he could see. He clawed away the dirt along the side facing him, digging another six inches before he could get his fingers beneath the box. Then, taking that final step that took him from archaeologist to grave robber, he thrust his hands beneath it, got as firm a hold as he could, and yanked.

He wasn't ready for it to come free without a fight, which was why he found himself on his backside when the box slid out of the ground as if of its own accord. It knocked the wind out of him, but the thrill of the find had him righting himself even before catching his breath again. He got to his knees while Espy scrambled to join him. He held the box out and examined it.

It was a plain metal box, with a simple hasp and staple lock. It didn't even require a key. Jack suspected the man who'd planted it there believed that if someone proved smart enough to find it, the person would be entitled to its contents without having to hunt for a way to open it.

He set the box down at the edge of the hole, twisted the lock, and lifted the lid. Espy, holding one of the flashlights, held it steady during the reveal. The first thing Jack saw was a dark cloth. Slowly he lifted the cloth from the box, and Espy's light beam fell on the brown leather of a book.

Jack carefully removed the book from the box. It looked like a journal or ledger of some kind, its size and binding common for the early nineteenth century. He opened it and found unlined pages covered in handwriting, the text neat and meticulous.

Espy drew closer, bringing the light to bear on the book. Jack opened it to the front. There was no title, no name, nothing to designate whose hand had left the words. So he started to read, skimming through the first paragraph. As he absorbed the information, as the magnitude of what they'd found became apparent, that tingle of discovery he'd felt earlier came rushing back.

"What is it?" Espy asked.

Jack didn't answer immediately. The truth was that he wasn't certain what it was he held. All he knew was that in the small portion he'd read, it appeared to be the writings of someone intimately involved with the society that had dogged Jack's steps for so long—someone who'd felt the need to pen a secret account of that association.

Then another thought struck him. Without answering his wife, he scanned the pages with increased intensity, searching for the one thing that had eluded him through the years. It was almost ten pages before he found it, and when he did, he placed his finger on the page directly beneath the words. At that moment he felt a sense of accomplishment that superseded even their improbable success in locating Henry Chambers's treasure.

For the first time, he had a name.

When Gordon Reese had hired him to locate Elisha's bones, and then as he began to unearth hints that an ancient secret society existed, he heard whispered names: Chevrier, Manheim, Fraternidad de la Tierra. But none of those names belonged to the society itself.

One of the things he learned during that period was that the guardians preferred to use others to handle the tasks associated with protecting the relics, including acting as their caretakers. Jack had always imagined that sort of subcontracting allowed them to protect their anonymity, or at least muddy the waters enough to make it impossible to determine the real power behind the scenes.

But now, as he paged through the handwritten thoughts of a man whose family had played a direct role in the protection of the bones, he finally knew the name of the ones pulling the strings.

"Sacerdotes Osiris," he said.

The words brought with them a sense of satisfaction, even as they raised a number of questions. Still, he allowed himself to enjoy the moment. The time would come when he would have to ask new questions, to consider what this discovery meant, but for now the name sufficed.

Because of her field of expertise, Espy didn't need a translation.

"Priests of Osiris?" she asked.

Jack nodded, then studied the book for a brief moment longer before standing, leaving the metal box in the hole where it had spent the last century and a half.

Now that he had what they'd come for, all he wanted to do was get out of there, to find someplace to sit and read, to absorb everything written on the pages. He was just about to say as much to Espy when he noticed that her attention was no longer on him. Her eyes had shifted to something over his shoulder, and then widened.

He started to turn and was halfway around when it seemed the largest flashbulb in the world stole his vision. The next sensation he felt was that of being lifted in the air. Then everything went dark.

11

WHEN JACK'S EYES OPENED, his first coherent thought was that he couldn't have been out long; his ears were still ringing from whatever had sent him flying. His second thought, the one that got him moving again, was to wonder what had happened to his wife.

He forced himself off the ground, rolling to his knees despite a sharp pain in his chest. He looked down at himself, struggling to see. He blinked a few times and his vision cleared a little. He saw that there was no blood, no torn clothing. The word *grenade* came to mind, except that a real grenade would have shredded him.

He looked around for Espy, not seeing her anywhere, and was amazed to find how far the explosion had lifted him from the dig site. He felt a wave of panic that he couldn't locate his wife, but he knew he had to keep it together, because whoever had attacked them was still out there.

As if on cue, Jack's vision returned enough for him to see movement among the gravestones beyond where he'd been digging—two figures coming toward him, moving fast. He couldn't see any details beyond dark clothing.

They were still a ways off. Jack thought he saw raised weapons. Yet he didn't budge. Instead he ripped his focus away from the dark figures and tried to spot Espy, looking for a prone form on the flat ground or someone running toward the tree lines on either side of the cemetery. But he didn't see anything, which meant she must have been able to get away. It only took one glance back at the ones striding toward him, and the now clearly discernible guns, to compel Jack to move.

As he scrambled through and around the bushes and trees separating one part of the cemetery from the next, his knee screamed in protest. With each step he could feel it on the verge of giving out. Still, he kept on, unable to tell if anyone was in pursuit. As he rounded a thick cluster of the ubiquitous rosebay willow herb, the tall stems and large purple blooms obscured his view of what was ahead, so he was unprepared for the ivy that rose up and grabbed his legs. He went down hard, a sharp pain shooting up his leg. He clamped his teeth together to keep from crying out. Ignoring the pain, he pushed himself up and pulled away the ivy wrapped around his ankle. He scrambled behind the rosebay willow, and froze.

His breath came in ragged gasps, and for a time it was all he heard, the night gone silent around him. As his breathing slowed, he strained to listen for any sounds of pursuit, anything to let him know the proximity of the men with the guns. He heard nothing but the tentative chirps of insects.

He spared a moment to sit on the ground and inspect his leg. The left pant leg was torn, and he could see the place where something sharp—maybe a rock—had sliced open the flesh. It hurt but it wasn't deep; he could ignore it for the time being.

He took a deep breath and considered his next move. Then, as he sat immobile in the quiet cemetery, something struck him—something unsettling enough that he almost bolted to his feet, his impulse to run back to the dig site.

He no longer had the book.

A sick feeling overtook him as he thought about what he'd held in his hands, what he'd now lost. He took another deep breath, forcing himself to relax, to set aside the emotion. He must have dropped the book during the assault, when the stun grenade, or whatever it was, sent him flying. But just because he'd dropped it didn't mean someone else had found it. It was possible it was still back at the site.

After listening for a while longer, Jack began to move again, staying low and following the rosebay around to the right. With a bit of luck, he thought he might be able to slip out of the cemetery unnoticed—once he found Espy. Even if he was alone, though, without knowing if the ones after him had anyone posted along the perimeter, leaving the cemetery was a risky proposition. Which meant the only course of action available to him, one that dovetailed with his need to recover the book, was to find his way back to the dig site.

Jack went to a knee and listened. After two minutes of not hearing anything, he started off. He picked his way as quietly as he could, watching his footfalls, trying to avoid fallen branches. He had a good idea of where he was in relation to the dig site, but he realized how easy it was to get turned around. So it was with some relief that he stepped around a tree and saw the unearthed grave twenty yards away. Nothing was moving in the area, yet the men who'd attacked them were wearing black, which meant Jack would have a hard time seeing them in the night.

While he was considering that, a figure stepped out of the darkness, causing him to nearly jump out of his shoes. He was caught in the middle of the fight-or-flight response, either a launch at the threat or a run on a bum knee, when something clicked in his brain: a recognition of the feminine form.

Without a word, Jack stepped forward and took her arm, pulling her back into the shadows from which she'd emerged. Once there, he told Espy everything he needed to tell her in a single look—one she reciprocated—before proceeding to give her as thorough a once-over as he could considering their circumstances. He didn't see any obvious injuries and breathed a prayer of thanks for that.

She was still holding her shovel, and she switched it to her other hand as she leaned in, her lips touching his ear.

"I counted at least three," she whispered. "Two went after you. A third circled back the way we came."

He nodded and turned to peer out at the dig site. The big question Jack had was whether or not their attackers knew the importance of this place, if they had any inkling about the book. If so, then they would have kept someone here, suspecting their quarry would have to come back. That meant someone could be out there waiting for Jack and Espy to step out.

As he looked around for the armed men, he also scanned the ground for their lost prize. The small brown book. But the grass was thick, and it was the middle of the night. The daunting prospect drew from him a heavy sigh. He leaned in close to Espy.

"I lost it," he whispered.

"Lost what?"

"The book. I must have dropped it."

He wasn't sure what he expected to hear in response, but it

wasn't what Espy supplied. Where he'd anticipated surprise or disappointment, there was calm.

Espy slipped a hand into her jacket pocket and pulled out the book. "You mean this?"

The only thing that kept Jack from laughing out loud was the prospect of being shot. The fact that Espy had the book changed things. Now the only objective was escape. He was about to motion for Espy to follow him when a voice called out of the darkness.

"Dr. Hawthorne, I'm Special Agent Bowers. I work for the American government."

The voice itself was enough to freeze Jack where he stood, but the identity of the man behind it was wholly unexpected. He frowned, wondering how McKeller's man had tracked him to this place. The man's voice had echoed, so Jack was unable to get a fix on his location. He looked to Espy, who shook her head.

"Dr. Hawthorne, there seems to have been a misunderstanding. You're not in any kind of trouble. You have information critical to national security, and we need you to come in so we can ask you a few questions."

And I've got a bridge to sell you, Jack said to himself.

He didn't answer Bowers, knowing the man would use the response as a way to locate him. At the same time, he was trying his best to reconcile the man's presence in the cemetery. Jack knew he'd taken a chance booking flights in his own name, as well as using his credit card while in London. He'd accepted the possibility that McKeller's people would find him. But this—the coordinated assault by what looked like a paramilitary team—was difficult to accept.

When Jack didn't reply, Agent Bowers tried again. "Dr. Hawthorne, we have a perimeter established around the cemetery. You can't get out. So all we have to do is wait for daylight. But where's the sense in that? The sooner you come in, the sooner we can all be drinking coffee and getting this thing taken care of."

Jack had doubts about the comprehensiveness of the agent's perimeter, knowing that he couldn't have more than a handful of people with him. It was more likely that his team was in the immediate area, waiting to close in should Jack make a mistake.

Espy moved in close and took his arm. "There's something wrong," she whispered.

"You're telling me," he said.

"I mean with Bowers. I don't think he's really with McKeller."

Jack looked at his wife, wondering how she could know that. But in all their years together, he'd learned not to doubt her hunches. "What makes you think that?"

"His accent."

Jack didn't remember the man having an accent; he sounded quintessentially American.

"It's slight," Espy said, "but I'm certain he's not native. Maybe French."

Jack parsed that, wondering what it meant. He knew it wasn't uncommon for the Company to use foreign nationals as agents. Except that he kept coming back to Duckey's small-team theory—and Jack would have bet that every member of that team was as American as apple pie.

"If they're not with McKeller, then this doesn't make sense," he whispered back. Except that it did. With the obvious choice removed, the next logical one presented itself. He didn't even pause to consider how the Priests of Osiris knew about Mc-Keller's interest in the bones, or about the ransacking of his home. They knew everything about him; they had for a long time.

He checked the shudder that went up his spine. While the man calling himself Bowers had been trying to get Jack to reveal himself, he'd only succeeded in allowing Jack to do the same. If he was right, Bowers was past the dig site, about twenty yards beyond it and off the path. But his team wouldn't be with him. They had either established or were in the process of establishing a gauntlet of some kind, hoping to flush Jack and Espy into running.

Jack put a hand on Espy's arm, and her eyes found his. He motioned for her to stay where she was and then reached for the shovel that she'd carried with her the entire time. She gave him a questioning look, but he didn't have the time to explain. Shovel in hand, he got his feet under him, shared one more look with his wife, and then did something stupid.

"As much as I want to believe you, Agent Bowers," he said, "it's hard to take the word of a man who walked into my house uninvited and probably went through my underwear drawer."

Then he was moving. As he started off, heading to his right around more of the rosebay, Espy was caught by surprise. She rose to follow, and again he gestured for her to stay put. He saw resistance on her face, but she didn't move. As he circled around the rosebay, he was careful to keep quiet. He'd attracted attention; now he just needed to see what it got him.

He found a spot about thirty feet away from Espy and crouched behind the rosebay at a place from which he could still see her. She was looking in his direction, and he could tell she was irritated. She had to understand she was being used as bait.

"Believe me, Dr. Hawthorne," Bowers called out, "it wasn't

my intention to enter your home like we did. Like I said, it was a big misunderstanding."

Jack smirked at that. He decided that if the man calling himself Agent Bowers was with the CIA, he would be better at this sort of thing.

He didn't respond, but instead waited. As it turned out, he didn't have to wait long. There was movement behind Espy. She didn't see it; her back was to the person stepping out from behind the trees. The figure stopped and regarded her for a few seconds, no doubt wondering where Jack was. But before long, the agent started to advance.

Shovel in hand, Jack left the cover of the rosebay willow and headed in Espy's direction, his steps faster now, gambling everything on surprise.

The agent didn't see Jack coming. He was almost on top of Espy when Jack hit him, the shovel striking him in the back of the head with a *clang* that was much too loud—loud enough for every fake CIA agent within a block's radius to know from where the sound originated.

When the shovel came down on the man's head, Espy, who'd been oblivious to the events playing out behind her, jumped up and gasped. Jack dropped the shovel and knelt at the side of the downed agent, only to discover it was a woman. He checked to see that she was breathing before, as quickly as he could, going through her pockets. Just as he expected, there was no identification. But she did have a phone. Jack made sure the power was off before slipping it into his pocket. The last thing he did was scoop her gun off the grass. He considered the weapon for roughly half a second before settling it in his hand and motioning for Espy to follow him.

They moved in a direction away from Bowers, and Jack

was hoping that by taking out one of the man's agents, he'd created a hole in their gauntlet. In removing the agent, even if he hadn't killed her, Jack had altered the dynamics of the game. The Priests of Osiris had left him alone for years, and up to this point, Jack had clung to the hope that he and Espy could end this most recent encounter in some sort of détente. He doubted that end was possible any longer. The people to whom Bowers was beholden would want something more, perhaps even blood.

They'd been so long on the cemetery grounds that it came as a surprise when he and Espy reached the edge of it as quickly as they did. He supposed spending a few hours in the dark, surrounded by a forest, while being hunted by armed men, served to make the place seem larger, more foreboding. So when he saw the first streetlight, it almost seemed surreal.

In spite of his relief at having made it out, caution slowed him. Espy was next to him and was doing the same thing, looking out past the last few trees, hoping their gamble had paid off, that there was no perimeter. At first glance there didn't seem to be. What there was, though, was a new vehicle parked behind their rental. It was a dark sedan with tinted windows. They'd probably already been through the rental.

After one more look around, Jack ran toward the cars, his knee screaming in pain. They reached the sedan first, and its windows were dark enough that there was no way to tell if anyone was sitting in it.

Reaching the rental car, Jack put his hand on the door handle, but then stopped. It occurred to him that he had no idea how much time Bowers and his team had spent going through the car. Perhaps long enough to place a tracker in it. There was no way to tell, which meant he couldn't take the chance. He let go another heavy sigh.

"We have to walk," he said.

So they started off on foot, heading away from the main road. But before they got more than a dozen steps, Espy stopped him.

"Wait," she said. She turned and ran back to the dark sedan. Standing at the driver's side, she hesitated for just a second before trying the handle. Jack was surprised when the door swung open, and even more surprised when Espy slipped into the driver's seat. He started to head that way as Espy searched the car. It was also a rental, so there wouldn't be anything in the glove box or in any of the other areas that normally accumulated junk. Espy didn't check a one of them. Instead he saw her feeling around on the floor. Finding nothing, she leaned over and checked the passenger side as well. When that returned nothing, she turned her attention to the dashboard. She leaned in close, her eyes moving to the lower left. She extended a finger, and he heard the trunk pop open. Then Espy was out of the car, but rather than going right to the trunk, she opened the rear door and bent in. When she emerged, she had something in her hand: a manila folder. She turned to Jack and smiled before moving to the trunk.

Soon she was hurrying toward him, the manila folder in one hand and what looked like a duffel bag in the other. She handed the bag to him, and then the two of them disappeared into the night.

12

✝

THEY WERE ALMOST OUT OF MONEY. After hours of digging, hiding, and running, they were both hungry, and they had spent a good portion of their remaining funds on the shoddy hotel room they now occupied. With the few pounds in Jack's pocket, they might have been able to find a sandwich to split, but he had his doubts about the edibility of any sandwich they could buy for the money they had.

Right now, though, he was thankful for something with which to occupy himself, to distract him from his empty stomach. Espy had the manila folder open on the bed while he'd placed the duffel bag on a wobbly table by the bolted window. It was a standard green duffel with no markings on the outside to indicate ownership. He unzipped the bag and was unsurprised by what he saw.

There was a handgun on top, a Glock, and two clips. Jack hoped that he wouldn't have occasion to use either of the guns, but he felt better having them. Still, he reminded himself that these weren't Gordon Reese's hired guns, or Victor

Manheim's. These were men and women working security for a well-connected secret society. In some ways, Jack suspected these people were as trained and as capable as the agents they were impersonating. So if he could avoid shooting off even a single round, it was in his best interests to do so.

He set the gun on the table and dug deeper into the duffel. There was a change of clothes, black trousers and a white shirt. Sandwiched between the two articles of clothing lay a passport. Jack shook his head when he saw the French seal. He flipped it open and looked at the picture. It was a young man, twenty-something, clean-cut, unsmiling. There was no way to know if the name was real. He put the passport and clothes on the table and reached for the last item in the bag, his mood immediately brightening. He flipped through the contents of the money clip, a decent amount of cash in euros. As if in acknowledgment of this good fortune, Jack's stomach made a rumbling sound. He pocketed the money and left the rest out on the table, then crossed to the bed to see how Espy was faring.

The folder lay empty, its contents spread out on the bed. Jack moved so he could look over her shoulder.

"There's nothing here about us," Espy said. She picked up one of the pieces of paper, extending it toward him. "Most of it is information about the Chambers. Genealogy, business activities, money trails." She looked up at him. "There's a lot here. They've either been watching these people for a long while or they're really good at what they do."

Given what they'd found in the false grave—what a representative of the Chambers family had seen fit to hide as some sort of insurance policy—Jack suspected the Priests of Osiris had been watching the family for a very long time. Because Jack was convinced that the Chambers family was intimately involved in the organization, he had no idea what this evidence of self-surveillance meant. It was simply another piece of the puzzle to catalog.

"What did you find?" Espy asked.

Jack pulled the money clip from his pocket and showed her. She gave an appreciative nod and then turned her attention back to the contents of the folder.

"How did they know we visited the Chambers estate?"

"I don't know for sure," he said, "but I'm guessing your new friend Olivia Chambers did a little investigating after our meeting. And somehow that tipped off our friends."

That was only a guess, and Jack knew how flimsy it was. Nevertheless, he wondered how, apparently, the organization had tracked them to Parkhurst and then on to Bath Abbey Cemetery.

Espy picked up a stapled packet of paper. "I found this one interesting," she said, handing it to Jack. While he skimmed it, she gave him the highlights. "From what I can tell, that report details every major business transaction the Chambers have engaged in since 1695. That's the year after the Bank of England was founded. The Chambers have had a good portion of their money there ever since."

As he looked through the pages, numbers with a great many zeros, payments and receipts, names of companies and financial institutions all jumped out at him. It was a dizzying array of information, but what he gleaned was that the Chambers had used their position, their permanence among the United Kingdom's most influential families, to wield incredible influence on the financial world.

"Okay, what am I supposed to be seeing?" he asked. He knew his wife well enough to realize she wouldn't have pulled these pages out for his review unless there was something significant he should know.

"Look at the third page," she said. "The bank ledger from 1844 to 1845."

He did as instructed, and when he found the section she'd mentioned, it didn't take him long to see what had caught her eye. The section detailed the monthly balance of the Chambers account with the Bank of London. Over the course of five months spanning from late 1844 to early 1845, the Chambers family took a serious financial hit, to the tune of millions in the one bank account alone. Jack looked up at his wife.

"It's not just the Bank of London account," she said. "If I'm reading this correctly, they lost almost three-quarters of their wealth in less than six months. It's as if every business holding they had tanked at the same time." She shook her head. "The Chambers were diversified before diversified was a thing. Yet they still lost almost everything."

Jack flipped through a few more pages and continued reading. In 1845, the family's financial situation had become so dire that they came close to losing even the land they'd held since the twelfth century. Then, just when it looked as if they were on the brink of losing everything, they began to recover. The record of that was almost as dramatic as the other, with whatever forces that had worked to bring the family to the brink of destruction seemingly putting on the brakes as they teetered on the edge of a cliff. Over the next several years, the family wealth grew again, investments proved successful, and businesses thrived. But Jack couldn't look at all this without seeing a coordinated attack, and perhaps a stayed hand.

"It looks to me like an attack on every facet of their financial identity," he said.

"I thought the same thing," Espy agreed. "Like the Chambers were being punished."

Neither of them had to vocalize who they believed to be responsible for the discipline of one of Britain's most powerful families. The fact that they could do something like this spoke of their power and ability to manipulate markets and financial institutions. It was frightening to consider.

"And Henry knew it was coming," Jack said.

What Espy had found shed new light on the purpose of the cemetery. Henry Chambers had some kind of advance warning that he'd earned the wrath of the Priests of Osiris—enough notice to commission Loudon to design Bath Abbey Cemetery. He meant it as an act of defiance, a way to get back at those he thought were set to ruin him.

That new revelation made Jack mentally salivate about what might be in the book he'd dug up. If a man in a spiteful frame of mind wrote it, it might be the equivalent of an exposé.

The book was sitting on the counter just inside the door, next to a coffee maker with a frayed cord. He'd set it there when they'd entered, knowing if he got into it right away—before going through the items they'd taken from the car—he would have been lost for the night. Now, though, there was no reason for him to hold off any longer.

Handing the financial papers back to Espy, he retrieved the book, found a chair as equally wobbly as the table, and settled back to learn as much as he could about the enemy.

Jack hadn't moved in two hours, but the time had passed almost without his notice. He'd read every word of Henry

Chambers's notebook twice, then gone back to reread certain sections a third time. His overarching state of mind was one of disbelief, as Henry had put flesh to a phantom. It was a bit unsettling seeing something that had existed on the fringes—something about whose existence he'd even harbored doubts—brought into the light of day.

Still, despite the wealth of knowledge there, Chambers was careful about what information he chose to share. The bulk of it was old history, such as the events that saw a small group of Hebrew priests, committed to protecting the holy relics, secret them to Egypt, only to see their coalition evolve over the centuries into a cross-national, multiethnic power that had wrought great, often terrible influence over world affairs. Yet, from what he'd read in the book, there was very little about the actual structure of the Priests of Osiris—no names, no seats of power. It was influence without much substance, at least historically.

Because of Jack's profession, there were parts of Henry's writings that provoked particular interest. An entity that had existed for as long as this one, in a variety of incarnations, and with so many different players, had to have had an impact on a great many cultures. Studying certain areas of the archaeological arena in light of what he was discovering could turn some established theories on their heads. It had certainly helped Jack better understand a few of the mysteries surrounding Quetzl-Quezo.

There was enough here that Jack had to take care not to get lost in it, not to give in to the urge to become the academic. If he and Espy and the boys made it through this, if they came out the other side with their lives and freedom, then he would have all the time he needed to explore the ramifications of this information. For now, he had to concentrate on the bits that he could use immediately.

He had to remind himself that there was no way to know how much of it was even true. Every bit of what he'd read could be fabrication—brilliant misinformation. What he needed to concentrate on was *motive*. After reviewing the report on the family's finances, Henry Chambers appeared to be a man with a motive for his actions. And Jack's gut was to accept all of it, which meant he had to decide where to go from there. And that was where one of the passages that had earned a third read played a prominent role.

While he'd read, Espy had done the smart thing, taking sleep where such could be found. What he'd culled from the book had him energized enough to want to wake her, to tell her what he'd learned, but he couldn't do it. In fact, he decided to join her. There was nothing more he could do at such a late hour, and he wasn't even sure that, even with the money that came from the agent's bag, they had enough to do anything substantial. He hoped that by getting some rest, as well as something good to eat, such things would aid their decision-making.

Setting the book on the table, Jack stood and stretched, feeling the effects of two hours of sitting there motionless. He turned off the light and moved to the bed, where he took off his shoes and slipped in beside his wife, trying to keep from waking her. Even so, he hadn't finished settling in when her voice came out of the darkness.

"An engrossing read?"

Jack didn't answer right away. He knew if he started talking about what he'd learned, he might not be able to stop.

"There's a lot in there," he finally said.

"I'm assuming that's the understatement of the year?"

He chuckled and rolled onto his side, his hand finding her shoulder. She was facing away from him. He slid over, closer to her ear. "The short answer is that the Priests of Osiris are more powerful than we realized. They probably have people highly placed in governments around the world. And if we had any sense, we'd give ourselves up to McKeller and take our chances. We could be facing our deaths if we keep moving forward. Beyond that, I didn't learn much."

He felt Esperanza's body move under his hand and he recognized a silent laugh. "Well, if that's all," she said.

"Oh, and I learned that Henry Chambers knew the meaning of the word *vindictive*."

"Which is a plus for us."

Jack went silent for a while, waiting to see if sleep would come or if the Chambers notebook would keep him wide awake. He heard steady breathing coming from Espy and assumed she'd returned to sleep, but then, as if reading his mind, she stirred.

"I'm worried, Jack. I need to talk to Alex and Jim, to hear their voices and know they're both okay." She paused, sounding on the verge of tears. A few moments later, she asked him, "What do we do next?"

Jack heard a weariness in her tone. He squeezed her shoulder and assured her the boys would be all right. Then he whispered, "I think tomorrow we need to figure out how to get to Saint Petersburg."

"We have to go where now?"

Giving up on any chance of sleep, Jack told her what he'd discovered, filling her in on the history of a band of Hebrew priests who'd fled to Egypt with Elisha's bones and co-opted a religious institution in order to protect the relics. He told her about the influence of the Priests of Osiris throughout history, of the things Henry Chambers claimed they'd done. He filled her in on the gaps—the things Chambers seemed intent on keeping from the reader. It was one of those gaps that made Saint Petersburg their next destination. It was the only path Jack could see that pointed them toward the true leadership of the Priests, not those members they conscripted to do their bidding.

"At three points in his writing, Henry talks about the Peter and Paul Fortress in Saint Petersburg," Jack said. "That struck me as odd during the first read through, so when I read through it all again, I found that each reference to the Fortress comes in a paragraph following a statement about the organizational hierarchy."

While he was talking, Espy had barely moved. He knew she'd absorbed every word, shifting bits of information around, joining seemingly unconnected facts and ideas. She was, after all, an academic at heart, and one of the most intelligent people he knew.

"And you're certain it's not just a coincidence?" she asked once he'd gone silent.

"The sentences that talk about the leadership are ten words long each. The ones about Saint Petersburg are seven."

At that, his wife shifted her position, turning so she could see his face.

"I double-checked it," he said. "I went three paragraphs above and below each reference, and there are no other sentences or sentence couplets that match that construction."

Even in the dim light he saw the spark of interest in her eyes, the intrigue of a puzzle in need of solving.

"One last thing," he said. "Each sentence couplet is separated by seventeen sentences, none of them the same length, but all totaling 123 words."

Espy started to speak, and Jack was fully expecting her to ask follow-up questions, to help come up with an agenda for when they arrived in Russia. He'd have to tell her that what they'd do when they reached Saint Petersburg was still an open question, and that for now it was enough to have a direction, a focus. He was unprepared, then, when she asked nothing of the sort.

"Will you pray for us? For the boys?"

Jack did. And as he took their circumstances before God, who had proven his power over and over again, he felt his wife relax. By the time he'd finished, he could hear the regular breathing that comes with sleep. He stayed awake for a long while after that, thinking about tomorrow. At some point, sleep came for him too.

13

✝

JACK AND ESPY WERE ON DECK to watch the approach into Saint Petersburg. The cerulean sea of the Gulf of Finland was dotted with the remains of the season's ice, but as the wind swept across the deck, Jack felt as if it were the middle of winter. Next to him, Espy shivered, and he put his arm around her and pulled her close.

Ahead of them was a recently completed lock, threading a new needle between Kotlin Island and the mainland. Beyond the lock was Neva Bay, the far end of which was their destination. From two miles offshore, all Jack could see of the land was a green strip that faded into patches of lighter green and brown in the distance. Yet as they neared the city, things began to take shape.

Saint Petersburg looked as if it were borne from the sea, as if its buildings were lifted from beneath the waves and set upon some sunken foundation. Indeed the city was beset by water, the Neva River bisecting the Russian metropolis, predestining the city to subsist on shipping and trade from its very inception.

They were still a ways out, so he couldn't see the city in much detail, but he could discern the solid wall of buildings lining the shoreline like a medieval sea wall, the taller buildings rising beyond like spires.

Their port of call was Lomonosov, outside the city proper. It was one of the largest cargo ports in Saint Petersburg—industrial enough to allow them a decent chance of going ashore amid the chaos that was a massive international trade hub.

He felt the ship begin to turn beneath his feet and he shifted his weight to compensate. To starboard he saw the greens and browns give way to gray as the ship neared Lomonosov. He could see the constant motion along the docks: ships, people, and equipment moving in organized bedlam, like the frenzied scurry of ants.

He and Espy moved to the rail, feeling the salt spray as the ship pitched forward. Before long, Jack saw a smaller boat approaching, and he could feel the cargo ship slowing until the boat came alongside. The crew dropped a ladder down as the boat tied off, and from his spot at the rail Jack watched a man climb the ladder and come aboard. The harbor pilot headed for the bridge, and not long after, the ship surged forward. Under the harbor pilot's guide, the 50,000-ton vessel approached a wharf, losing speed as it closed the distance. Soon the cargo ship had stopped, and crewmen above and dockworkers below busied themselves tying off the massive vessel.

The two passengers did their best to stay out of the way, remaining on deck until the captain approached them. Jack hadn't seen the woman much during the voyage, which had made him a bit uncomfortable. It was hard to know for sure, to figure out if she was the sort who would accept a sum of cash to carry two strangers between countries, or if she would pocket the money and turn the undocumented travelers over to the port authority.

She was a small woman, yet there was a hardness to her. Jack guessed her age to be around sixty, but he also knew that years of work on the ocean could weather a person beyond her years.

"We'll get a visit from customs in a few minutes," she said. Her English was good, if heavily accented. Espy, who'd heard her bark orders to her crew, said she was Ukrainian. "That can take anywhere from ten minutes to a few hours, depending on what kind of mood they're in."

She stopped speaking and watched as two crewmembers passed by with a dolly. Once they were out of earshot, she turned back to her passengers.

"You can wait in my cabin until they're done. After that, we'll find a way to off-load you with the rest of the cargo."

Her piece said, she turned and walked off, leaving Jack to wonder if the offer of her cabin was the act of a captain trying to hide something from prying eyes or a way for her to find them when she served them up on a platter. When he shared a look with Espy, her expression told him she was wondering the same thing.

He led the way belowdecks, locating the captain's cabin from a quick tour soon after boarding. Once inside, Espy shook off her heavy jacket and collapsed into a chair. Jack did the same. But as he thought more about what was happening above deck, he found he couldn't relax.

He'd considered flying into Saint Petersburg, but since the Priests of Osiris had been able to track them to and around England, he'd become leery about traveling in any way that could be tracked. The flip side of traveling as smuggled cargo was the uncertainty that they would reach their destination. He and Espy had argued about it, but in the end she'd come to agree with him. It was because of her initial opposition to the arrangement, though, that he wouldn't share his current misgivings with her.

As luck would have it, they didn't have to wait long. Perhaps ten minutes after entering the cabin, the captain opened the door.

"They're checking us against the manifest now," she said.

She advanced into the room and closed the door. Once it was shut, she turned to her two charges, regarding them with the kind of stare that was absent even a trace of self-consciousness. She had the eyes of a woman who'd spent a lifetime at sea, forever trying to find something out among the waves.

"One of the things you learn in a job like mine is not to ask too many questions," the captain said. "But I think I'd feel bad if I didn't try to convince you not to do whatever it is you're about to do."

Jack wasn't sure what he was expecting the woman to say, but that wasn't it. "What, exactly, do you think we're going to do?"

She was shaking her head before he finished. "I don't know. And I don't think it really matters. What does is that I can tell by looking at the two of you that you're not prepared to be here—not without papers. Or proper clothes."

She said this last to Espy, and Jack looked over at his wife, expecting to see offense. Instead she gave a warm smile and began to speak, addressing the woman in near flawless Ukrainian.

The reaction Espy's words provoked from the captain was immediate, and for the next several minutes the two women were engaged in animated conversation. Jack had no idea what they were talking about, only that their Ukrainian captain appeared engaged, once looking in Jack's direction and laughing. He simply smiled back and allowed his wife to do her thing.

Eventually the captain glanced at her watch, and what she saw there was enough to cause her to put on her captain face again. Her last few words sounded gruffer than the previous, and then she nodded and left them alone again in her cabin.

Jack allowed the resulting silence to linger, waiting for Esperanza to fill him in, but she seemed content to wait for whatever came next.

"I assume the two of you have worked out a shopping excursion of some kind once this business is over with?" he prodded.

"Yulia is a dear," Espy said. "She talked about all sorts of places we need to visit in Saint Petersburg."

"Yulia?"

"I know," Espy said. "I'm not sure she looks like a Yulia."

Jack answered with a smirk. "So I'm guessing she's not going to turn us in?"

Espy shrugged. "I have no idea. I think she thinks we're spies, so there's really no telling what she'll do."

"She thinks we're spies?"

"Maybe it was the whole South American woman who just happens to speak fluent Ukrainian that did it."

"Of course it was."

Not long afterward, the door opened again, revealing Captain Yulia. Jack was relieved to find her standing there alone, rather than with others with drawn guns. She held two coats that looked like the ones worn by her crew—thin, gray, and waterproof. She extended the coats and waited without a word while they shrugged them on. Then she led them topside. The deck looked different, several piles of lashed cargo now gone.

There was also significantly less activity, and nowhere near the number of crewmen.

Yulia led them to a set of stairs that had been rolled up to the deck. Jack looked down at the dock, not seeing a single person below. Some people in orange vests were moving around farther down the dock, none of them seeming to pay attention to the cargo ship. Yulia's was just one of almost a dozen docked there, with one ship heading back out into the bay even as Jack watched, and what looked like two more in line to come in.

Before they descended the stairs, Yulia reached out a hand to Espy. She placed something in Espy's hand and then took a step back. The Ukrainian captain nodded, regarding them for a short time before turning and walking back to whatever work awaited her.

When she was gone, Espy turned to Jack and opened her hand, revealing a roll of euros, about the size of the one Jack had handed over to secure their passage.

"So I'm guessing she's not going to turn us in," he said.

Espy gave him a disapproving look before slipping the money into her pocket and starting down the stairs. Jack smiled at her back and followed.

14

✝

AFTER TRADING THE EUROS for rubles, it was a simple matter to find lodging in a Russian city of nearly five million people. That didn't mean, though, that the accommodations were going to be comfortable. Jack's back let him know it disagreed with the choice to bunk down in a place near the water, a small hotel in the Petrogradsky district, in a line of like establishments there to serve the tourists who came for the White Nights festival in June.

Jack had grumbled a bit about what the bed with the metal bar down its center had done to his back, while Espy, who'd slept next to him, seemed unbothered by it, awaking fresh the next morning. It wasn't long, however, and Jack found his sour mood giving ground as they headed out to visit the Peter and Paul Fortress.

He'd not had occasion to visit the city before this and so he'd never seen the Fortress in person. As he and Espy approached it, he found himself having a dichotomous reaction. On one hand, the bell tower that rose four hundred feet was the kind of structure that could stop a person where he stood, evoking wonder and awe at the vision of the builders. But there was also a part of him that thought the Fortress looked like a college campus.

Peter and Paul Cathedral stood as the center point for the grounds, while several much smaller buildings of tan stone and red brick did a passable job of imitating the residence halls and classroom buildings of Evanston University. The sight caused Jack to feel a pang of nostalgia for the increasingly large number of classes he'd missed over the last few weeks. Nearing the entrance, they bypassed a tour group and crossed over Saint John's Bridge. They then paid the fee to spend as long as they wanted within the Fortress's walls.

Once stepping through the gate, their next challenge showed itself right away. With the Fortress being so vast, with the large number of buildings and rooms, a century of construction and three centuries of occupancy and abandonment, Jack had no idea what he was supposed to do. The only thing he had to go on was what Henry Chambers had written in his book, and Jack's study of it had shown Henry to have been quite circumspect when it came to divulging any information that could be considered useful.

Espy studied the map they'd picked up at the gate. It was in Russian, which made her the map reader. While she read up on the Fortress, Jack's attention went to the thing that had drawn the eyes of every visitor for the last three hundred years. The Peter and Paul Cathedral towered over the Fortress's interior, its construction showing off features reminiscent of Arabic architecture. The exterior was pale gold—the color of a desert. That, as well as the domed cupolas and faux minarets, signified without a doubt that the building was of the Eastern Orthodox tradition. His eyes followed the spire up to the very top, where an angel stood, wings spread as if about to take flight.

Jack glanced over at his wife, whose head hadn't lifted from the map. He reached over, took her hand, and pulled her toward him while pointing up at the cathedral. He watched as her eyes found it.

She stood in silence for a moment, gazing at its magnificence. When next she looked at him, she smiled. "Thanks," she said.

"Don't mention it."

Five minutes later, they started off across the cobblestone, intent on getting a look at the cathedral's interior from a tourist's perspective before being forced to shift gears and regard the Fortress as a riddle.

A stream of people entered and exited the cathedral, and Jack and Espy stepped in among them, heading toward the entrance, a portico ringed by eight massive columns. Moments later they were inside. From the outside, the cathedral possessed an elegance and stark beauty, despite a plainness common in the Eastern motif. Inside, though, Jack and Espy were treated to something entirely different. They looked up and were awestruck by the giant chandeliers hanging from the ceiling, lights ablaze to illuminate the mosaic tile above as well as the marble columns and gilding details.

He and Espy took in the stained glass, the royal tombs, and the iconic imagery. It was a lot to absorb, and after a while they found seats so they could rest their feet and gather their thoughts—and turn their attentions back to what had brought them to Russia.

From where Jack sat, he had a good view of the unusual iconostasis, the tower rising high over the altar. He was certain he'd never seen one quite like it. Remembering the map in his pocket, he pulled it out and opened it, curious as to the reason for the strange design. But he'd forgotten the text was in Russian. He was about to ask Espy if she could find anything relevant to the iconostasis when something caught his eye, something he *could* read.

He brought the map closer, looking at the notes beneath the cathedral drawing. Most of the characters were Cyrillic; there was no chance of him reading even a single word. It wasn't the Russian, though, that had attracted his attention. Rather, it was a line of numbers.

"What does this say?" he asked, handing the map to Espy, a finger on the line in question.

"It says, 'The cathedral's spire is 123 meters tall and is topped by the iconic image of the Fortress, the angel.' Why?" When finished, she looked at Jack, who was smiling back at her.

"One second." He reached into his jacket pocket and pulled out a small notebook where he'd jotted what he believed were the relevant bits from Chambers's notebook. The piece of information he was looking for was on the first page. He handed the notebook to Espy. "See there," he said, showing her where it was written. "Each of the three priestly couplets is separated by a total of 123 words."

"So Chambers was referencing the bell tower."

"That's one number down," he said.

Espy frowned and looked back at the paper, trying to decipher his notes. "'Each of the sentences dealing with organizational leadership is ten words long,'" she read. "'Each dealing with the Fortress is seven.'"

Jack considered the only other repeating number he'd found—the seventeen sentences of varying lengths totaling 123 words. He didn't have a good feel for that one, unsure if it was a number they needed to factor in or if it was just coincidence. "And the 123 words between each sentence in a couplet is made up of seventeen sentences," he added.

Espy absorbed the numbers. Jack could see her moving them around in her mind like Scrabble tiles, looking for the proverbial seven-letter word.

"A ten, a seven, and a seventeen," she said, "with the tens and sevens probably tied together somehow."

"That's possible," Jack said. "But I don't want to exclude the possibility that they're supposed to remain separate."

Espy nodded. "We have three numbers that may end up being two numbers—where does that leave us?"

"I think it leaves us taking a tour," Jack answered. At Espy's puzzled look, he continued, "I don't see any of our numbers on your map. I suppose we could just walk around the cathedral and hope we spot something, if what we're looking for is even in the cathedral. Or we can find someone who knows the history."

Espy had to concede the logic, so when the next tour started fifteen minutes later, they were in the party. One problem was that the tour guide spoke only Russian, which meant Espy was forced to provide a running commentary in order for Jack to keep up. This earned them a few sour looks from other members of the group, but Espy did her best to keep her voice low. Over the next half hour they gathered much information, including the background on the iconostasis that had piqued Jack's interest earlier. But neither of them heard anything that might relate to the numbers.

As the tour neared its end, it became apparent the tour guide had saved the best for last: the bell tower. The stairs to the tower's carillon were located next to the main entrance of the cathedral, which had enthralled Peter the Great enough to commission its creation and installation.

The guide led the way up the stairs, tossing facts over his shoulder as the group followed. Jack was perhaps halfway up the narrow staircase when he saw Espy stiffen. A moment later, her hand was on his arm, gripping it tightly as she stared at the back of the guide's head. She interrupted the man, saying something in Russian. He gave a short reply, and Espy asked an immediate follow-up question. The guide responded again, this time speaking longer. When he'd finished, Espy seemed satisfied, but when they reached the top of the stairs, she pulled Jack aside.

"It's up here," she said, her voice an excited whisper.

"What is?"

"Whatever we're looking for. I think it's in this room. The carillon was installed in 1720. Apparently, Peter the Great traveled to the Netherlands and heard ones like them and commissioned a set for the cathedral."

Jack nodded. "Go on. What else?"

Espy gestured to the guide. "He tells an interesting story about Peter, who first heard the bells in Amsterdam in the late seventeenth century and the experience stayed with him. So much so that he made a return visit in disguise, climbing the bell tower of a cathedral there to get a better look."

She stopped and shifted her eyes to the carillon. Jack followed her gaze, studying the tower's bells.

"He climbed the tower in 1717," Espy said.

When she said it, Jack looked on the carillon in a new light. Chambers had pointed them to the height of the tower. Now the number seventeen. There were no coincidences.

The carillon above them was made up of perhaps two hundred bells, all arranged in rows and levels. And Henry Chambers's notes implied there was something here to find.

Jack glanced around the small space, searching for an access to the bells. He spotted one beyond the tour guide. It was a ladder—rungs built into a recess in the wall. Jack's eyes followed the ladder up until it reached a circular platform surrounding them. He looked at the guide again, then at the crowd in the room, then back to Espy.

"I think we may need some privacy," he said.

15

✝

AN HOUR PASSED AS THEY SAT in near darkness, hoping an untimely entrance by a staff member or groundskeeper wouldn't undo what they had accomplished, secreting themselves within the cathedral.

Jack looked at his watch. It was almost nine in the evening and he hadn't seen or heard anyone in at least forty-five minutes.

"Ready?" he asked his wife.

"If I stay here a minute longer, I'm not sure I'll be able to straighten again," Espy said.

Jack pushed himself up and peered down to ground level. When he didn't see anything moving, he worked himself into a sitting position and swung his legs over the lower portion of one of the twin frames of the iconostasis. They had waited until as late as possible before going into hiding, and it had been a gamble choosing to do so atop the iconostasis. Had anyone looked down at the right angle from the upper level, they would have been spotted.

They lowered themselves to the floor and then proceeded

to the front entrance, to the stairs leading up to the bell tower. Before long, they had climbed the steps and were once again looking up at the carillon.

"We started with four numbers," Espy said. "We've used two of them. That leaves the seven and the ten."

"If I didn't miss anything," Jack said to himself.

Mindful that security could do a walk-through at any time, Jack headed to the wall and began to climb, the metal cold under his hands. Espy followed, and once he'd reached the platform, he gave her a hand up. From there, he could see the narrow walkways between the rows of bells, allowing the staff access to each of them. He looked down, surprised at the distance to the floor below.

Three levels of bells spread out in front of them. Now that he could see all of them, he counted two hundred forty, with three levels of eighty, in eight rows of ten. He was puzzling over how to figure the two remaining numbers to their best advantage when Espy stepped past him and onto one of the walkways.

Jack didn't follow her. Instead he viewed the arrangement as a whole, trying to understand what Chambers had wanted them to find. As he pondered the riddle, Espy reached the other side. She ran a hand along one of the bells, careful to keep it from sounding. Then she turned around, facing Jack across the chasm.

"It's a grid," he said.

"Congratulations," Espy said. "I figured that out before we climbed up here."

Jack smirked. "The grid is ten by eight. The numbers Chambers built into his book are ten and seven." He paused and looked at the lines of bells. "But where's the starting point?"

With no obvious answer, he stepped closer to the nearest bell. The one he was studying hung in the middle level, its rigging directly in front of his face. The bronze bell wasn't large, maybe six inches. There was a molded ridge around it, an ornate line that looked like leaves and ribbon.

Out of the corner of his eye, he could see Espy doing the same thing. "Anything?" he asked.

"Nothing. It's a plain bell. The ornamentation seems purely decorative."

That was Jack's take as well. He stepped back and looked around at the more than two hundred like bells. Then he stopped himself. The best way to approach a difficult task was to break it into more manageable pieces. The first piece he had to deal with involved finding their starting point.

The only way up to the bells was the ladder behind him. Logically, the starting point would be either of the two bells on the ends of the first row. The more likely candidate was the one to Jack's left, which better simulated a genuine grid. And if that was the case, then counting ten bells down and seven across put the target on Espy's side.

"Take a look at the second to last bell on your left," he told her. "The first row."

Espy made her way across the walkway, holding on to the bell rigging as she went. Her steps were careful, her hand light on the rigging. When she got to the right place, she studied the bell in question. After several moments, she shook her head. "Nothing."

Jack frowned, even though her answer wasn't unexpected. Had she said anything else, he would have thought it too easy. He headed back to the ladder and leaned on the wall, pondering the next step. While he did, Espy reached a hand under the bell, grasping the clapper. Then, with no danger of sounding the bell, she used her other hand to tip the bell up.

Jack was lost in thought, trying to make sense of Chambers's clues, when he noticed a change in the way Espy was looking at the bell. He was intrigued enough to want to get a better view of what had attracted her attention. He started across the walkway but didn't make it halfway before Espy lowered the bell. There was no mistaking the excitement on her face. When he reached her, she tipped up the bell again. Jack leaned in close, but there was little light, not enough for him to see anything of the bell's underside. Espy shifted the bell then so that it caught the light. Even so, it was hard to see the engraving along the inner wall. It looked like Russian script.

"What does it say?"

"Ducal four," Espy said.

Jack raised an eyebrow. While he didn't know a great deal about the Fortress beyond the little he'd picked up over the last day or two, he knew that *Ducal* had to refer to the Grand Ducal burial vault on the Fortress's grounds.

He reached for the bell adjoining the one Espy was holding. Securing the clapper, he tipped it up and peered in. When he saw nothing along the inside, his excitement began to grow. Quickly he checked two more bells, neither of which turned up anything. He was about to give in to a genuine feeling of accomplishment when, almost as an afterthought, he reached for the bell just above the one Espy was still holding. When the light caught the interior of the bell, he was almost dismayed to see something inside.

"What about this one?"

Espy leaned close and peered in. "Trubetskoy seven."

Jack frowned. He knew he'd heard that word before, but

where? Releasing the bell, he pulled the map of the Fortress from his pocket, unfolding it while Espy looked on. He located the bastion, an old prison, on the map. He sighed and checked the bell at the bottom of the sequence.

"Naryshkin five," Espy said when he showed it to her.

Jack went through the motions of checking a number of other bells, both around the three with confirmed writing and at other points around the carillon. As he worked, he was mindful of how much time they were spending, knowing they couldn't count on lax security forever. So after a while, he returned to Espy.

"We have three other places to check," he said. He knew there was a hint of irritation in his voice that shouldn't have been there. They had, after all, successfully followed clues written by a man more than 150 years ago—clues they'd discovered buried in a cemetery more than a thousand miles away. He should have been giddy. Instead he understood the amount of work three additional clues represented.

Espy didn't seem to share his feelings. In fact, she was smiling. "How many couplets were there in the notebook?" she asked.

"Three."

"And on a three-dimensional grid, where we've already accounted for the first two dimensions . . ."

Before she finished, Jack's smile matched her own. According to that logic, the one they wanted had to be the top one: Trubetskoy seven.

"Have I told you today that I love you?" he said.

"Nowhere near as often as you should," she answered with a grin.

Trubetskoy Bastion, a part of the Peter and Paul Fortress, had a notorious history. At one time, it was the premier political prison in Russia, housing prisoners considered to be the most serious threats to the social and political order. Now it was a museum. The interior was built to resemble a tunnel, to limit the light, and from the cells he'd seen, to create a feeling of supreme isolation. Trubetskoy had more than sixty prison cells, but Jack was only interested in one of them—number seven.

He'd found it on the lower level. It was a corner cell with solid stone walls. He could almost feel the loneliness and despair a prisoner must have felt in the cramped space. However, the fact that it was small worked to his advantage, as it didn't take him long to find what he was looking for.

Inch by inch, he and Espy began going over the stark cell number seven. Jack found two gaps in the stone at floor level—holes barely wide enough to fit a finger. He found the one in the corner of the window wall with relative ease. The other, though, had taken a while, causing him to mentally tip his cap to whoever thought to sink it vertically into the ridge of stone running just above the cement floor. It was the separation that made it an ingenious tripping mechanism, because it took two people to make it work.

Espy balked about being asked to slip a finger into a hole that, after the passage of so many years, could have been home to all sorts of different creatures. But she did it, and when Jack did the same with the second hole, they were rewarded with a click and a movement of a portion of the wall.

Standing, Jack investigated what they had uncovered, finding that a small part of the wall slid out, revealing what looked like a door handle. Grasping it, he gave it a turn and then took a step back as a much larger section of the wall began to move.

As he watched, a seam came into view along what appeared to be a natural line in the rock, and a door of stone swung slowly open. The free edge had been shaved at an angle to ease the opening and shutting motion. When the door opened, it revealed a short tunnel about four feet long, and at the end of it was a second door.

Jack fumbled for the pitted metal latch, feeling the resistance of untold years. It wouldn't move, so he shifted his hold and tried again. This time he was rewarded with the barest hint of movement—a millimeter of something shifting. He glanced at Espy. She seemed hopeful, if not buoyed by the marginal success.

Releasing the latch, Jack adjusted his grip and tried a third time, putting as much of his weight into it as he could. Even so, it didn't move right away. It took several seconds of straining before he felt a repeat of the motion that marked this part of the wall as something separate from the rest of it.

Less than sixty seconds later he'd moved the second wall some eighteen inches to his right. In reviewing his work, as well as the seam that showed up much clearer with separation, he guessed the door was three feet at its widest, before disuse and weathering had mangled the mechanism that at one time probably allowed it to slide with ease.

Jack and Espy stood in the hall, staring into the darkness. A moldy smell emerged from the opening, and there was no way to know if it was the odor of age or of death. Jack hadn't thought to bring a flashlight and didn't know how comfortable he was entering a tunnel that may not have seen human steps in more than a century.

"We need some light," he said.

They stood in the hallway and thought about it for a while,

until Espy got a look that told Jack she'd thought of something he hadn't.

"Wait here," she said before disappearing back up the hallway.

Jack waited for maybe two minutes before prudence told him to close the outer access lest a security guard surprise him. But as he moved to do that, Espy returned. She was carrying one of the torches from the audience chamber.

She offered it to him, and he couldn't help but smile, despite the probability that any fuel the torch had once held was either spent or ruined. That was when his wife proved that her resourcefulness extended past the mere finding of the torch. Around the top of it she'd wrapped some white fabric, and as he studied it, he saw it was one of the shirts they were selling in the gift shop. Espy held out her hand, showing him more of the shirts.

"I got five of them," she said. "I'm guessing you've got a way to light them?"

Jack fished around for the lighter in his pocket. With it in hand, he started back into the tunnel. The stagnant smell strengthened the farther they went. He paused and lit the fabric wrapped around the torch. It went up quickly, letting him know they didn't have a great deal of time, regardless of the extra shirts. So, making use of the light they had available, they stepped through the second door and into another world.

The first thing Jack noticed was the slope of the ground. It headed downward, at an angle that told him it wasn't simply following the natural grade of the land.

Before going any farther, he handed the torch to Espy and, turning back, retraced his steps to the other door. He examined it until he made certain that he could open it again from this side. Satisfied, he shut it. As stone contacted stone, the hall was plunged into a darkness that would have been absolute but for the burning of the *I Love St. Petersburg* T-shirt wrapped around the medieval torch. Jack did the same for the second door and then turned to venture forward.

He ran a hand along the rock as he walked, feeling the cold beneath his fingers. Because the tunnel was narrow, the light did a passable job illuminating their way, showing perhaps a dozen feet before them with clarity. They descended for a long while. The first shirt burned down to cinders, until it was casting only the barest light on the walls. Once it had gone out entirely, Jack and Espy went on walking in darkness, trusting the path to continue along the same lines. It wasn't until he noticed the slope begin to lessen, to return them to what felt like a horizontal path, that Jack lit the second shirt.

The tunnel had widened as they walked, and the walls, once smooth stone, were now rough-cut and irregular. It was as if they were entering a true subterranean cavern rather than anything made by human hands. It made Jack wonder if Peter the Great chose this location for the Fortress for reasons lost to the history books. It made him wonder how many more secret tunnels existed beneath the place.

The torch burned lower, and Jack was considering using another shirt while also calculating how much light they'd need for the walk back when his hand touched something that felt different from the rough wall. It was a peculiar enough sensation to make him stop and backtrack a couple of steps. He ran his hand over the wall again and found it—the smooth spot surrounded by rough. He brought the torch in closer. But while he could pick out something pale in the rock, he couldn't see it in any detail. So he took out another shirt and wrapped it around the torch.

It took a few seconds to catch, and then for the flame to build, to bring the hidden thing into the light. Espy gasped. Jack's reaction was only silence as he looked at the skull staring back at him.

There was no way to tell for sure how many years it had been there, but Jack guessed it to be a long while. He reached out and touched the place where it met the wall; the stone had been hollowed out to fit the skull.

"Jack," Espy said. It was the way she'd said his name that made him turn away from the skull and look back at her. She'd taken a step back away from the wall, but her eyes were on it, staring past Jack, around him. When he looked back to the wall, he held the torch up higher. And in the light, the rock wall resolved into a thousand or more black eyes. The torchlight didn't reach far, but as he peered at the edges, as he followed the upward run of the wall, the skulls seemed to go on forever.

Jack took a step back, regarding the macabre spectacle with awe, revulsion and . . . wonder. The shirt wrapped around the torch had started to unravel, a section of it falling off. He grabbed for it and wound it around the torch's weak flame. As it rekindled, as the light reached into the distance, Espy gasped again.

The wall of death facing them went up at least a hundred feet, with the evidence of brutality disappearing into the darkness with it. There was a part of Jack's brain that was having a difficult time processing what he was seeing, and it took several seconds before he could grasp the reason. It was because there was nothing in the culture of the area to suggest this sort of thing, nothing in the history that spoke of this kind of cruelty. What he saw in front of him was an ancient evil, something that came from some other place and found a home here.

"What is this place?" Espy asked.

Jack didn't have an answer for her, especially because, as he forced himself to turn away from the wall, he saw the impossibility of it. They had entered an enormous chamber, a cavern large enough to swallow the torchlight before it could strike the far wall. But as he followed the curve of the wall with his eyes, he saw no break in the lines of skulls. There were thousands of them. Maybe more than that.

He advanced along the wall, his steps slow, wanting to take it all in and yet rebelling against the idea. The level of mass murder here was nothing he'd ever seen, not even in sites from ancient civilizations where emperors would take their soldiers with them to protect them in the afterlife. No, this was something closer to Mayan practices, although Jack thought that even the Mayan might have blanched at this level of human slaughter.

The torch was fading again. Jack knew that only two shirts remained with which to keep the flame going, and seeing what was around them, there was no way he was going to get stuck here in the dark. Thus motivated, he shifted his attention to the rest of the cavern.

He and Espy moved along the wall, not looking at it, until after a while Jack began to see a shadow up ahead—an object that stood out from the wall. He stopped and held the torch aloft, but the flame was low enough that he couldn't see the object clearly. He debated putting a new shirt to the flame, but held off, choosing instead to approach the object.

They were still yards away when he thought he knew what it was. He stopped, taking hold of Espy's hand.

"I have to go take a look," he said, "but you don't have to."

"If you think I'm going to stand here in the dark with all

those skulls looking at me while you walk away with the only light we have, you're out of your mind."

"Good point," Jack said, taking her hand in his.

They closed the distance to the object, an expanse of stone maybe seven feet by five feet. It was entirely flat, and as Jack leaned in closer, he understood that his original thought was wrong. With the multitude of silent witnesses around them, his initial thought had been that the stone was an altar, a sacrificial slab. Now he didn't believe that to be the case, if for no other reason than the fact that he could find no discoloration on the surface, no stains of dried blood. Instead, the colors he saw on the slab were vivid. And intentional.

"Please tell me they didn't perform sacrifices here," Espy said.

"They didn't," he assured her.

He turned his attention back to the slab. The entire top surface of the stone was covered with crude-looking images—pictographs really. Jack tried to make sense of them. They seemed to be organized in rows, four of them across the stone. In the low light, it was almost impossible to make sense of the images, but his experience told him he was looking at a story, a progression of ideas and events.

"This is very old," he said. When Espy didn't answer, he looked up. "Too old for this place."

Jack looked back at the stone. He could feel his heart beat faster as the importance of their discovery hit him. Running a hand along the stone, he felt the channels cut by ancient artisans.

"These are petroglyphs," he said, unable to keep the excitement from his voice. He went to a knee, bringing the fading torch in closer. He could see that he was wrong. The slab wasn't uniform; it was irregular. And the striated edges confirmed a fledgling thought. "This was brought here from somewhere else."

The light continued to fade, and Jack knew they didn't have enough fuel. Nowhere near enough to stave off the darkness for as long as it would take for him to examine the slab, to give it the study it deserved.

He looked at Espy. The dying flame of the torch gave his features a flushed appearance. "We need *real* light," he said.

Jack was worried that it had taken them the better part of an hour to find another light source. The fact that they hadn't yet been discovered—that some security guard hadn't noticed the new seam in the cell wall and then the door—was the kind of luck he couldn't count on continuing. The problem was, his need for haste was running headlong into his desire to go over every inch of the stone slab.

He and Espy each held a flashlight—large industrial ones taken from a utility closet near the bastion entrance. Both beams were focused on the slab, and the longer Jack looked at it, the more excited he became.

"It's at least 700 BC," he said. The carvings occupied four rows, and it was now apparent that they told a story. "These look like the Häljesta petroglyphs," he added. Then he paused, spotting something in the top corner. "Except here they look more like the Ughtasar set."

"And I assume there's something peculiar about that?"

"*Peculiar* is a good word for it." The longer Jack looked, the more influences he spotted on the slab—petroglyphs in a half-dozen styles. It was a remarkable discovery, but one that presented a real puzzle. "I'd bet my life these carvings were done more than twenty-five hundred years ago. But I'm finding at least six different regional influences—none of which I'd expect to find occupying the same stone."

"You're saying they all tell the same story?"

Jack shined the light over what he determined to be the start of the story, then worked his way along, following the progression of it. He was halfway through when he decided to move the light to bear on the first image. He hovered there for a few seconds before shifting the light slowly down the line. When he stopped, the portion of the slab bathed in light showed several lines, forming an image that Jack recognized.

"It's . . . it's Elisha's story," he said. He moved the light back to the start and progressed again, this time stopping at the end of the fourth row. He saw nothing to make him doubt his theory. "It's telling a linear story, using petroglyphs from six different cultures. Incredible . . ."

Espy stepped closer to the stone, running her hand over it. "That doesn't make sense. It was the Israelites who took possession of the bones. They're the ones who formed the order. So why are there so many different cultures showing up here?"

"Except that I'm pretty sure the Israelites lost possession of the bones, or at least sole possession of them, not long after they reached Egypt," Jack said. "Think about it. We've seen evidence of this organization's influence across a number of cultures. Egyptian and Mayan for starters. How many more cultural or religious histories have stories that could be better understood by placing a global priesthood having magical bones in the midst of them? I think what we're seeing on this stone is that the religion practiced by the Priests of Osiris is a set of philosophies and practices they've accumulated from other people groups over the centuries."

"Or maybe it's the other way around. Maybe the cultures and religions were influenced by the ones who did this." Espy gestured toward the slab.

He considered that and, in doing so, realized it was the sort of academic question that could send him into months of research—the sort of question that had been missing for so long at Evanston. The stone slab in front of him was a snapshot in time, a record of the order when it was still relatively young. To study it—to take it apart piece by intellectual piece—would give him the kind of insight into the organization that he'd been searching for.

Such a realization, though, reminded him that he didn't have the time it would take to properly address the question. As fascinating as the slab was, it spoke of the Priests of Osiris as they were more than two thousand years ago. He had to believe that Chambers's notebook had led them there for something else. Grudgingly he stepped away from the stone slab and he and Espy continued walking along the wall.

They didn't have to go far. Perhaps twenty yards past the slab was a door that opened into the wall. For a subterranean door in the middle of a cavern of horrors, it was surprisingly nondescript. It looked to be made of a single piece of wood set on simple hinges. The handle was a lever, and there was no lock. Jack looked at Espy, who returned a shrug. He turned back to the door and tried the handle.

The door opened easily, although the action produced a squeal as hinges that had not seen use in a very long time were awakened. When Jack crossed the threshold, he frowned because, while he wasn't sure what he was expecting, what he saw wasn't it.

The place had the look of a small lecture hall. The room was twenty feet square at the largest and was filled with chairs. There were six rows of six, all facing toward a point in the room where a podium stood. Jack couldn't pinpoint the date of the chairs with the accuracy Romero might have, but he thought they were of the Shaker style, which would place them around 1850.

Espy came in and stopped next to him. "It's like hell's conference room," she remarked.

Jack smiled, yet he couldn't dismiss the comparison. It was precisely what the place felt like.

He walked deeper into the room, heading for the podium. It was large, about the same time period as the chairs. He couldn't help but wonder who in the past had stood at this podium. What was discussed here?

It wasn't until he walked around to the front of it that he felt his breath catch in his throat. The top of the podium was bare, its surface scratched and pitted. But there was a shelf on this side, a slot from which a book protruded. He bent down and carefully pulled the book out. Straightening, he set it on the podium. He could tell right away it was very old. The leather cover was cracked and worn, the pages yellowed. As he opened it, the spine creased.

Espy was at his side in seconds.

There was no cover page, but he wouldn't have expected one. Neither was there any preliminary information—no date, publisher, edition. The reason for that became clear as he saw the print. "This is Gutenberg type," he said.

Espy leaned in close. "I can hardly read it."

"I wouldn't have expected you to be able to. Even in English, some of those early typefaces are almost impossible to read. This looks German to me, and really old. Maybe the mid 1400s."

Espy whistled.

Jack couldn't read German, so he moved a half step to the left, allowing Espy to view the book.

In the conference room of an ancient organization, adjoining an enormous underground cavern with a horde of muted witnesses, Espy read from a book that was likely more than five hundred years old, a book that could well contain secrets about what might be the oldest and most influential group of men and women defined by a particular ideology.

Jack moved away from the podium, giving his wife the time she needed to decipher old German in Gutenberg type on aged paper. He walked the perimeter of the room, not really looking for anything but keeping an eye out should something strike him. He didn't know how long he waited. At some point he took a seat on one of the old chairs, absently wondering who might have sat in the same seat. He watched Espy. She was bent over the work, oblivious to all else.

Jack rose and went to the door, looking out into the darkness. He took a deep breath, the air of centuries come and gone filling his lungs. In the silence, he pondered the existence of a benevolent God who might have ignored whatever evil happened in this place. A God who would allow powerful men to alter the course of history and exploit others was a God whose worth some people might call into question. Yet Jack couldn't bring himself to do it. He'd seen enough to understand that the evil that men did was theirs alone, and that God acted as the redemptive force in the midst of evil.

Even after all these years, after adopting the faith and trying to raise his children in it as best he could, it was still a difficult position to take. But he didn't see how he could do otherwise. The best that humanity had to offer—the love, the willingness to help others, the push to reach for things that seemed unattainable—was evidence that the human condition was more than just self-preservation, more than kill or be killed. There was a spiritual aspect to existence that mandated the existence of God. It was the same thing that allowed Jack to look out on the evidences of human depravity, the silent witnesses in the walls, and imagine a people who could be saved from all of it.

He snorted at his own musings and reached into his breast pocket, pulling out a cigar. He lit it and then stood in the doorway for several minutes, until Espy called for him. When he joined her again at the podium, her face was flushed, even in the limited light. It appeared that she was about halfway through the book. He didn't bother looking at the place her finger was pointing; he wouldn't have been able to read it anyway. Instead he looked to his wife, whose face glowed with satisfaction.

Jack raised an expectant eyebrow.

"We're going to Paris," Espy said.

16

✝

THE SKY OVER SAINT PETERSBURG was a slate gray the next morning, a leaden overlay that met a city of similar color at a point in the distance. Old weather-beaten buildings rose up on each side of the street, everything gray, even the snow that formed a dingy blanket over streets and buildings.

Jack and Espy followed a broken, uneven sidewalk as they walked back to the hotel from the tiny café where they'd found breakfast, their collective mood standing in stark contrast to their somber surroundings. Despite the number of times it had happened over the years, Jack was always surprised when he succeeded in discovering something hidden from the rest of the world for an untold number of years. It left him with a sense of exhilaration, a rekindled fire that more than balanced the struggles he'd faced along the way. There always came a time when there were additional hurdles to cross, plans to make, but for a little while he could enjoy the feeling of having done something near impossible.

He and Espy had said little since leaving the café. Suddenly Jack realized how tired he was. He looked over at Espy and saw the same weariness on her face. Like him, she desperately missed the boys.

They traversed another block before Jack first recognized that something was wrong. As he and Espy walked down the street, joining the streams of people that gave the city life, he began to grow uneasy. He couldn't explain why exactly, but he felt an urge to look over his shoulder. He had the feeling they were being watched.

"What's wrong?" Espy asked.

Jack forced a smile. "Nothing. I'm just a little anxious, that's all."

Around them, the people they passed gave every indication of being oblivious to what he was sensing. They were walking a street lined with small storefronts, eateries, clothing stores, coffee shops, and bookstores—all packed tightly together. It was the sort of area where a pair of foreigners could lose themselves.

Jack put a hand on the small of Espy's back and smiled. "Let's go into one of the stores up ahead," he said. "Just as casual as we can."

"Okay," Espy said, looking a bit worried.

Jack searched for the right place, something with a narrow door, a dark interior. Then he spotted it, a bookstore, just ahead. They slipped inside the small shop, which was so crammed with used books that the two of them could barely walk side by side. So Jack and Espy switched to single file and moved toward the back, where they found a more open area.

There was no proprietor in sight. Jack used the opportunity to pause and take stock of their situation. He looked back up the main aisle, past the stacks of old, musty books. Through the dirt-glazed window facing the street, he saw people passing in both directions. He didn't see anything out of the ordinary.

"What's going on?" Espy asked, her eyes also on the window.

"I'm not sure." Just when he was starting to wonder if he was losing his mind, a man in a dark coat walked by, and there was something about the way he glanced into the store as he passed that sent a shiver up Jack's spine. Then the man was gone, continuing down the sidewalk, out of Jack's line of sight. Jack's hand moved to the gun behind his back, but he didn't pull it out.

"We're being followed," he said.

"Are you certain?" Espy asked.

Jack nodded and looked around the store, now wondering if entering it had been a wise move after all. In such a small establishment, hardly fifteen feet from wall to wall, there were few places to hide. He looked toward the back. Several more stacks of books occupied the space between where they stood and a doorway that led into a back room.

"Let's go," he said. "Follow me."

He started for the back, negotiating his way around bookcases and customers browsing in the tight space. When he reached the doorway, he peeked into the back and found a storage room—more books stretched floor to ceiling, the arrangement even more haphazard than the layout on the sales floor. But what he didn't see was the proprietor, which was starting to puzzle him. He began to wonder if whoever ran the place was not around but had stepped out for some reason.

At the other end of the back room was a metal door, probably leading to the outside. Espy moved first, reaching the door and giving it a push. Jack followed, and soon they were outside, the chill breeze feeling welcome after the mustiness of the bookstore. They were standing in an alley between multi-story buildings. There was a smell like rotten food.

Jack and Espy hurried down the alley. Before they reached the end of it, Jack spotted a cut-through that led to a street parallel to the one they'd been walking on prior to ducking into the bookstore. He got Espy's attention and took the cut-through, emerging onto a street that looked like a twin of the other.

Jack started off in the opposite of their original direction. After traveling a block, he no longer had the impression they were being followed and so he slowed, not wanting to draw attention to themselves.

"Do you think it's McKeller?" Espy asked.

Jack considered the question. He was inclined to think their tail was courtesy of the organization whose secrets Jack was unearthing. They had already displayed a propensity for finding Jack and Espy, no matter how carefully they tried to cover their tracks. But McKeller had also demonstrated an ability to have people in place. The man had proven his re-sourcefulness, and Jack didn't doubt his motivation. But what swayed Jack, what made him lean toward his older enemy, was the evidence that pointed to a substantial presence here in Saint Petersburg.

"I don't think so," he said.

Espy was quiet for a time. Jack knew what she was think-ing, because he suspected he was in the same place. The fact that the Priests of Osiris had a man on them had to mean they already knew what Jack and Espy had discovered. The moment Jack and Espy opened the door in Trubetskoy seven, they'd probably signed their death warrants. Up to that point, everything Jack knew about the organization was conjecture and hearsay. Now, having seen for himself the underground cavern, he had proof not so easily rebutted.

As he considered the gravity of their situation, Jack wondered how much the current leadership of the Priests of Osiris knew about their own history. Nothing in the cavern had given Jack the impression it had seen use in a very long time. The fact that the book was there seemed to imply the place had been abandoned. Jack wondered if, in discovering the book, he and Espy had found something lost even to its original owners.

"When we decided to come for the bones, we knew we'd be putting ourselves in danger," Jack said. He caught Espy's eye and smiled. "So I guess we're right on schedule."

Espy shook her head. "What's the point of finding the bones for the sake of the boys if we end up dead and they become orphans?"

"Well, a lot of people have wanted me dead over the years, and I'm still here. So they'll have to get in line."

Even as he said it, he could see that he wasn't helping matters. Instead of saying anything else, he simply stopped walking so he could regain his bearings.

The hotel was back in the other direction, though Jack wasn't certain they could go back there. If the Priests of Osiris had someone following them, it was likely they knew where Jack and Espy were staying. The problem was, most of their belongings were at the hotel. What little money they had, Jack had on him, as well as their passports and one of the guns. But their clothes and research were at the hotel. Espy was carrying the Chambers notebook, along with the book they'd brought with them from the cavern.

Jack ran a hand through his hair, absently looking at a street sign he couldn't read. He'd started to turn to Espy when his peripheral vision caught something coming from his left, something moving a good deal faster than any of the vehicles or pedestrians around them. Jack hardly had time to twist his neck before he heard the squeal of tires. Acting on instinct, he spun around on his bad knee and lunged at Espy. He hit her hard, his shoulder in her ribs, coming down on top of her. He felt a rush of air behind him and heard the screeching of brakes. Someone started to scream, but the sound was suddenly drowned out by the crunch of metal on metal.

The pain in his knee was overwhelming. It was all he could do to keep from crying out. Beneath him, Espy was struggling. Despite the pain, Jack had to move. He rolled off his wife, the motion sending fresh jolts of agony through his leg. He blinked twice to clear his vision and to bear witness to how close he and Espy had come to being in the path of the car—a car that had come to an abrupt halt against the steel base of a streetlamp. The front of the car was crushed, its windshield shattered. He couldn't see the driver. People were approaching the car. He saw a few moving toward him.

Jack turned to Espy. She was pushing herself to a sitting position while trying to come to terms with what had just happened.

"We have to go," Jack said.

She didn't speak, but after glancing at the crumpled car, she nodded and rose to her feet. Her nose was bleeding, yet she didn't seem to realize it. She grimaced and touched her nose, pulling back fingers covered in blood.

Following his wife's lead, Jack tried to stand. But the pain was too much and his knee buckled when he went to put weight on it. He fell back onto the pavement. Espy rushed to help, supporting him as he attempted again to stand. With his arm around Espy's shoulders, Jack rocked onto his leg, testing the knee. He could feel it start to give way.

"I can't walk on it," he said.

"Then we'll have to see how fast you can hop."

She took hold of the hand Jack had on her shoulder, then tightened her hold around his waist. Jack leaned into her. Just before they started off, he chanced a look back and saw a man struggling to get out of the wrecked car. He was fumbling with the door handle, but it wouldn't open. He looked up, meeting Jack's eyes.

"Oh no," Espy said.

Jack expected to see her looking at the man inside the car. Instead she was looking somewhere else. He followed her line of vision but didn't notice anything right away. Then he saw it, the leg just visible under the front of the car. There was a woman's shoe. Jack saw blood. There was no movement under the car, no sounds. The woman couldn't have survived. A few good Samaritans were at the front of the car, peering underneath it.

"We have to go," Jack repeated.

Espy hesitated for just a second before walking back the way they'd come. She was carrying a lot of Jack's weight, and try as he might, he couldn't put more than the slightest pressure on his leg. The going was slow. They made it half a block before a gunshot cut through the city noise. Jack glanced back at the car wreck.

The man in the car had shot out one of the side windows. He reached a hand through and opened the car door from the outside. Jack noticed the crowd had taken cover, and the streets were now quiet. He didn't see a soul but for a couple of people on the other side of the intersection, running in the other direction. Beyond that, everyone had either ducked into nearby businesses or dived behind parked cars or other large objects.

Espy was trying to move them along, but Jack knew they wouldn't be able to outrun the shooter once he'd climbed out of the car.

"We need to hide somewhere," he said between pained breaths. He frantically looked around, searching for a place in which they could disappear, something like the bookstore.

Espy saw it first. Farther down the street, the storefronts had sunken entrances, three or four steps below street level. On their left was one such storefront, also having the benefit of two low cement walls lining the steps to its entrance. Above the store hung a green sign with the number 24 on it. When they reached it, Espy lowered Jack none too gently down the steps, then quickly followed. Just as Espy stepped within the cement walls, a shot rang out, followed by an impact with the cement barrier.

The door of the business was open, and Jack motioned for Espy to enter. When she stooped to help him up, he waved her off.

"Go on," he said. "I'll be right behind you."

"Not on your life," she said, trying to slip her arm around his waist again. "I'm not leaving you here."

While she struggled to find a hold, he reached around and pulled out the gun. When Espy saw it, she paused.

"We can't get away with me weighing you down," he said. "I'm not asking you to leave without me. I'm just asking you to wait inside."

Right then, a woman Jack assumed was the store's owner came to the door. She scowled at Jack and Espy as if they were loitering in front of her place of business. It looked as though she was about to come out and shoo them away when she saw the gun and then jumped away from the door. Her secondary reaction, though, was almost as quick. She was reaching to lock the door when Esperanza leaped for the handle, pushing the door open before the storeowner could slide the bolt.

The storeowner began to scream. Espy tried to communicate to the woman that they weren't a threat, but the owner only screamed louder as she turned and ran for safety deeper into the store.

Espy looked at Jack, shrugged, then started after the frightened woman. Once she was gone, Jack shifted position, putting his back against the wall, facing the direction of the man shooting at them. It didn't take long before he appeared, his head coming into view first. He was in a full run, only slowing to negotiate the turn into the store. But when he saw Jack, he stumbled.

Jack had a clear shot. The other man was at the top of the stairs, just a few feet away. Jack looked up at him, the gun in his hand steady. The shooter's own weapon was held low, pointing at the pavement.

He wasn't the same man who'd walked by the bookstore. He was much younger. His eyes—wide with exertion and surprise—were the same gray as the Saint Petersburg sky.

There was a frozen moment during which neither man moved. Jack was the first to speak.

"If you put the gun down and walk away, I won't have to shoot you."

The man didn't budge. "You won't get out of Saint Petersburg," the man said, his accent thick.

"That may be so, but unless you put that gun down, you're not going to make it off this street."

Jack saw calculation in the other man's eyes. He was wondering if he could get his gun up before Jack could fire off a shot. He was also probably wondering how long he had before the police showed up in response to the accident, and to investigate reports of a man running down the street with a gun.

It happened so fast that Jack almost missed the man's gun rising up. And as he watched the muzzle swing toward him, it seemed like forever before Jack could bring his own finger to pull the trigger. In the confined space, the roar was deafening, and Jack couldn't tell if it was coming from his own gun or the other man's. There was a shower of dust as the cement next to Jack's head was blown apart. He didn't even have time to close his eyes.

When it was over, the man was lying on the sidewalk, clutching his leg.

Using the cement wall as leverage, Jack tried to stand while still keeping the gun trained on the fallen man. He was moving, one hand holding the place where his knee used to be. The man writhed on the pavement, his injured leg bleeding profusely. He shouted in what Jack could only assume was Russian. His gun lay on the sidewalk next to him.

As Jack struggled to work his way up to the next step, the man opened his eyes.

"I don't want to kill you," Jack told him. It wasn't just a platitude. Despite all that had happened, Jack had no desire to kill this man, which was why he'd aimed low.

With a snarl the man turned to look for his gun. Seeing where it lay, he reached for it, his fingers brushing the grip.

Jack pushed away from the wall, throwing himself up the two steps that separated him from the other man. He didn't quite make it. Instead of landing on top of him, the best Jack could do was to bring an arm down on the ruined leg. It was enough to make him stop reaching for the gun. The man convulsed and released a scream and then rolled into Jack. Interlocked, they tumbled down the stairs. During the fall, Jack dropped his gun. He heard it clatter on the steps.

When they reached the bottom, the man was on top of Jack. Jack's gun was only a couple of feet away. The man strained to grab it. Jack tried to struggle out from under the man, using his free hand to pull back the man's reaching arm, to grasp his shirtsleeve.

But the man whipped his head around and brought his forehead down hard on Jack's. The blow took away Jack's sight momentarily, and he released the man's arm. Jack felt the weight on him shift. His vision cleared in time to see the gun coming around, the man's grip sure. He almost had the gun to Jack's temple when the man jerked backward, lost his balance, and collapsed to the pavement, again clutching his leg. Jack saw a startled look on his face.

Only then did Jack hear the yelling and cursing in Spanish. He looked to his left, where he saw Espy standing above him. Her face was contorted in anger. She stepped over Jack, went to the downed man, and brought a knee down on his chest. The man brought his arms up to protect his face from the blows she rained down on him. He tried to crawl away, groping around for the gun he'd dropped.

Espy, though, slapped away the man's hand and snatched

up the weapon. Breathing heavily, she pressed it against his head. "Is this what you want?" she spat. "Is this what you're looking for?"

Instantly the man stopped his struggling. Once he was subdued, Espy looked over at Jack. "Are you okay?" she asked.

Jack was anything but okay, but he nodded all the same. He pushed himself to a sitting position. Espy turned her attention back to the man pinned beneath her.

"Who sent you?" she shouted. Despite the gun pointed at him, the man's only response was to glare up at her. She leaned in closer, her face only inches away from his. "Last week my sons were taken from me. Since then I've been chased through four countries, I've been shot at, and I haven't been able to take even one bath. And this one"—she gestured to Jack—"made me desecrate a grave. So if you think I'm not willing to shoot you, I urge you to think again."

When she finished, Espy didn't pull back. She kept her face close, eyes boring into his, until a flicker of doubt crossed the man's face. At that, Espy pushed the gun harder into his temple.

The man swallowed. "Her name is Olivia Chambers," he said, casting a glance in Jack's direction.

"Olivia Chambers?" Espy said, looking shocked.

Jack was just as surprised as his wife. "Why does *she* want us dead?"

The man shook his head. "She didn't tell me. She never does." He winced in pain. "Please . . . I need a doctor."

Espy turned to Jack. "What do we do with him?"

He was pondering their dilemma when he saw movement to his right. The storeowner had gathered the courage to come to the door. She was holding a cell phone.

"Excuse me," Jack said. The woman's eyes moved from

Espy and the man lying on the ground to Jack. "Would you happen to have any rope?"

Her expression didn't change—not until Espy, with the gun still pressed to the other man's head, translated. Afterward, the storeowner gave a nod and disappeared into her store.

17

✝

ESPY CHECKED THE WINDOW AGAIN, lifting the shade to scan the street. It was the fourth time she'd done so, and Jack couldn't blame her. The people after them—both sets of them—had demonstrated an uncanny ability to determine their whereabouts. For all he knew, a member of the Priests of Osiris might have watched Jack and Espy leave the scene of their altercation with the assassin.

Leaving the window, Espy returned to the bed, where Jack sat against the headboard, a pillow shoved behind his lower back. His knee was wrapped in a towel with ice cubes sandwiched between the fabric and his bare skin.

"How are you feeling?" she asked.

Beneath the towel he tried to move his leg. It responded to his commands, but the pain was extraordinary. The knee had been the bane of his existence for years. He always knew it would give out at some point; it just couldn't have picked a worse time to prove him right.

"Not bad," he lied.

Her smile told him she was aware of the lie. He reached for her hand and pulled her near. She curled up next to him, her head on his chest.

"I miss the boys," she said.

"So do I."

They lapsed into silence, and after several minutes Jack realized that she was asleep. He remained still, knowing how desperately both of them needed rest, but his mind wouldn't shut down to allow him to join her. He lay there awake for a long while as his wife slept.

The words of the nameless assassin came back to him, that he and Espy would never be able to leave Saint Petersburg. Jack knew the man wasn't making it up. Every dock, every airfield, every taxi service—all of them would have eyes watching. And Jack had no reason to doubt the resources available to accomplish that sort of surveillance. By mentioning Olivia Chambers, the man had confirmed for Jack that they were up against an entity with unlimited clout.

And what did he and Espy have available to them? They had less than five hundred dollars. They had questionable passports, especially with McKeller demonstrating his ability to hijack the surveillance power of the CIA. He had two guns—one with fourteen rounds and a second, tucked away in the duffel as a backup, with much less. They had archaeological and linguistic currency, and an old book that was pointing them toward Paris.

Espy had explained to him how everything she read in the book led to Paris as the base of operations for the Priests of Osiris. The organization identified Paris early on as a place where it could sink its roots. There was an entire chapter devoted to analyzing the appropriateness of the city as a staging ground for their activities. Jack hoped the book had more to go on, because Paris made Saint Petersburg look like a hamlet. Without any additional information, they could go no further than poking around the Eiffel Tower.

Their list of assets had them coming up woefully short. He didn't know how they were going to get out of Saint Petersburg, much less get to Paris. He weighed the possibility of walking into the nearest police station and telling them everything he knew. But considering where they were, and with the forces that had seen him and Espy holed up in a hotel that wouldn't have appeared in anyone's travel guide, he suspected the Priests had the resources to make sure any report Jack made to the Russian police would be swallowed up in paperwork and bureaucracy.

So once again he was back to their assets. He was contemplating their options going forward when he felt himself nodding off. When he awakened with a start, almost an hour later, the question about how to escape Saint Petersburg was still heavy on his mind. But the answer seemed close to presenting itself.

As he settled back, putting an arm around his wife, he found himself thinking about Duckey, and Romero, and all the other people who'd helped him along the way—offering guidance, money, information, a place to stay. The question now was who could he call on to help them with the present dilemma? Several minutes passed as he considered this, and at some point he fell asleep again. When a movement from Espy roused him, the answer was as obvious as it was insane.

The disposable cell phones had been left at their last hotel—a place they couldn't return to—the phones with numbers that either Romero or Duckey would recognize. The only phone Jack had available was the one in his pocket, which had about ten prepaid minutes left on it.

He rose and walked to the other side of the small room, fishing the phone from his pocket. He powered it on and, before dialing the number, rehearsed what he needed to say. He had ten minutes to make three calls.

Duckey answered before the first ring had completed. "Where in the world *are* you?"

"Hey, Ducks. Listen, I only have a minute or so and I need you to do something for me."

Jack could feel the exasperation coming from his friend. It had been days since they'd gone silent in response to McKeller's tap of Duckey's phone, days since Jack had taken down the numbers for Duckey's own disposables, and Jack couldn't begrudge Duckey his irritation over his not making use of those numbers. Yet he didn't have time to explain his hesitance at dragging Duckey in any further. For now, Duckey would have to content himself with hearing Jack's voice and knowing his friend wasn't dead.

"What do you need?" Duckey asked.

"When Martin Templeton had me in Libya, I called the Israelis to broker a deal. I need their number."

Duckey went silent. Jack could imagine him pondering the weight of his request—along with the idiocy of it.

"How do I find the number?" Duckey asked after a time.

"I called them from Templeton's phone, but I entered the number in my own. Can your friends at the Agency access my phone and give me the number I've saved as Mossad?"

"You have the Mossad's phone number saved in your directory?"

"Doesn't everyone?"

Jack could sense Duckey's silent grumbling through the phone.

"Just so you know, my contacts are running a bit dry at the moment. This McKeller thing has everyone pretty spooked. So I can't promise anything."

"I know, Ducks," Jack said. "And thanks." When he disconnected, Jack felt better than he had a few minutes ago.

He fell asleep again, and woke when the phone rang. He fumbled for the phone.

"Do you know how hard it is to get a phone number that someone has entered into their cell phone but never called?" Duckey asked.

"I'm guessing not very hard?"

"Wrong," Duckey said. "Because now the technical geniuses I've always counted on to help me with these little favors of yours are wetting themselves at the thought of getting caught providing information to an ex-agent."

Jack felt his heart sink. "So you didn't get it."

"No, I got it. I'm just saying it wasn't easy."

Jack snorted and shook his head. "You're pretty pleased with yourself, aren't you?"

"Very much so," Duckey said. "You have a pen and paper ready?"

Jack opened the desk drawer and found a notepad and pen. "Ready."

When he was finished giving Jack the number, Duckey said, "You do realize you're about to call a group of people who almost killed you, right?"

"I'm aware of that."

"And you think that's a good idea?"

"At this point, Ducks, I'm out of ideas. So if you can suggest anything that might get us out of Saint Petersburg without drawing anyone's attention, I'd love to hear it."

"Did you say Saint Petersburg?"

Jack was about to fill him in when the phone beeped. He pulled it away from his ear and read the display. "It looks like this phone is going dead soon."

"Call me on the next one," Duckey said. "I have the list."

"Unfortunately, the Priests of Osiris have overrun our last hotel," Jack said. "So they have the other phones now."

"The Priests of who—?" Duckey asked.

But before Jack could respond, the phone went dead. He tossed the phone in the trash, then went to the bed and woke up Espy. "I'm going to get a phone," he said.

She blinked a few times and then nodded. Jack wasn't sure she heard him or grasped what he'd said, but he didn't press the issue. She was asleep again by the time he opened the door, the number for the Israelis in his pocket.

He found a store not too far from the hotel, which was good because his limp made it an arduous journey. There was some minor difficulty when the language barrier kept him from discerning the amount being charged for the phone, but he worked it out by handing the clerk too much and hoping he didn't get ripped off. Then, with the phone activated, Jack headed back to the hotel. He made the call from outside so that he didn't disturb Espy.

Despite his nonchalance with Duckey, Jack experienced some trepidation as he made the call. The last time he'd called this number, it was to negotiate a trade for his life. By his reckoning, the Israelis still owed him. If they didn't feel the same, however, then he was setting himself up with another adversary.

They picked up on the second ring, using a language Jack guessed to be Hebrew.

"Hello," he said. "This is Jack Hawthorne. Can I speak to whoever it was I spoke with about ten years ago?"

He had no idea who was on the other end of the call. For all he knew, it was someone fresh out of whatever passed for the Israeli spy academy. That was why the lack of an immediate response didn't make him nervous. It took almost a full minute before someone answered. It was a new voice.

"Dr. Hawthorne, I was under the impression that our business was concluded," the man said in English.

"As was I," Jack said. "But sometimes extenuating circumstances change things. I'm afraid I need another favor."

Silence fell again, and Jack could only imagine what was going on in the man's mind.

"You delivered something to us, and in return we allowed you to live. A simple transaction, one that left no debt on either side."

Jack couldn't argue the man's point. Years earlier, when he'd attempted to find the Nehushtan—the serpent staff of Moses—he was taken prisoner by someone working for the Israeli government, a man who'd decided to allow a personal vendetta to get in the way of delivering the Nehushtan to the Israelis. In the process, the Mossad marked both of them for a hit. It was only because Jack was able to deliver the staff to them that they allowed him to live.

"What if I can offer you another something?" Jack asked.

"I doubt you could offer us anything of significance" was the reply.

Jack smiled. "What if I told you that I could help you locate the bones of the prophet Elisha? That I could give you the name and address of the super-secret ancient society that's had them in their possession for more than two thousand years?"

After yet another long moment of silence, the man said, "You're saying the bones of Elisha still exist? I'm sorry, Dr. Hawthorne, but I find that very hard to believe."

"They still exist. I can give your people information on the whereabouts of an underground chamber where the bones were once kept. They're not in the chamber anymore, but I imagine you're smart enough to figure things out from there. But in return, I'm going to need something from you. My wife and I are currently stranded in Saint Petersburg. We need to get out of the country and the usual avenues are closed to us. You get us out, give us enough money to survive on for a little while, and the location's yours."

This time, it wasn't silence Jack heard. Instead he heard the muffled sounds of people talking behind a phone not properly muted.

"I'm sure you understand what will happen if we discover you're being disingenuous," the Israeli said.

"I understand. If I'm lying, you'll kill me. But, just between you and me, you're going to have to take a number on that one."

With that, he told the Israeli the hotel address and then ended the call. He'd played his hand. Now it was up to them.

18

IT HAD BEEN THIRTY-TWO HOURS since Jack made the call to the Israelis, and his phone had remained silent since then. He and Espy had left the room only to get food. Jack was starting to wonder if the Israelis had decided to decline his offer, if the help he'd hoped for wasn't coming. He said as much to Espy.

"They'll be here," she said. "You were right when you called their interest in Israeli artifacts a mandate to reclaim their cultural identity. Beyond the Ark of the Covenant and the Grail, I'd be hard-pressed to think of something more desirable than the bones of one of their most important prophets." She frowned. "Well, I'm not sure they'd be interested in the Grail, but you get my point."

"What about Noah's Ark?"

"Alright, I'll give you that one," she said.

"Moses's staff?"

"We already found that."

"Not that one. The other one—the one he used in Egypt to bring down the ten plagues."

"Maybe . . ."

"A salt shaker holding Lot's wife?"

That last was met with a thrown pillow, and Jack found himself smiling for the first time in hours. He picked the pillow up from the floor and prepared to return fire when there was a knock at the door. Jack froze and shared a look with Espy. He tossed the pillow on the bed and went to the door. He didn't see anything through the peephole, as if whoever was on the other side had pressed a finger up against the hole. He sighed and reached for the handle. Just before he opened it, he wondered about the possibility of it not being the Israelis, but then opened the door anyway.

The open door revealed two men, similarly dressed in dark pants and dark shirts. They were about the same height and build, and had the same hair color.

Without saying anything, one of them stepped forward, took Jack's arm, and ushered him back into the room. Before the door shut behind him, the man was looking around the room. His eyes stopped at Espy, giving her the same clinical once-over, and then he turned his attention to Jack.

"I trust you're ready to leave, Dr. Hawthorne?" He asked the question in a pleasant tone, but Jack knew that his answer meant nothing to the man.

"Suitcases packed," he said.

Espy rose from the bed and joined them. There was a moment, the briefest instant, in which Jack saw something genuine on the Israeli's face as the man watched her approach. Even after everything she'd been through, and the fact that she'd worn the same clothes for three days, there was a certain kind of beauty that was not easily hidden.

She gave the Mossad agent a warm smile.

"The understanding is that you will provide the information you promised," the Israeli said. "In exchange, we will take you to Paris and provide sufficient funds for you to survive there for a week."

As he spoke, Jack looked past him, taking in the second member of the team. He hadn't moved since the moment he shut the door and turned around. What bothered Jack was how the Israeli was staring at him. Jack didn't think he'd blinked even once the whole time.

"You get us to Paris and I'll tell you whatever you want to know," he said.

The Israeli shook his head. "You will provide the information first, and then we will fulfill our part of the deal."

"But if I tell you now, what's to keep you from walking out of here without us? My way, we get what we want and so do you." The Israeli opened his mouth, but Jack beat him to it. "If we get to Paris and I don't tell you what you want to know, you're going to kill us. I think that's pretty good motivation for me to talk, don't you?"

As if to punctuate the question, Espy gave the Israeli a sweet smile.

The man stood there motionless for a while, his face revealing nothing. And just when Jack thought he might call the whole thing off and leave, he turned to his companion and extended a hand. The other man pulled something from his back pocket and handed it to his partner. "Please gather your things," he said.

It took less than thirty seconds for Jack and Espy to do that, and Jack cast a sidelong glance at the Israelis when his hand hovered over the gun on the bedside table. Yet neither of them made a move to stop him, so he scooped up the weapons and slid them behind his back. When they'd gathered everything, the Israeli manipulated the thing in his hand, separating it into two things. He handed one to each of them. It looked like a stocking cap, one with no eyeholes.

"You will put these on before we leave this room," the Israeli said. "You will not be allowed to remove them until we reach our destination."

Jack caught Espy's eye. He could tell she didn't like this, but he didn't see another option.

"I apologize for the inconvenience, Dr. Habilla-Hawthorne," the Israeli said to Espy. "I'm sure you understand our need for secrecy."

Espy seemed to appreciate the man's attempt at kindness. She gave Jack a smile, then slipped the stocking cap over her head. Jack did the same and, in doing so, yielded control to two men he didn't know, men who would kill him in a second if doing so met their needs. He decided not to consider that too deeply.

One of the Israelis wrapped a hand around Jack's arm. He heard the door open and then he was led outside. They hustled him along quickly, Jack doing his best to manage the pain in his knee. He stumbled once, the knee shifting, but his escort caught him, propelling Jack forward. The Israeli pushed Jack into the back of a car, guiding his head. Espy came in after him; Jack could smell her shampoo. Soon they were being driven down the road. He reached over and felt for Espy's hand. When he found it, he didn't let it go for the next hour, not until the car came to a stop and he was once again being led through the open air.

After perhaps twenty paces, the same strong hand on his arm stopped him. The Israeli took Jack's hand and placed it on a railing.

"There are six steps," he said. "At the top, keep your head low and walk forward."

Jack did as instructed, and when he'd reached the top and walked a few feet, another pair of hands grabbed him and turned him clockwise, then led him on a short walk. They guided him into a seat. As before, Espy took the seat next to him.

"I hope we're in first class," Jack said to no one in particular. Espy shushed him.

Jack wasn't certain how long they were in the air. He thought perhaps three hours. During the flight, he didn't hear a single word from anyone. There was no way to tell how many people were aboard. At some point he dozed off, and when he awakened, they were landing.

The next part was a blur. Jack and Espy were rushed from the plane, dumped unceremoniously in a car, and driven for at least an hour. Jack gave up trying to count distances and turns and simply sat back and let it all happen. When the car finally stopped, he and Espy were led up more stairs and through a door. Before it shut behind them, he heard city noises.

When the stocking cap was pulled from Jack's head, the light made his eyes water. He blinked several times before he could make out the same two Israelis, as well as Espy, whose rapid blinking had to look a lot like his own.

The room was dimly lit and devoid of furniture save three chairs. There were no pictures on the walls, no potted plants. The lead agent—the only one who'd spoken—gestured to the chairs.

"Now it's your turn," the Israeli said.

The other man moved to the door, taking a position next to it, his eyes on Jack.

Jack moved to one of the chairs. Espy did the same.

"Even if you're not the religious type, I'm willing to bet that you did your research before you got to Saint Petersburg. So my guess is you know about the story in Second Kings where someone tosses a dead body onto the bones of Elisha and the man comes back to life."

The Israeli nodded. Jack suspected the man's friend at the door hadn't blinked since leaving Russia.

"As it turns out, Israelite priests took possession of the bones immediately after that. Then, in order to protect the bones—from what, I don't know—they took them to Egypt." He stopped and offered the man a crooked smile. "And that's where things get interesting."

Over the next hour, Jack told the Mossad agent all he'd promised and more. He told him about the Priests of Osiris and their guardianship of the bones through the ages. He told him about the power of the bones—power that he'd personally witnessed. And he told him about the underground cavern below Trubetskoy Bastion. At some point during the monologue, Jack wondered if anyone within the Israeli government was connected with the other organization. He decided it didn't matter. His immediate aim involved more than giving the Mossad something in exchange for their assistance. His goal was to tick them off, to give them enough to make them want in. Simply put, he wanted them muddying the waters while Jack did what he needed to do next.

He knew the plan wasn't without its risks. By revealing the secrets he'd uncovered to the Israelis, Jack was taking one more step toward ensuring continued enmity between the Priests of Osiris and his family. But what other choice did he have? The guardians of the bones had already demonstrated a desire to have him killed. In Jack's opinion, there were no levels of antipathy higher than that.

Once he finished, the Israeli didn't say anything for a long while. In fact, now that Jack thought about it, he was certain the man's expression hadn't changed the entire time.

"That's an incredible tale," the Israeli finally said.

"Incredible, yes. But also verifiable," Jack said. "You can check names and dates. You can get someone into the Manheim estate in Australia to confirm the existence of the old display room. I'm certain they would have sealed it off by now, but the room will still be there. You can check the associations of Manheim and Chambers and see what connections you can find. But, most important, you can stick your finger in a hole in cell number seven of the Trubetskoy Bastion and win the chance to see a truly amazing piece of Paleo-religious history." He paused. "And about a thousand dead people."

Jack thought he saw his interrogator's mouth turn upward just a hair. Or maybe that was just wishful thinking. Without a word, the man rose and pulled a phone from his pocket. When the other party answered, the agent said something short and ended the call. Jack glanced at Espy, but she shook her head.

Less than a minute later, the door opened and a new man walked in. He looked just like the other two except that he was heavier. He was carrying a duffel bag, which he handed to the lead agent. The agent set the bag on a chair and opened it. He began to pull out clothes, handing Jack a pair of dark trousers and a sweater. Digging in the bag again, the Israeli produced a pair of shoes. Jack took them with a nod of thanks.

Next, the agent pulled out clothes for Espy. "We guessed a size four," he said as he handed them over.

Espy thanked him and accepted a similar pants-and-sweater combination.

Once again, the agent reached in the bag. "Here is ten thousand euros," he said. He flipped through the bills and then set the stack on the chair. "I trust this will see you through your first week in Paris?"

"It'll do," Jack said.

Minutes later, he and Espy, wearing their new clothes, descended the steps and headed out into the Paris evening. Jack looked back only once to see a run-down brick building, trash strewn on the ground. A car pulled around even as Jack and Espy walked away. He suspected if he went back in ten minutes, no sign would remain of anyone having been there.

"You know they have a tail on us, right?" Espy said.

"If they want to follow us into the mouth of hell, they're welcome to come along," Jack said. "The more, the merrier."

Espy's eyed widened. "You *want* them involved?"

He turned and smiled at her. "Force the enemy to expend resources engaging another threat, and there are fewer resources to spare on us."

Espy gave a nod, yet a hint of concern followed on its heels. "Aren't you worried things will get too crazy, with too many players to keep track of?"

"Actually I'm not sure we have enough ingredients in the soup yet," Jack said.

He didn't elaborate, but instead raised a hand to hail a passing cab.

19

JACK HAD THE BOOK IN HIS HANDS—the one removed
from the cavern beneath Trubetskoy Bastion. In the day and a
half they'd waited for the Israelis to make their appearance,
Espy had translated a great deal of it for him, especially those
parts that had convinced her of the need to go to Paris. Once
she turned those parts into something Jack could understand,
he found himself agreeing with her.

Even without the book, there were few cities that made
more sense than Paris, few that boasted of such continuous
history, and fewer still that had served at various times as the
social, artistic, political, and economic capital of the world.
To imagine a long-lived organization like the Priests of Osiris
selecting Paris as their permanent base wasn't a stretch of the
imagination.

Jack and Espy had taken up temporary residence in Le
Marais, the district in which the book suggested they concen-
trate their investigation. They had a room at Le Pavillon de la
Reine. While Espy made use of the hydro-jet shower, Jack took

a seat in a rattan chair and began going over all his notes. His new laptop, bought with Israeli money, helped him research some of the questions raised by the aged book.

In her reading, Espy had found two pivotal words: *Flamel* and *Stone*. Those two items, listed as chapter headings in consecutive chapters, told Jack's historically minded wife—who'd spent more time in Paris than most non-natives—where to concentrate their efforts.

Fortified by a strong cup of coffee, Jack tapped a key on the laptop, advancing to the next screen, which resolved into a picture of a house; 51 rue de Montmorency held a distinction among Paris homes as the oldest stone dwelling in the city. Built in 1407, the small structure had outlasted most everything else around it, riding out wars, plagues, and multiple owners to stand alone among Paris dwellings. From the picture, it didn't look like much, but it was the history that fascinated him—especially the history that centered on its builder.

Alchemist Nicolas Flamel read like an odd duck, but Jack couldn't diminish the man's accomplishments. Over the last half hour Jack had learned a great deal about the man. Aside from the legends that tied him to alchemy, he was also a manuscript seller. In other words, he owned a bookstore, and at a time before Herr Gutenberg made such an occupation financially tenable.

Jack leaned back in the chair, allowing his doubts to have their say. According to his wife, the book did little to elaborate on the references to the property. So, in investigating the structure, not only was Jack lacking a starting point, he was missing an expected end result.

One of the interesting things about 51 rue de Montmorency

was that, while it qualified as a historical site, it was also a functioning restaurant. And while taking a table for two would be a good way to gain access to the place, the setup wasn't conducive to the kind of fieldwork he needed to do.

When Espy finished getting dressed, they headed out for a late supper, taking the few blocks on foot. The restaurant was in a quaint area with a lot of foot traffic. As Jack had gathered from the pictures, the exterior was unassuming: faded stone and simple wood trim. Entering, Jack was both charmed and disappointed. Charmed because the restaurant was that perfect combination of quaint and elegant, disappointed because it seemed sacrilegious to renovate the interior of the oldest house in Paris in order to serve from a high-end menu.

Even without a reservation, it didn't take long to get a seat. The server filled their wineglasses. Jack glanced at the menu, though most of his attention was focused on the room, his hopes fading that he and Espy would find anything there. Little of the original room remained. Despite the gaucheness of it, Jack opened up his laptop on the table, looking for the floor plan. When the server came, Espy ordered for them.

Several minutes of fruitless work left Jack worrying about their chances of finding anything. He suspected that if Nicolas Flamel was a member of the Priests of Osiris, as he was beginning to suspect, then whatever message he might have left in this place was probably gone forever. The only way anything might have been preserved was if Flamel had possessed the foresight to plan for the survival of his message across six hundred years, which might have entailed secreting something within the foundation or behind one of the many original stones that framed the place.

When their food came, Jack closed the laptop and moved it to the floor.

"It's not here, is it?" Espy asked.

Jack sampled the wine for the first time. Whatever Espy had ordered for them was very good.

"I don't know," he said. "Maybe it was once, but I think this level of continued use may have destroyed it."

Elements of the original house remained, mostly decorative pieces. The exterior façade was still intact, as were some columns and most of the molding. Jack had taken all of it in when they'd entered, then later dismissed every bit of it.

The lobster was excellent. Espy chewed thoughtfully. "What about the man himself?" she asked.

"Flamel?"

"We're only assuming whatever we're meant to find is in this building. What if we're supposed to be looking at Flamel instead of at the house?"

"Then why make a reference to the first stone house in Paris a chapter title?"

Espy shook her head. "I don't know. It's possible I'm wrong about this being the place."

"Nicolas Flamel builds the first stone house in Paris and it's just coincidence that his name and the word *stone* are consecutive chapter titles?"

Espy shrugged. "I wasn't the one who spent two hours researching the guy."

Her comment gave Jack pause because, in truth, his research on the man paled in comparison to the time he'd spent studying the structure—the layout, the construction, the list of owners through the centuries. Without answering his wife, Jack retrieved the computer. Fifteen minutes later, his Breton lobster cold, he pulled his chair around to Espy's side of the table, showing her what he'd found.

"I glossed over the fact that Flamel was an alchemist," he said. "And what are all good alchemists looking for?"

Espy had been skimming the text on the screen, so she had the answer at the ready. "The philosopher's stone."

"It's not the house," Jack said.

"No," Espy agreed. "It's something that doesn't exist."

They spent the next half hour researching, much to the consternation of their server, who made periodic appearances to check on them. But after a point, Jack and Espy leaned back in irritation.

"I have no idea," Jack admitted.

The declaration came just as the server arrived again at their table. Jack had no idea if it was genuine interest, or if she felt that by assisting she could get them out of the restaurant, but she glanced at the computer. "What are you trying to do?" she asked in decent English.

Jack pondered how to ask their server if she could make a connection between a dead alchemist, his lifelong dream, and a secret organization walking around modern-day Paris. "By any chance, does the restaurant's owner ask the staff to learn about the history of the house so you can answer dumb questions from tourists?"

"*Oui*," she said. "What do you want to know?"

"Nicolas Flamel was searching for the philosopher's stone—"

"Not searching. He found it," the server said, interrupting Jack.

"Okay, he found it," he agreed. "But beyond finding it, is there anything else he did that would have had anything to do with the stone?"

The server gave him a puzzled look.

"What my husband is asking," Espy said, stepping in, "is if Flamel kept any records of his work, anything that documents the steps he took to create the stone."

The woman brightened. "Yes. He documented everything in *Le Livre des Figures Hiéroglyphiques*. How do you say? . . . *The Book of Hieroglyphic Figures*."

At the mention of the book, Jack frowned. "Wasn't that published almost two hundred years after he died?"

"From his writings," the server said, and Jack knew enough not to question her further. In payment for her help, he left a twenty-euro tip on the table. Jack and Espy gathered their things and left the restaurant. They found a nearby coffee shop and again set to work.

Jack found a PDF copy of the out-of-print work in its entirety. The book was short, a mere twenty-eight pages. Espy read it aloud, but Jack was more interested in the pictures. There were several, all ornate representations of religious or mystical scenes, fascinating and even haunting. But as he looked at each of them, and as Espy read the text, nothing of significance jumped out at him. After Espy finished, Jack sat back and sipped his coffee. Neither of them spoke. After a while, Jack leaned forward.

"Let's go through it again," he said.

Espy started to read. Ten minutes later, Jack asked her to stop. On page four were three pictures, labeled with Roman numerals. Picture III had caught Jack's attention. He leaned in toward the screen but couldn't make out the details. Seeing him squint, Espy pulled the laptop away.

"Wait a minute," she said. She punched a few keys and increased the magnification, and the details jumped out. The image was strange, resembling a medieval chess set. The pieces were laid out in quadrants, twisted figures, malformed and grotesque. From the center of the board rose a gnarled tree, towering over all else. It was the quadrants, though, that caught Jack's eye.

"What does that look like to you?" He pointed to one of the spots, partially obscured by the piece on top of it.

Espy leaned closer. "It looks like the image we saw in the Chambers painting," she said, her voice growing excited.

"And this?"

She looked at another spot on the board. Her eyes widened. "That's Gordon Reese's family crest."

Only when she confirmed the discovery did Jack allow himself a moment of exultation. If he was right, the pages of the book contained the crests or sigils of all the major players within the Priests of Osiris at the time of Flamel.

"That's interesting." He pointed to the spot identified by the Chambers crest. The chess piece there was larger than all but one. The figure, a male with no armor or weapons, was shown kneeling in submission to the adjoining piece—a figure with a sword, ready to attack. "I wonder who this is."

Espy shook her head and read the explanatory text next to the picture. "According to this, the picture is titled *Rousseau's Victory*." She looked at the picture, at the victorious piece poised to smite its enemy or grant mercy. "I'm guessing that's Rousseau."

Jack raised an eyebrow, then proceeded to Google the name—and returned far too many results. He sighed, stretched, and took a few sips of cold coffee. While he rested his eyes, Espy performed a second search, checking the name against the book it came from.

There were only a handful of results, most of which dealt with a study of the picture itself. But there were two references to something much more intriguing: short articles about a 2003 auction of rare books. One of the bidders was a man named Rousseau. According to auction records from Sotheby's, Alain Rousseau owned *Le Livre des Figures Hiéroglyphiques*, the original manuscript.

20

✝

THE ROUSSEAU BUILDING TOWERED over them, casting an imposing midday shadow over La Défense district. Jack stood on the sidewalk, staring up at its glass façade, wondering where what he planned to do ranked on the list of the dumbest things he'd ever done. What kept him from turning around and walking away, though, was the woman next to him. She knew what he proposed to do and she hadn't tried to talk him out of it. It told him he hadn't entirely lost his mind. He turned to Espy.

"Any way I can convince you to walk up the street, find someplace to get an espresso, and wait for me? If we're right about who this man is, then when I walk out of that building, I won't be alone. It would be helpful to have someone in place who can spot the tail."

Espy frowned, unable to argue the logic of the request, even as she knew his explanation didn't touch on the real reason Jack didn't want her with him. "And if you don't walk out of there?"

"Then you get ahold of Duckey and let him know what happened. The two of you will have to come up with a plan B for getting the boys back."

Espy went silent, and Jack could see fear behind her calm. Everything they'd done so far had been with the singular goal of getting Alex and Jim back. The retrieval of the bones, the escapes, the refusal to engage McKeller. And all their actions came down to this one choice, a walk into the lion's den. If it went badly, Jack knew that the small bit of control he and Espy had wrested from the situation would evaporate. He knew all this and still he had to walk through the door of the magnificent building in front of him.

He saw the weight of it settle on her, and the only gift he could give her was to avoid acknowledging it.

"When you get your coffee, get one for me too, okay?"

Then he turned and stepped through the revolving door and into the lobby, finding perhaps the cleanest, brightest, most welcoming lion's den he'd ever seen. A recurring theme permeated the corporate press releases of Rousseau-Beckett Industries: that of environmental consciousness. They were key players in the area of renewable resources. Most of their buildings operated near a zero-energy deficit. As he walked toward the elevators, taking in the great lighting and modern lines, Jack couldn't help but feel genuine appreciation for the vision behind it.

But he didn't have to feel the same way about the man. After spending the better part of a day gathering information about Alain Rousseau, Jack was convinced the man was somewhere near the top of the food chain. Like Gordon Reese, George Manheim, and Quinn Chambers, Rousseau was a captain of industry, a buyer and seller of people, a man of near unlimited power. But none of the others had a picture of their family in a six-hundred-year-old book—except for Chambers, and Jack doubted the family would care to trumpet their status within that etching.

One of the things Jack had found as he studied Rousseau was how often the paths of those two families crossed, almost always to the detriment of the Chambers clan. In fact, in taking a new look at the financial tragedy that befell the family in the 1850s, Jack could see a Rousseau hand in much of it. Even after the most recent tragedy in the Chambers family, the death of their head of household, Alain Rousseau had swooped in and bought out a number of the family's business concerns before Chambers's body had cooled. With all he now knew, Jack was certain the written history hinted at a familial conflict within the confines of the hierarchy of the Priests of Osiris.

No one stopped him as he crossed to the elevator. He joined a half dozen other people and punched the button for the top floor. When the elevator deposited him onto the sixty-third floor, the security absent from the lobby was plainly visible there. A uniformed guard eyed Jack as he stepped into the hall and made his way toward a set of double glass doors and the reception desk beyond.

The receptionist looked up with a feigned smile. *"Bonjour. Comment puis-je vous aider?"*

"Good morning," he said. "Is Mr. Rousseau available?"

The receptionist returned a cool look. When she spoke again, it was in perfect English, without a hint of an accent. "I'm sorry, sir. Mr. Rousseau isn't available right now. If you'd like, I would be happy to take your name and number and see if I can get you on his schedule."

Despite her perfect smile, Jack knew he'd never make it

onto that schedule. He put his hands on the divider between them and leaned in, giving the woman a conspiratorial wink.

"My name's Jack Hawthorne," he said. "And I'm guessing Alain will stop whatever it is he's doing and fit me in."

Indecision crept onto the woman's face. Jack saw her glance over his shoulder, probably at the security guard in the hall. When she looked back at Jack, his smile hadn't wavered.

"I'll wait over here while you call him," Jack said, pointing to a couch in the corner. Without waiting for a reply, he did just that. From his seat on the couch, he watched as she picked up the phone. She sent a furtive look in his direction and made a half turn so that all he could see was her back. When seconds later she lowered the phone, she looked Jack's way again, genuine surprise showing in her eyes.

Two minutes passed before the lord of the manor emerged from his office.

"Good morning, Dr. Hawthorne," Rousseau said.

Jack stood and extended a hand. Rousseau's handshake was solid and friendly.

Alain Rousseau was a slight man, but he had the air, the confidence, of someone of a much larger frame. His sharp, angular features highlighted a patrician nose. He didn't look a day over fifty. Although he was completely bald, his smooth head bespoke intention.

"It's a pleasure to meet you. I've followed your work for years." His tone carried a genuineness that almost caught Jack off guard. "To what do I owe the pleasure of a visit?"

"The pleasure's mine, Alain," Jack said, deliberate in his use of the informal. "Do you mind if we talk someplace more private?"

There was the slightest break in Rousseau's graceful exterior, though it didn't last long.

"Of course. Let's go to my office."

Once seated in his office—a large but not ostentatious one, considering how much wealth the man commanded—there was a palpable difference in the level of charm the man evinced.

"Now, what can I do for you, Dr. Hawthorne?"

Jack leaned back in the comfortable leather chair. "Alain, I'm here because there's a member of my government who wants something I no longer have, something I believe is now in your possession."

Surprise flickered in Rousseau's eyes. "I'm not sure I understand. I have something of yours?"

"In the interest of full disclosure, they weren't really mine," Jack said. "I stole them from you a number of years ago and you just stole them back. I can't fault you for that."

"I don't know what this is about," Rousseau said. "But I can assure you that Rousseau-Beckett Industries does not engage in theft of any kind."

Jack let that statement hang there. He sat in the guest chair and looked at a man who he believed had the power of life and death over his family. To his credit, Rousseau didn't appear uncomfortable under the gaze. After a moment, Jack reached into his jacket pocket and pulled out the book. He held it up but didn't extend it to the Frenchman.

"I found this deep beneath Saint Petersburg. Just a few days ago, in fact." Jack made a pretense of flipping through the book. He watched Rousseau's face, seeing the surprise claim him. "It makes for some interesting reading."

In that moment, as Jack studied the reaction of the man sitting on the other side of the desk, he wondered if Rousseau even knew what the book was. Perhaps in an organization that had spanned as many generations as had this one, there were secrets lost even to them.

"This helped fill in a lot of blanks," Jack said. "It's what ultimately led me to your office."

"What is it that you want?" he asked.

"When this all started, I had one organization after me. My intent was to find the bones and trade them for the safety of my family. But somewhere along the way, I woke a sleeping dragon." He paused and nodded to Rousseau, a kind of apology. "So now I have two organizations after me, one of which has shown no qualms about wanting me dead."

"You've produced some of the background," Rousseau said, "yet you still have not told me what it is you want. What do you think I can provide for you, Dr. Hawthorne?"

"I want you to call off the dogs," Jack said without hesitation.

Alain Rousseau's response was a slight smile. "You're assuming I have dogs to call off."

"You're right, I am. After what happened in Australia, I fully expected your organization to come after me. But for some reason, you decided to let me live. I can't pretend to understand why. All I'm asking for now is a return to that détente."

"And if I agree to this, if I 'call off the dogs,' as you say, on your promise to stop looking for the relics, how will you deal with the other individuals who chased you from the comfort of your home?"

Jack offered Rousseau a smile in acknowledgment of what he'd admitted. "How does someone eat an elephant?" Jack asked him.

"One bite at a time," Rousseau returned.

"We end our squabble and I'll find another way to deal with the CIA," Jack said. "As far as I'm concerned, the Priests of Osiris don't exist."

As the words left his lips, it occurred to him that he hadn't yet said the name. He wondered if he'd made a serious error, but Rousseau's expression hadn't changed. Instead he leaned back in his chair and studied Jack for a moment.

"Thank you for stopping by, Dr. Hawthorne. I'll consider your request." Rousseau stood and started for the door, gesturing for Jack to follow. Before reaching the door, he said, "There's one thing I can grant you. In honor of your boldness in coming here alone, you can be sure no dogs are waiting to pounce on you. At least not today."

With that, Jack was back in the hall, the door closing behind him.

When he stepped out into the sunlight, he breathed a sigh of relief. Then he set to the task of shaking the dog that Rousseau would have most certainly set on him.

———

Jack kept his pace slow, not wanting to lose whoever was following him. As he walked, he had second thoughts about asking Espy to watch from afar. The plan hinged on her spotting him as he left the meeting with Rousseau, then following until she could identify a tail. But the whole plan would fall apart if she'd missed his exit.

He knew he was taking a chance getting rid of whoever Rousseau had put on him, especially after asking the man for a favor. If Rousseau was at all inclined to consider Jack's proposal, interfering with one of the Frenchman's operatives was counterproductive. Yet the risks of being followed outweighed those that might come from angering Rousseau.

Another issue with Jack's plan was where he would go after

leaving the meeting. He couldn't go back to the hotel—not until he was certain they weren't being followed. But unless he stopped somewhere, the tail would never get close. He looked around, trying to find something that would work, when he saw a café sandwiched between two other buildings. The front window was dark; the place seemed quiet. He crossed the street and entered.

In less than a minute, Jack was enjoying a Pelforth and chatting with the proprietor, an older gentleman who spoke good English. The man said he'd learned it during the war. Jack didn't ask him which war. Once the man left him, Jack watched soccer on the television, wondering when he should start worrying about Espy.

Ten minutes later, the door opened and Jack turned to see his wife's familiar smile. She crossed the room to the appreciative looks of the rest of the early-afternoon crowd and slid into a seat next to him. The proprietor gave her a smile much larger than the one Jack had received, but Espy waved him off.

"Having a nice time?" she asked.

"Nice enough," Jack said. He took another sip of the Pelforth.

"Good. How about hurrying a bit so we can get away from here before the man with the gun wakes up?"

Jack looked at Espy and tried to determine if she was joking. What he saw on her face caused him to stand, toss five euros on the table, and follow her outside.

21

SINCE THE MOMENT THE BOYS were taken from them, Jack had known that his best chance of getting them back rested on his working independently, to avoid becoming beholden to the man who had them. He'd relied on his ability to compartmentalize to see him through to Paris. But now he just needed to hear the boys' voices, and he needed them to hear his.

The phone rang three times before McKeller answered. In the instant before the man spoke, Jack found himself listening for background noises—children's voices. He heard nothing.

"Who is this?" McKeller asked.

"This is Jack Hawthorne."

He walked slowly along Port des Tuileries, Espy at his side, the Seine running along beside them. Espy's shoes sounded on the cobblestone walkway, the only sound beyond the lapping water and the hum of traffic coming from beyond the wall that separated them from Quai François-Mitterrand.

Silence was McKeller's only response for several moments, and Jack waited patiently, his eyes on a boat passing beneath a viaduct. He suspected McKeller was trying to trace the call, which was why he'd initiated the contact from the section of the city busiest with tourist activity. McKeller could get a hit on Jack, but in a city the size of Paris, there was no way for the man to get any closer.

"You're playing a dangerous game, Dr. Hawthorne," McKeller finally said. "First avoiding my associates in Australia, and then breaking contact after our initial conversation. Neither were wise moves."

"I'm inclined to disagree," Jack said. "You want the bones, and I'm the one best positioned to find them. And I can do that a lot easier if I'm not encumbered by you or your hired thugs."

Espy, who could only hear one side of the conversation, frowned at her husband. Jack gave her a reassuring smile.

"You seem to be operating under the assumption that this is a game without rules," McKeller said. "Let me disabuse you of that notion. The safety of your sons depends on your cooperation."

Jack's hand tightened around the phone and his eyes narrowed, but he kept his voice even. "Believe me, I know that. But there *are* rules and they're very simple. I recover the artifacts and then make arrangements for a swap. And you don't see a thing until I see my children."

"Make no mistake, Dr. Hawthorne, I *will* kill your sons if you don't deliver the bones of Elisha to me," McKeller said.

The sound of the man's voice did much to convince Jack that McKeller spoke the truth. Jack stopped walking as the anger he'd been able to keep at bay since the call began came to the surface in a rush. Along with it came hatred, which threatened to cloud his thinking. The man on the other end of the line was threatening what was dearest to Jack, and he wanted to make him pay for that. But he couldn't. Not now.

Espy saw the change come over him. She put a hand on his arm.

"Here's what's going to happen," Jack said. "You're going to let me speak with my children. Or I swear to you, you will never see the bones."

"I don't think you're in any position to make demands, Dr. Hawthorne."

"That's where you're wrong. I know your wife is sick. I know that's why you need the bones. So the way I see it, I'm holding her life in my hands. I think that puts us on equal footing."

"If you know about my wife, then I'm sure you understand that I'll do whatever I need to in order to secure the bones."

"You may be desperate, but you're not stupid. The only way you'll see them is through a trade. And if you so much as lay a finger on my children, your wife dies too." He paused, but McKeller didn't challenge what Jack had said. "I'm going to call back in an hour. It will be a different number. Have the boys ready to talk."

He ended the call before McKeller could say another word, tossing the phone into the river. He and Espy stood there for some time, their eyes on the water, not saying anything. Then Jack took her hand and they started walking.

———

Jack sat with his back to the building, looking out on the traffic that navigated the busy intersection of rue Raymond du Temple and rue de Fontenay. The sidewalk table of Le Marigny allowed him to relax, giving him at least the illusion of normalcy. Espy sat beside him, her coffee untouched.

It had taken them forty-five minutes to walk to Vincennes,

where he was comfortable they could blend in amid the many shops, as well as the cars and people filling the streets and sidewalks. If McKeller had pinpointed the origin of the earlier call, any people he had in Paris—a possibility that Jack had his doubts about—would be wasting their time.

He glanced at his watch. This time the rogue agent answered on the first ring, only it wasn't his voice that Jack heard.

"H-hello?" came the tentative greeting.

Jack felt his heart catch in his throat. "Alex," he nearly shouted. Next to him, Espy straightened as if an electric current had rushed up her spine. She leaned in to hear their son's voice.

"Dad?"

The sound of his voice, the mixture of fear and excitement in it, nearly brought Jack to tears, but he held them in check. "Alex, it's me. Your mom's here too."

Jack heard something like a strangled sound through the phone—his son bravely choking back his own emotions.

"Alex, I know you have a lot of questions, but right now I need you to focus, okay?"

"Okay," Alex said, his voice quiet.

"How are they treating you? How's Jim?"

Jack heard an intake of breath, Alex gathering himself.

"They haven't hurt us," his son said. "They're keeping us in a house—"

Alex's words were cut off. Jack heard muffled sounds. But before panic could find a foothold, Alex was back on the line.

"He said I can't tell you anything about where we are," Alex said.

"Okay," Jack said. "How's Jim?"

"He's fine. They have his medicine here. And a nebulizer."

A wave of relief washed over Jack. "That's good," he said,

then paused, wondering how to explain things to Alex so he would understand and not be afraid.

"Dad, what's going on?" Alex asked.

"I wish I could tell you everything, but we don't have time right now. All you need to know is that the man who has you and your brother is holding you until I can deliver something to him, something that's taking me a while to get my hands on. But it's going to be alright. We're coming for you and Jim real soon, but for now I just need you to hold tight and take care of each other, okay?"

"I know," Alex said, and Jack couldn't help but smile at the certainty in the boy's voice.

Jack looked at Espy, saw the tears running down her cheeks.

"Can you give the phone to Jim?" Jack asked.

He heard more fumbling and then handed the phone across the table. Over the next brief minutes, Jack watched as Espy spoke with their younger son, watched her soothe the boy in a way only a mother could.

Then, as if a switch had been flipped, Espy's expression changed. Her eyes first widened, then narrowed. She handed the phone back to Jack.

"Hello?"

"You've spoken to your children, Dr. Hawthorne," McKeller said. "Now it's your turn."

"I'll hold up my end of the bargain," Jack said.

"You're in Paris," McKeller said.

"I am."

"I'm sending someone."

"You won't find me," Jack said. "Remember, I work alone. You just have the boys ready to move the next time you hear from me."

22

✝

JACK SHIFTED HIS POSITION on the too-soft bed, already feeling the soreness in his back that would increase exponentially by morning. Next to him, Espy seemed content, the sound of light snoring signifying her adjustment to their third Parisian hotel room. Their temporary residence, positioned at just the right point along the parking lot, allowed the headlights of every car making a left turn at the neighboring intersection to briefly turn night into day. He was tired enough that he should have been able to sleep through it, but thus far sleep had eluded him.

He shifted again, his movements causing a short stall in Espy's snoring, and tried to unmoor his thoughts, to let go of all the things clamoring for his attention. He found it an impossible task, especially considering what they had only tonight discovered—something that would shape their next steps.

They'd almost missed it. So focused were they on the chess-set images, so absorbed by the chance to identify the key players, that they'd overlooked what had to have been Flamel's main objective in writing the book: to provide a signpost, pointing the reader to the bones themselves.

In retrospect, it made sense that the Priests of Osiris would have established a final resting place for the bones, a place they could fortify and defend.

When Gordon Reese first hired Jack to find the relics, he was surprised to learn that custodial responsibility for them was a fluid thing, that the Priests selected individuals or organizations and charged them with the responsibility of protecting the bones for a finite period. Even at the time, it seemed a strange system, one rife with security risks. Viewed now, though, in light of what he and Espy had learned over the last several days, it made perfect sense.

Over the course of three millennia, few things remained constant. People and ideas came and went; philosophies and religions gained and lost influence; whole empires crumbled to dust. It was reasonable to believe those conditions would have forged an agile system, one where the sacking of a city didn't mean the loss of the relics. It was a logical evolution of that first flight, which took the Hebrew priests to Egypt.

But at some point, the guardians had to have a permanent resting place for the bones—a place to hold them in the event no suitable guardian could be found, or as a refuge in times of great unrest. That place would have to be well hidden and well protected, and able to be sealed off should the land around it shake and fall. And yet it had to be easy to access, so long as one knew its secrets.

It was Espy who found the reference—a mention of a mass disinterment and transfer of the dead from one city cemetery to the Church of the Innocents. A few hundred years later, the

Church of the Innocents saw its own mass transfer of remains, this time to the new ossuary: the Catacombs of Paris.

It wasn't this minor mention, however, that focused their attention on the Catacombs. Rather, that occurred after Jack and Espy began a more thorough investigation into the other pictures in the book, the ones identified as the main panels, the ones that shared size and thematic constants.

What they uncovered was what charted their next course of action. It was a pair of photos, shots taken belowground—exact representations of two of the images from the book. What Jack found fascinating were the dates. Flamel's book was published in 1612, based on material the alchemist compiled prior to 1418. The Paris Catacombs did not see its incarnation as an ossuary until the 1800s. According to experts, the pictures carved into the rock beneath the city dated to the middle of the eleventh century. He and Espy had found the signpost; now they had the road.

All he needed was a good night's rest so that he had the strength to take that road. As he thought that, and as he tried to focus on falling to sleep, his efforts were stymied by the glow of headlights filtering through the inadequate shade. He opened his eyes and blinked against the glare. Next to him, Espy stretched, looking undisturbed by the lights outside their window. Jack had to admit a small amount of annoyance at the ease with which she slept. He glanced at the clock, seeing it was nearing two in the morning.

With a sigh he rose from the uncomfortable bed and went to the bathroom, where he ran the water cold and splashed it over his face. When done, he rested his hands on the counter and studied the man looking back at him in the mirror. Lines under the eyes bespoke a lack of sleep over the last week. When he leaned in closer, he could see a few gray hairs in the mix. It hit him that he was a lot younger the last time something like this had happened to him, and he could do without sleep for a lot longer back then.

He ran a hand through his hair, yawned, and left the bathroom. Instead of rejoining his wife, he settled himself in a chair and dared sleep to force him back to the bed. As his eyes once again grew accustomed to the dark, he saw the outline of the ancient book on the table. His fingers went to it, the aged leather rough in his hand. Yet even as he touched something truly extraordinary, something bordering on priceless, he found his thoughts elsewhere.

He replayed the phone call in his mind, the talk with his sons. He felt better about things after hearing their voices, but he couldn't shake the guilt of leaving them to their abductors for so long. He still believed his best chance of seeing the boys again hinged on his recovering the bones. And his best chance of recovering the bones meant working without someone watching his every move.

As thoughts of the boys circled in his head, he found it difficult to keep his eyes open. Weary, he stood and was starting for the bed when light once again came through the window. He looked up and, a few seconds later, the light was gone. Focusing on it a bit longer, though, it seemed the light had been different somehow.

Instinctively, Jack moved to the table and reached for his gun. His fingers closed on it just as he heard a sound at the door. Gun in hand, he turned toward the door, but the noise—something that sounded like a hand on the doorknob—didn't repeat. Jack stood barefoot in the darkened room and listened, a rush of alertness tensing every muscle. Yet as the seconds passed without a repeat of the sound, or another strange light through the window, he found his breathing slowing, the adrenaline receding. He took a deep breath and brought the gun down.

He turned to put the gun back on the table when the door behind him exploded inward. As Jack whipped around, the shattered door dominated his line of sight, but in his peripheral vision he saw Espy bolt upright. The thought of his wife, vulnerable, moved him forward. When the first dark-clad figure stepped through the door, Jack pulled the trigger without a second thought.

He had to have missed because the man kept advancing. Then there were two of them, and before Jack could get off a second shot, the one in front shouted something in French. Jack saw the man's gun hand come up, but the weapon wasn't aimed at him. Espy, frozen in bed, offered a clear and easy target for the intruder. The man, face hidden behind a ski mask, barked a command—one that even Jack's poor French could interpret. But still he kept the gun up, even as the second intruder took a step deeper into the room, finding an angle that allowed him to target Jack.

Jack's heart raced; he could feel the vein in his neck throbbing. While he couldn't tear his eyes from the men in front of him, he could see Espy awakening to the reality of the situation. Jack's finger began to tighten on the trigger. But the lead man had a clear shot at Espy; he wouldn't miss. Jack lowered his arm. He dropped the gun at his feet.

The man nearest the door started toward the bed. Espy, watching the masked man approach, began to free herself from the blankets, moving away from the threat. Jack took a step closer to the bed, but the man halted Jack where he stood, pointing his gun at Espy and telling Jack to stay put.

Movement near the door pulled Jack's attention away from Espy. It happened almost faster than Jack could register it. A third man, one not wearing anything to conceal his face, stepped into the room, swiftly crossed the two steps to the man barking orders, and put a gun to the back of his head. The report of a single shot filled the small space, and a mist of blood sprayed out over the wall. The new arrival then turned to the second man, who only now was turning from the bed, and put two bullets in his chest. The masked man collapsed against the foot of the bed. The gun fell from his hand.

For what seemed an eternity, both Jack and Espy were frozen. Then, as if someone had shouted in her ear, Espy scrambled from the bed. Jack rushed toward her, gathering her up and moving her behind him. He cast his eyes about for the gun he'd dropped. But the new arrival had already turned away from his second kill to face Jack. He had a shock of blond hair, with bright blue eyes.

He quickly lifted his coat and secreted the weapon in a concealed holster. That done, he turned for the door. When he reached it, he spun back around. Jack thought he saw a hint of a smile. "Compliments of Monsieur Rousseau," he said, and then he disappeared into the night.

Already Jack could hear sirens, which spurred him into motion. "Get dressed," he said to Espy while grabbing for his shirt.

Espy took one look around at the carnage, as if struggling to process what had just happened, before reaching for her clothes.

Jack gathered up their few belongings, retrieving the gun from the floor and the book from the table. Once Espy was ready, Jack, after a moment's hesitation, headed for one of the bodies. He found the man's wallet and slipped it into his own pocket. A further pat-down yielded nothing. A mirror examination of the second man ended with a second wallet and a set of car keys.

Jack stood, nodded at Espy, and together they fled into the Paris night.

It was almost dawn. Jack parted the blinds and looked out onto the parking lot, where as far as he could see, there were no cars other than the three already there when he and Espy arrived. He scanned the street, the darkened building across from their own, and then let the blinds fall.

They'd driven their potential assassins' car for miles, heading deeper into the city, before abandoning the vehicle along Rue de Lourmel. Before leaving it, Jack had checked the registration but hadn't recognized the name on it. His time spent reviewing the contents of the two pilfered wallets had a similar result—a handful of euros and two French driver's licenses that might have been legitimate or fictitious.

After leaving the car, they'd taken a taxi to Le Marais, where they'd paid two teenagers for their coats, entered a dance club where they'd traded their newly purchased garments for different ones, then left thirty minutes later with a half dozen men and women in their twenties, only separating from the group once they were blocks away from the club. Another taxi ride, a cut through an alley, and a third taxi had created at least the illusion of distance between them and anyone who might have been watching. Their fourth room in Paris was the kind of place where, once inside, Jack had promptly slid the dresser in front of the door for an extra measure of security.

Now, stepping away from the window, Jack picked up one of the candy bars they'd gotten from the run-down hotel's vending machine. He went over and sank down on the bed next to Espy. Although he was exhausted, he was way too wired to fall sleep.

He and Espy had talked little since leaving their last room, but now, in the relative safety afforded by a solid, heavy dresser, Espy opened the floodgates.

"What *happened* back there?"

Jack had spent the last hour processing that very question. "The only thing I know for sure is that they weren't McKeller's men."

Espy sighed, picked up a candy bar, and gave it a critical look before unwrapping it. "Well, it's clear the one who killed them is with Rousseau."

Jack nodded. "On the surface, it looks like our meeting might have bought us a bit more than the détente I asked for."

Espy chewed thoughtfully. "But why?"

Jack considered his answer before giving it voice. It sounded absurd, even to him, and yet it was the only thing that made sense.

"Civil war," he said.

Espy gave him a questioning look.

"Think about it," Jack said. "When we uncovered Chambers's book, we agreed it seemed to have been written and then hidden as a safeguard against an internal threat. And when we studied his finances, we found periods where the Chambers empire was under some sort of attack by an entity with very deep pockets.

"Then you have Flamel's book, the picture showing the Chambers family in subjugation to the Rousseaus." He paused as he ate the last of the candy bar. "In Saint Petersburg, the man who tried to kill us said he was working for Olivia Chambers."

Espy took it all in. She stood and walked to the window, where she moved the shade and looked out through the blinds. Letting the blinds close, she turned her back to the window. "You're saying we've walked into a conflict that's been going on for at least a hundred and fifty years, where we've become a couple of pawns?"

Jack gave a half smile in response. "That may be a good position to be in." At Espy's raised eyebrow, he explained further. "We've always wondered why we weren't pursued after Australia. We knew too much for them to allow us to live. Except they did. Now I'm wondering if one side kept us alive just because the other side wanted us gone."

Espy frowned. "So we owe our lives to spite?"

Jack shrugged. "I guess spite's as good a reason as any."

"The people who came after us in the cemetery—maybe they weren't sent by the organization as a whole, but by the Chambers family." Espy returned to the bed and sat, leaning back against a pillow.

"It's their book we stole," Jack said. "They're the ones with a motive. The Rousseaus have been at the top of the food chain for a long while, and the Chambers have been a threat to Rousseau supremacy for hundreds of years. And what we're involved in now is just one more skirmish in a long line of them."

"The question, then, is how do we remove ourselves from the battlefield?" Espy asked.

As far as Jack was concerned, that was the big question. Rousseau had allowed them to live because they were useful, a thorn in the paw of the Chambers family. But the closer Jack and Espy got to the bones, the more likely it became that

Rousseau would start to see them as a threat. And Jack could think of no better reason for the two old enemies to put aside their differences than for the purpose of protecting their secrets.

"I told Rousseau we'd stop looking for the bones," Jack said. "And now he knows we haven't done that. At some point he's going to decide that keeping us alive just to irritate the Chambers clan is no longer worth the payoff. Then he's going to try and kill us too."

Espy turned to her husband and gave him a tired smile. "If they're going to kill us, they can do it after we get some sleep."

Jack thought that was as sound a plan as any. He reached for the lamp on the bedside table, and within minutes the sleep that had avoided him for so long claimed both of them.

23

THE HISTORY OF THE PARIS Catacombs was a study in pragmatism, with the growth of the city and the overwhelming of its cemeteries, the fouling of the water and the smell prompting church and city officials to find another place in which to house Paris's dead. The miles of abandoned mining tunnels beneath the city proved to be the perfect place so that, over time, Parisians saw the systematic growth of their own personal underworld. There were more than six million people interred beneath the streets of Paris, and miles of uncharted tunnels and caverns beyond those in use. It was those less charted sections, specifically where the rock carvings began, that interested Jack.

The air cooled quickly, then dampened. The smell of stagnant water filled the air. Lights placed at intervals revealed the steps as Jack and Espy descended into the earth. Soon Jack heard water running somewhere close.

Up ahead, disappearing into the long tunnel at the bottom of the stairs, were three people, teenagers. Behind Jack and

Espy were two women. They looked like tourists, here to gawk at the dead, in a place that seemed so unearthly precisely because of its baseness, its nearness to the very stuff of which everyone was made.

The Catacombs were a tourist destination, with areas gated off to guide the curious through chambers holding bones in numbers sufficient to form entire walls, some with designs fashioned through judicious placement of the bones.

When they reached the bottom of the steps, Jack and Espy followed the long tunnel through the rock, the evidence of the old mine showing in tool marks and bore holes. They walked for a long while, until the tunnel opened up into a chamber. There, Jack was struck full force by what had been in the back of his mind since they'd made the decision to come here. The similarities that existed between this place and the massive chamber beneath Trubetskoy Bastion could be no coincidence.

The similarities left him wondering about the possibility that the creation of the Catacombs was perhaps less about city planning than about recreating a motif—of fashioning a replica of something that already existed in the organization's history. It was an interesting question, but ultimately an academic one. At the moment, he and Espy had more hands-on concerns.

Fortunately there were fewer visitors than he'd anticipated, which meant they were able to distance themselves from others' eyes in short order. That accomplished, Jack pulled out a packet of folded papers from the pack slung over his shoulder. Stepping under one of the lights, he unfolded the paper and tried to get his bearings.

Most of the tunnel system was off-limits to tourists, with gates serving to direct visitors along approved paths. Past those barriers existed a less organized ossuary, areas not suitable for public viewing. Even beyond those sections, though, were tunnels that extended far beyond the influence of the macabre role forced upon them—places where few had explored, miles of winding tunnels, caverns and drop-offs, which had remained mostly intact since the ceasing of the mining operation.

The pages Jack held constituted a series of maps, none complete, most with sections entirely speculative. He hoped that by using pieces from all of them, he could establish a more or less accurate path.

He started off in what he thought was the right direction, choosing a tunnel to the right, following the track lighting until the tunnel emerged into a smaller chamber, where several skulls atop an ossuary wall watched their passage.

They walked for a long while, negotiating the labyrinthine system. The air seemed to grow thicker the farther they went. Water seeped from the stone. Finally they came to a rusted iron portcullis that blocked their way. Beyond it, the meager light tapered to nothing. Jack slid his pack to the ground, pulled out a flashlight, and handed it to Espy. When Espy shined the light past the iron grating, Jack saw a tunnel much like the one they were in.

A double loop of heavy chain secured the portcullis, a rusted padlock holding it together. Even with bolt cutters it took a few minutes before Jack could remove the lock. Once the chain was unwound, he grabbed hold of the grate and pulled. It didn't budge. Espy placed the flashlight on the ground and, coming alongside him, added her hands to the task. Even so, it took a good bit of straining before the gate moved.

Once through, Espy kept the light in front of them, the beam picking up little beyond stone and more stone. But as the tunnel emerged into one of the ossuary chambers, Jack saw why visits from the general public were discouraged. As Espy sent the light around, it revealed a scene from some dark story. Entire skeletons lay haphazardly across one another, some still clothed, others with patches of flesh visible, mummified by the conditions of the Catacombs.

Sobered, they continued on. Before long, Jack could tell they'd left the graveyard far behind. The tunnels they were now passing through were the suspect ones on his maps. They came upon forks and branches that followed no particular pattern. Not long after that, he found it.

The rock carving looked old, yet the workmanship was solid, the lines clean. But it was the image itself that aided the dating. The shepherd and crook image indicated the beginning of the High Middle Ages.

Jack ran his hand along the edges, feeling the weight of years. But he didn't linger. After a quick look around the tunnel, he and Espy moved on. They found the next one maybe a hundred steps farther on—an exact representation of the image of the three angels on page seventeen of Flamel's book.

"They're distance markers," Espy said. "They have to be."

The only way to test that theory was to keep walking. Not long after leaving the second wall carving, they reached a place where the path before them forked. Jack looked down at the map.

"That's not supposed to be there," he said.

Espy smirked and took the right fork, and since she had the flashlight, Jack followed. When the light picked up a third image, roughly the same distance as that between the first two, he and Espy exchanged grins.

The next hour passed in much the same fashion, Jack's only concern the possibility of losing the flashlight. At times, the going was slow, the ground uneven. He took Espy's hand as they navigated their way around a pit, the bottom of which Jack couldn't see, even as his wife shined the light straight into it. By the time they reached the eleventh image, Jack felt as if he'd walked the entire length of the city. Still, he felt his energy level rise as they started off again because he knew they were nearing the end of it.

But when the appropriate distance passed and the last rock carving failed to appear, he frowned.

"Did we miss it?" he asked.

"Maybe there aren't twelve," Espy said. "It was guesswork on our part. For all we know, the eleventh was the final marker."

"It's possible," Jack said, though what his wife was suggesting didn't feel right. "At least half of the carvings have New Testament subject matter. And the number eleven isn't significant in Christian numerology." He looked around but didn't know what he was looking for. "Let's keep going."

They began walking again and, almost as if they'd passed some final test designed to demonstrate their commitment to the task, the last of the wall carvings solidified before them. Jack knew it was the last because it wasn't alone. Around the edges of the carving—that of a pair of dragons entwined—were smaller versions of the previous eleven.

He and Espy moved closer, drawn to something that few eyes outside of the Priests of Osiris had ever seen. Flamel saw it. Jack guessed the alchemist was of their ilk.

"Look," Espy said. She pointed at one of the smaller carvings, where a hole about the size of a finger looked to have been drilled through the bottom of the panel. Jack looked at the others and saw the same thing. Jack was reminded of his earlier premise—that this place was a replica of sorts, simulating the older holy place of the order in Saint Petersburg.

"A finger key," he said. "Like the one in Trubetskoy Bastion."

Espy had started to reach toward a panel when Jack grabbed her hand.

"This isn't exactly like the other one," he said. "They can't expect someone paying them a visit to have eleven fingers."

Understanding came to Espy and she withdrew her hand. "So how does it work?" she asked.

Jack weighed the options, comparing the locking mechanism with others he'd seen, and those that would have been appropriate for the time period. It had to be a simple mechanism.

He considered the available data, most of which had come from a man who believed he could discover something that would produce an unlimited quantity of gold. Flamel was a mystic, a dreamer. Yet Jack knew he was also technically minded. He was once a chemist. There was his work as a scrivener; he did the exacting work of preparing and preserving manuscripts. His directions in *Le Livre des Figures Hiéroglyphiques* were clear and precise, everything orderly.

"It's a tumbler lock," Jack said. "It requires the right combination."

"And we're supposed to get that how exactly?"

Jack thought it a good question, but he was becoming convinced that Flamel had wanted someone to know the answer. Maybe Flamel, like the Chambers family, was on the outs with the organization he served.

"I think somebody told us the combination," he said.

He didn't have the laptop and he doubted he would get a signal anyway, but he remembered the pages of the book. He knew the order. The panels were arranged differently on the wall.

He inserted a finger into a hole corresponding with the first picture featured in the book, gratified to feel something slide in. He repeated the process with the next nine holes, his excitement growing with each accepting slide. When he'd depressed ten of the sliders, he stopped. Espy, waiting for him to finish the job, gave him a puzzled look.

Jack looked at the wall. There was no way to tell what was on the other side. It was possible—even probable—that he and Espy were walking into a trap. But if he'd only learned one thing about himself over the years, it was that he would always open the door.

He raised his hand and slid a finger into the eleventh hole.

For a moment, nothing happened. Jack frowned and traded a look with Espy. Then, just as he was about to take a step closer, the wall in front of him shifted, the panels that made up the tumbler lock sliding away, drawing back to reveal another layer of stone.

At first, Jack didn't know what it was he was looking at, only that it wasn't a secret chamber holding the bones of the prophet Elisha. Instead he saw a single panel circled by markings—carvings that Jack couldn't identify, much less read. The carvings surrounded a small, narrow opening—a slit into the stone. Jack reached into his bag and pulled out a cloth, using it to wipe the dust from the markings. He took a step back.

"Can you read that?" he asked.

Espy moved closer and studied it. Finally she shook her head. "I don't know what that is."

Jack grumbled to himself and stepped up to the wall again. He'd been expecting a big reveal, not another puzzle, and he found his patience wearing thin. He ran his fingers along the markings. They looked vaguely hieroglyphic, but he could tell they weren't Egyptian. He stood there for a long while, the silence of the cavern creating a bubble in which he was free to think, free to try to make—even force—connections between the volume of data he'd accumulated over the years. He was too close to be denied by a line of characters he couldn't decipher.

He lost track of how long he stood there. Neither could he have identified when the first vague recollections began to touch at his consciousness. What came first was the image of precious gems: rubies, a black opal. Even with these, though, it took a while longer before he made the connection. And when he did, he started to laugh. In the silence of the chamber, the sound was overly loud, yet Jack didn't care. There was no one around to hear him.

He moved his hand from the markings to the hole in the rock around which they circled. And as he touched the place, his laughter grew.

Espy was watching him, a puzzled, even concerned look on her face. Jack shook his head, eyes glittering. He turned away from the wall and took Espy by the hand. He began to lead her back the way they'd come.

"Let's go," he said.

The look Espy gave him was one of disbelief, and the only thing it did was bring a fresh round of mirth to Jack. Once he could speak, he squeezed her hand.

"We have to call your brother," he said. "He's never going to believe this."

"You're joking," Romero said.

"Not even a little," Jack said.

After so long belowground, the open air seemed fresher than Jack remembered. He and Espy stood near the Catacombs' entrance, the sights and sounds of Paris descending into evening unfolding around them.

"You mean to tell me that you need a dagger I purchased almost twenty years ago so that you can recover ancient bones hidden beneath the streets of Paris?"

The doubt in Romero's voice almost made Jack laugh again, but he kept his emotions in check.

"Do you believe in providence?" Jack asked.

"Of course," Romero said. "No one could spend as much time with you as I have and not believe in it."

Jack didn't begrudge Romero his doubt. While he'd seen it with his own eyes, it was difficult to believe that the markings on a subterranean lock in Paris matched the markings on a dagger he and Romero had tried to purchase in Brazil almost two decades ago. It was that sort of synchronicity that buoyed Jack's faith, that made him believe in a God for whom nothing was an accident.

"It's the dagger you bought—or stole—from Paulo," Jack said. "I'm certain of it."

He heard Romero muttering. Jack knew his friend still had it. It was one of the highlights of his collection, difficult to part with because of how hard it'd been won.

"The dagger's the key," Jack said. "I need it if I'm going to find the bones."

Romero went silent, and Jack knew the man was searching for a reason to argue. Jack waited while the process worked itself out. He had no doubt Romero would send the dagger; he would send it for the betrayal of telling Quinn Chambers where to find the bones.

"How could the Cavalcanti dagger be the key?" Romero asked. "It's been in my possession for almost twenty years. And before that, it spent the better part of two hundred years in a grave. If it's the key, then no one has been in that room in a very long time."

"Unless there's more than one," Jack said. "The Cavalcanti dagger is either the original or a copy."

Jack heard more grumbling, but he knew he'd won. Romero owed him.

"And how do you propose I get the dagger to you?"

"FedEx," Jack answered. "They have a next-flight service. If you have it ready for pickup within the hour, I can have it in my hand within twelve."

He heard a snort through the phone.

"It will cost me near five hundred at next-flight rates," Romero said.

"So I'll owe you," Jack came back.

He gave Romero the address and, after ending the call, kept the phone in his hand. After thinking things through, he looked at Espy.

"How do you feel about inviting the boys to this party?" he asked.

Espy nodded. "I think they'd like Paris."

Jack quickly called another number. "I've got them," he said when McKeller answered. "I'm sure you understand that I can't get them through customs. You're going to have to come to Paris."

McKeller responded with a sardonic chuckle. "You must think me a fool."

"The CIA doesn't hire fools," Jack replied. "But I do think you're desperate. And I think you need the bones badly enough that you're willing to bring my children here so that we can make the exchange."

"You've overstepped, Dr. Hawthorne. You're playing fast and loose with your sons' lives."

"I don't think I am. You bring the boys to Paris by tomorrow. I'll call you and arrange for a very public meeting place. I give you the bones; you give me my boys. You can have as many people with you as you think you need to make sure I don't pull anything. Believe me—you won't see the bones if Alex and Jim aren't with you."

He ended the call before McKeller could speak again.

"Now we wait," he said to Espy.

24

✝

JACK THOUGHT IT SEEMED STRANGE to activate the tumbler lock a second time. It was almost as if he knew where the key was beneath the welcome mat. He keyed the sequence in the right order. When the eleventh panel slid into place, the wall once again worked its magic, showing the single panel waiting expectantly for the final key.

Jack reached into the bag and withdrew the dagger. Earlier, when he met the FedEx man at the National Library, he'd been mindful of watchful eyes and so delayed opening the package until he and Espy were back in their hotel room. Pulling it from the box and removing it from its protective wrappings, Jack was returned to the day when Paulo had handed it to him across a table along the Brazil/French Guiana border. The jewels sparkled even under the bad fluorescent lighting of their hotel room. As he turned it over in his hand then, and as he did the same standing now before the lock, as he reacquainted himself with the markings on the hilt that matched those on the Parisian wall, he found that he could muster little excitement.

For the real treasure was behind the wall that the key in his hand was meant to open.

He extended the dagger and set the point in the slot made for it. He slid the dagger in, the sound of metal on stone punctuating the moment. As the hilt came into contact with the stone, Jack felt the weapon click into place, some unseen lever sliding in response to the dagger's proportions.

The response was immediate. There was no rumble of stone, no portentous movement of the earth. Instead, Jack heard a quiet popping noise, and then a seam that he hadn't noticed before separated to reveal an opening into a once-solid rock wall. There was something almost anticlimactic about it. After all the work he and Espy had done, he'd hoped for something a bit grander.

The opening wasn't large, perhaps two feet wide and half again as tall. The natural darkness of the chamber made it difficult to see inside, so Jack took the flashlight from Espy and aimed it into the opening.

Nothing but rock, the hole extended into the wall following the same proportions as its width. Jack had no doubt that it was meant as a storage area. The walls were smooth, straight, finely chiseled. At the bottom, where Jack could envision the bones resting, was a raised area, a small dais. But it lay empty. Whatever it had once held was now gone.

As he took in the absence of what he'd hoped to find, Jack felt defeat hovering in the shadows, and the weariness of the last few days washed over him. He looked away from the hole and made eye contact with his wife. She could read everything on his face; she knew what he'd discovered without having to look in herself.

She moved closer, taking Jack's hand. She took in the empty cavity and released a deep sigh.

"Okay, so we've narrowed down the list of places it's not," she said.

The comment brought a semblance of a smile from Jack. But before he could respond, he noticed the tunnel was gradually lightening. Turning, he looked back the way they'd come and watched as the light grew. Espy saw it too. Jack realized that it probably didn't matter who owned the light; it couldn't bode well for them. He turned to survey the path that would take them deeper into the Catacombs, noting the lack of cover in that direction.

He hurriedly unfolded his collection of maps and tried to make sense of the winding passageways recorded on them. He knew their biggest issue involved the accuracy of the maps; he thought it a miracle he and Espy had come as far as they had. Beyond this point, the truth of the maps was even more questionable. A single wrong turn, or an unseen pit, or a broken flashlight was all that separated him and Espy from a life of aimless tunnel wandering.

In the end, he lowered the maps, slipping them into the bag. The light was getting closer, and they were almost out of time. He took out the gun, wishing he'd thought to bring the second one from the duffel bag.

"It's going to get dark," he whispered. Then he switched off the flashlight, allowing the darkness to close in around them. He reached out, found Espy's arm, and pulled her toward the far wall, the one opposite the wall with the tumbler lock. He put her behind him, positioning his body so that he was as flush with the stone as he could be. He watched the light approach.

It occurred to him that the locking mechanism was still tripped, the Cavalcanti dagger still shoved into its slot. He supposed it didn't matter now.

Before long, the diffuse light resolved into a trio of beams and Jack heard footfalls. The small cavern in which he and Espy stood had a slight parabolic shape. It kept the occasional flit of a beam of light from falling on them.

Jack had the gun up, but he didn't have a target. That changed when three shapes materialized from the shadows, forms hovering at the edges that teased him before darting ahead. Jack kept his eyes aimed past the lights, trying to pull details from the gloom.

If he shot first, he knew that he and Espy might survive, that the element of surprise could be the thing that saved them. But he also knew he couldn't pull the trigger until he identified the threat. He couldn't shoot until he ruled out the possibility that the ones approaching were teenagers exploring past the boundaries of the Catacombs.

The decision cost him his opportunity. An instant later, light fell on the tumbler lock. Jack heard one of the newcomers say something unintelligible in a sharp tone, followed by other lights moving to further illuminate Jack and Espy's handiwork. Then the three figures stepped into the chamber.

Jack couldn't make out many details, only that the newcomers were men, all of them wearing dark clothes and warm jackets. It didn't take long before one of them panned a light around the chamber, and for that light to find the two figures tucked against the wall. When that happened, when the light hit Jack full in the face, he raised his own flashlight and hit the switch, sending the strong beam back at the intruders. He heard a curse, registering the delivery in English.

In the next moments, in a cavern beneath a bustling European city, time froze. Jack blinked against the glare of the light in his face. He kept his own light trained on the intruders, his gun at the ready. But each of the men now fully illuminated had a weapon pointed back at him. He'd run out of options.

"You must be Dr. Hawthorne," one of them said, the accent decidedly British.

Jack answered with a nod. "You seem to have the advantage over me."

"More than you realize," the other man said. He took a step forward. Jack brought his gun up in response. "Dr. Hawthorne, if we wanted to kill you, we'd have already done so. Please lower your weapon and allow us to escort you out."

"I think we can find our own way," Jack said.

He felt Espy's hand on his arm, a gentle squeeze.

"While that may be true," the Englishman said, "these tunnels can be dangerous if you're not careful. I would hate for anything to happen to you."

A retort came to Jack's lips, but he let it pass unspoken. Jack was smart enough to know that, ultimately, it wouldn't change anything. It was the message Espy's arm squeeze was meant to convey. What it came down to was that he had one gun against their three.

He lowered the gun and then dropped it at his feet, the metal making sharp contact with rock. "Live to fight another day," he said.

The two men who'd remained silent thus far crossed the chamber. One picked up Jack's gun while the other divested him of his flashlight. Jack's attention, though, was fixed on the Englishman. The man turned to the repository and reached for the dagger. He withdrew it and held it up to the light, turning it over in his hand. With the dagger removed, the inner panel slid back into place, the lesser panels moving to cover it. Soon nothing remained of Jack and Espy's work.

The Brit ran a reverent hand over the icons before turning away from the wall. He gestured at his compatriots, who began to guide Jack and Espy back the way they'd come.

Jack gazed out a second-floor window, taking in the view of the property: the cobblestone courtyard and fountain, the ancient trees, the manicured grounds that seemed to stretch for miles. The villa, tucked into a secluded area in Versailles, was large and opulent while at the same time preserving a provincial, even earthy, feel. The room in which their escorts had installed them was large and airy, with several tall windows that let in the day's waning sunlight. A pair of comfortable couches, along with matching chairs and a couple of tables, were the room's only furnishings. As Jack sank onto one of the couches, he considered that he'd been held in worse prisons.

He'd checked the door not long after arriving, and while it wasn't locked, the two guards posted in the hall did much to keep him in his gilded cage.

When he sat, Espy glanced up from the book she'd picked up from an end table, although she didn't say anything. They'd covered what ground they could during the twenty-minute ride from Paris, and during their first few minutes of solitude in the villa. Jack had come to the conclusion that Rousseau hadn't been responsible for their detainment. Rather, he believed that another potentially more dangerous adversary was hosting their stay in Versailles.

As if in silent confirmation of that belief, the door opened to admit a woman whose patrician smile was ice and contempt.

Olivia Chambers stopped only a few steps past the doorway, giving her guests the once-over.

From his spot on the couch, Jack regarded her with an expression that bespoke boredom, while Espy didn't bother to look up from her book. Jack saw a hint of a frown touch Olivia's lips, but it vanished quickly. The lady crossed the room, choosing a spot at the armrest of the other couch from which to address them.

"It's a pleasure to see you both," she said.

Jack responded with a smile, and Espy, still absorbed in the book, hadn't given any indication she was aware someone had entered the room. Olivia stared at Espy, as if taking in the indifference.

"Especially you, Mrs. *Manheim*," Olivia said. "I was so hoping I'd have a chance to talk with you again."

Jack saw the corner of Espy's mouth rise a fraction. Casually she closed the book and returned it to the table before returning the other woman's gaze.

"Thank you for having us," Espy said. "The villa's lovely. Yours?"

The complete calm—the absolute confidence—in her voice seemed to give Olivia Chambers pause, as if she were suddenly reminded of how their last meeting had ended.

"It is. One of my more quaint residences."

The comment elicited no response from Espy.

Olivia smiled. "Yes, Dr. Habilla-Hawthorne, I imagine a place like this is quite something compared to your cute little Colonial Revival in Ellen."

Espy took the jab in stride, annoyance only showing in her eyes, and mild enough that Jack doubted if Olivia had even noticed it.

Olivia shifted her attention to Jack.

"The intrepid Dr. Jack Hawthorne," she said. Olivia ran her eyes over Jack, adopting a pleasant smile that he knew was intended solely to vex Espy. "I've been wanting to meet you for quite some time. I only wish I'd known who you were when you visited me in London."

Jack's patience for pleasantries was long spent. "If you'd known then who we were," he said, "you would have had us killed there rather than having to come to Paris to do it."

Olivia frowned, but instead of answering right away, she circled the couch and took a seat opposite him. "Why would I want to have you killed?" she asked.

"Maybe because I killed some of your operatives a few years back. Because I stole the bones from George Manheim, and I buried them in the desert. And because I know far too many secrets involving the Priests of Osiris for you to allow me to live." He paused, inviting her to deny any of it. When she didn't, when her face revealed nothing, he leaned forward and looked her in the eyes. "And let's face it, Olivia, the only reason Rousseau's worked so hard to keep us alive is because it ticks you off."

His words pushed Olivia Chambers to drop the veil long enough to show genuine anger. It told Jack he was right about the long history of enmity between the two families. But like the well-mannered aristocrat she was, the lady quickly recovered.

"Dr. Hawthorne, surely you don't think you're the first one outside of the organization who has been able to learn our secrets." She shook her head and chuckled. "You're not as special or as resourceful as you think."

"That may be so, but how many outsiders have been able to witness the power of the bones?"

As with the previous comment, he saw this one do its work.

It made Jack wonder how many members of the Priests of Osiris had been given the opportunity to see Elisha's bones harness the power of God.

"Our internal affairs are just that, internal," she said. "What's more important is the work we do, and the disturbance you represent to that work."

Espy snorted. It was her turn to lean forward, to engage the enemy. "From what I've seen, it seems the bones have done more harm than good."

"And how do you come to that conclusion?"

"I'm sure you know we've been to Saint Petersburg," Espy said. "And you may also be aware that we found the meeting hall beneath Trubetskoy Bastion."

She allowed time for Olivia to acknowledge that, which she did with a nod.

"The thousands of skulls in the walls surrounding your history stone testify to the brutality of your little priesthood," Espy remarked.

At first, Olivia appeared to be surprised, but then she immediately composed herself and said, "I can't speak to whatever it is you're assuming. But your accusation tells me that despite knowing more of our secrets than most, you have yet to grasp our longevity, as well as the breadth of our influence. The Priests of Osiris is almost three thousand years old, and countless people have committed themselves to protecting the relics. Every skull in that chamber represents someone who died in that service. It's a place of honor."

Jack thought it was the first genuine thing the lady had said, and that alone made him accept every word of it as truth. Although he'd read enough of their literature—uncovered in the treasure room of the Manheim estate—to know the power of the bones had been used throughout history to the detriment of many. Olivia Chambers certainly couldn't claim altruistic intent, and that lack of altruism extended to him and Espy.

"I imagine the only reason you're confirming all this is because you're going to kill us," Jack said.

Even as he said the words, he found it wasn't fear for himself that consumed him. It wasn't even fear for his wife. Instead, it was the thought of Alex and Jim, who, if McKeller had done as Jack instructed, were somewhere in or near Paris. They were waiting for their father to come rescue them, and he couldn't even save himself.

"Yes, I'm going to kill you," Olivia said, "and I'll tell you why." She looked at Espy, then back at Jack, and smiled. "I'm going to kill you because it will *tick off* your friend Rousseau."

A second later, one of the windows exploded.

Jack jumped, whirling around just in time to see whatever had shattered the glass come to rest against the leg of the table. Instantly smoke began to pour from the object. He leaped toward Espy, yanked her off the couch, and headed for the far corner of the room.

Olivia's reaction was almost as quick as Jack's. After taking stock of what had happened, she stood and began rushing toward the door. That was when they heard small-arms fire coming from the hallway.

Olivia froze, her eyes on the door. The gunfire was growing louder. They could hear shouts. Jack pulled Espy behind a table. It was flimsy protection, but it got them out of the line of fire if someone fired a shot through the door. Olivia, on the other hand, stood in the center of the room, gaping at the door as if unable to comprehend that danger could find her in her own house.

Jack heard another shot, closer now, and Olivia turned her head, her eyes filled with fear as she found Jack across the room. Despite what she'd done to them, and that she planned to kill him and Espy, Jack couldn't help feeling sympathy for the lady.

She broke eye contact first, turning back to the door. It didn't take long for the conflict taking place out in the hallway to reach them. By then, the smoke grenade had made it hard for Jack to see. He crouched, pulling Espy closer to him, positioning himself between her and the door.

Jack heard a loud thud and then the door burst open, the jamb splintering. Through the smoke he saw men streaming into the room, their weapons drawn.

Olivia remained still, even as the first man through the door ran to her and roughly forced her to her knees.

Then they came for Jack and Espy through the smoke, and all he could do was watch them approach, and look on as they dragged Olivia Chambers through the shattered doorway.

25

JACK TRIED THE DOOR HANDLE once and found it locked. He didn't bother trying to get anyone's attention on the outside. At some point, both he and Espy fell asleep. Later, a sound at the door woke him. His wife was already alert.

Alain Rousseau's entrance didn't surprise Jack. The man offered both of them a smile and then turned his attention to Espy.

"Good evening, Dr. Habilla-Hawthorne," he said. He took her hand in both of his. Jack looked past him. There was at least one other man in the hall. "My apologies for making you wait so long. I had some things to attend to."

Despite the circumstances that had brought them there, it was difficult to avoid being charmed by this man. Something about him drew a person in.

Espy smiled. "I understand. You must be a busy man." She paused and, without a break in her smile, added, "I mean, all the killing alone has to take up most of the workday."

Jack couldn't help but chuckle. Rousseau didn't react but instead released Espy's hand and turned to Jack.

"You're an incredibly resourceful man, Dr. Hawthorne. Very impressive." He spun around and headed for the door. "Now, if you'll follow me, please."

After exchanging a look, Jack and Espy did as they were told, walking behind Rousseau while his associate took the rear. Jack didn't see a gun, but he didn't doubt its presence. They walked to the end of the hallway, where Rousseau gestured them through another door, which opened into an office more luxurious than the one at his workplace. Jack had watched their approach to the mansion through the window of the sedan that had carried him and Espy from Versailles and knew they were in Rousseau's private home.

A large desk sat to the left, but Rousseau did not move to it. Instead he invited his guests to sit on a leather couch along the far wall. He took a seat on a matching chair.

"So what do you propose we do now, Dr. Hawthorne?" he asked.

"I vote for letting us go," Jack said.

Rousseau smiled at that, albeit with a hint of sadness in the expression. He didn't have to say anything for Jack to understand that their previous arrangement was no longer valid.

"I believe we've tried that already," Rousseau said. "You said you would stop pursuing the relics and work something out with the CIA."

"In exchange for you calling off your dogs," Jack responded. "And we both know how that worked out."

Rousseau leaned back in his chair. "All I said was that my people would not harm you. I never said they wouldn't follow you."

"Well, they did more than 'follow' us."

"Perhaps," Rousseau said. "However, you seem to forget

that without my help, Olivia's people would have killed you in your hotel room." He fell silent, staring at his guests. When he spoke next, he addressed Espy. "What about your son? Jim, is it? Aren't you the least bit interested in seeing what the relics can do for him?"

Jack saw Rousseau's words find their mark. Of course Espy was curious. Over the years, as they'd watched Jim's condition deteriorate, they'd often wondered about the powerful relics they'd once held in their hands, how they might be used to heal Jim. Yet they'd always drawn a line in the sand in that regard.

"They're not our bones to use," Espy said.

"Then whose?" Rousseau asked. "If not you, who have shown your worth, who have succeeded where few have, then who has the right to use them?"

"As hard as it is to say this, especially as a mother who loves her son, who wants him to be healthy and happy, what it comes down to is that it isn't our call to make."

Rousseau looked unconvinced. "Since you seem disinclined to answer the question, what about this one? If the bones of the prophet Elisha still contain the healing power of God after such a long time, why would that be so? Would you not think the bones must have some ultimate purpose, something as yet unfulfilled?"

It was another question Jack had asked himself over the years—another for which he didn't have a satisfactory answer except to recall something Gordon Reese—the man who'd hired him to find the bones, which had forever altered the course of Jack's life—once said.

"The power of God doesn't fade over time," Jack said. "Haven't you considered that maybe the bones don't have an ultimate purpose? That they just contain the residual power of an all-powerful God?"

The man's smile told Jack that he wasn't framing the debate in any new way.

"Would it surprise you to learn that we have theologians in our association?" Rousseau said. "That we have an exegetical history as robust as your own?"

Jack mulled that over, then offered a headshake. "The Priests of Osiris is older than Christianity, has either influenced or been influenced by countless religions, and has survived on an oral and written history that has to have left many of your beliefs, your tenets, open to interpretation. So it doesn't surprise me that you have people performing in that role."

The answer seemed to amuse Rousseau. He smirked as if enjoying some private joke. "Oh, the priestly tradition is mostly vanished now, yet those old questions still evoke some passion."

"Why are you telling me this?" Jack asked.

"So that you'll understand," Rousseau said.

"And what is it that I'm supposed to understand?"

Rousseau allowed the question to hang there. He rose and went to his desk, removing a bottle from a drawer. It was a Macallan scotch, a single shot worth half of Jack's yearly salary. He placed three glasses on the desk and then looked to his guests. Both of them declined. Rousseau poured himself two fingers without ice. Only after he sampled the drink did he speak again.

"What I want you to understand, Dr. Hawthorne, is that there are no more temples. The boardroom is our temple now. The country club our sacred cloister. The CEO our high priest."

At Jack's silence, Rousseau laughed again.

"The bones do serve a purpose," he said. "A two-fold one,

in fact. The first should be obvious. By holding the power of eternal life in our hands, what heads of state can we not control? What captains of industry? The second . . ." He trailed off, finished the last of the scotch. "I'm sure you've heard that trite phrase about keeping your enemies close."

"You mean control of those within your own organization," Espy said.

"Unify men in a great task, a quest if you will, and you stand a better chance of controlling those men."

Jack couldn't help but find the conversation fascinating. What he was hearing from Alain Rousseau was an account of how one of the world's oldest religions—and he had no doubt that's what it once was—inherited the secular mantle. The idea enthralled him.

"And which of those two purposes has resulted in all the many deaths your organization has been involved in?" Espy asked.

"Asks someone whose own church fathers sanctioned the Crusades, the Inquisition, the burning of heretics and witches, and an untold number of other atrocities," Rousseau countered. "And yet I don't accuse you for the ancient misdeeds of your faith."

"Except it's not a faith to you," Espy said. "Your god is money."

Rousseau shrugged. "Then I suppose I'm little different from most of your televangelists." He set his glass on the desk and refilled it. "You already know that I was the one who saved you," he went on. "I'm the one who made everything that happened in Australia disappear. Who has allowed you to live in peace ever since."

"I'm well aware of that," Jack said. "And I suppose I owe you thanks for it."

"It was self-serving," Rousseau said.

"Your house has been at war with the Chambers family for a long time," Jack said.

"Generations, except I wouldn't call it a war. It's more accurate to call it corporate politics, but on a grand scale."

"You had him killed," Jack said.

"Of course I did," Rousseau said. "There comes a time when even long-lived skirmishes have to end. When the risks of allowing it to continue are too great. So it was time to end the Chambers influence within the organization for good."

"But Olivia Chambers wasn't about to let that kind of power just slip away," Jack said.

"Another thing for which I owe you thanks. It was your presence that brought Olivia Chambers to Paris. Your presence that forced her to risk leaving the protection of London and travel with limited security."

Jack saw that Espy was troubled, although she kept herself in check. She was smart enough to know that Alain Rousseau would have killed Olivia Chambers regardless of their involvement.

"If I understand correctly what you've said," Espy began, "the original purpose of the Priests of Osiris was to preserve and judiciously use the bones of Elisha."

Rousseau nodded agreement.

"But then over time, as the organization grew, it became more about amassing wealth and power."

Rousseau nodded again.

"So what's the purpose of the Priests of Osiris today? What's the twenty-first-century vision of a band of Israelite priests who only wanted to protect the bones of one of their greatest prophets?"

The question was a weighty one, and Rousseau pondered it before answering. "At its peak, the Priests of Osiris was comprised of twenty-two families, all of whom took the responsibility of protecting the bones quite seriously. Of course, each of them also knew what the power of the bones could do for them personally and often acted accordingly. Today it's a coalition of six families, five now with the withdrawal of the Chambers family. And the purpose at this point is simple economics. The bones are a tool, a means toward continued prosperity for the people who have proven strong enough to protect the claims inherited from ancestors long dead."

"Yet you mentioned priests and theologians," Jack said.

Rousseau smiled. "As you said, the Priests of Osiris is the world's oldest religion. Our influence extends into churches and governments; we own both priests and prime ministers. But make no mistake, our religion is now run by five families. And our catechism is economic theory."

While the reality of it didn't surprise Jack, the hearing of it left him feeling hollow—to learn that whatever mystery, whatever good, had once existed had been supplanted by gold. He found that he didn't have anything left to say, no more questions to ask. Rousseau, however, seemed ready to fill the gap.

"I lied earlier, Dr. Hawthorne. When I told you that I only kept you alive to vex Quinn Chambers? That wasn't entirely accurate."

Jack didn't answer, but just sat quietly beneath Rousseau's appraisal.

"One of the axioms of any successful business is that one should make use of all available resources," Rousseau said. "And you've certainly proven yourself on that score."

He lapsed into silence again, took a sip of the scotch. Jack shook his head as he pondered what the man had said. He had an idea about where the conversation was headed.

Rousseau set his glass down and pulled the desk chair back. He opened another drawer and reached for something. When he pulled his hand back, he held the Cavalcanti dagger. He lifted it, studied the jewels. He looked at Jack, an appreciative smile on his lips.

"You have me in a quandary." Rousseau shifted his gaze to take in Espy too. "Both of you do. On one hand, you both know too much for me to consider you anything but a grave risk to our organization. On the other hand, failing to make use of your talents, your respective skill sets, almost seems a crime."

"What are you saying?" Jack asked.

"I'm saying I'm prepared to welcome you into my employ. That I'd rather have you using the tenacity you've so clearly demonstrated to protect the bones of Elisha rather than forcing me to have to kill you."

Of all the things Jack had expected to hear, the extension of a job offer wasn't on the list. His eyes widened and he looked at his wife, her expression the same as his. Years ago, perhaps even as far back as his first hunt for the relics, Jack wouldn't have considered the offer, wouldn't have considered sacrificing his principles to work for an organization with such a dark history. Now, though, he found that his decision had to view the boys as a framework. If Jack and Espy declined, the boys would likely be orphaned. If Jack and Espy sacrificed principle and signed on with the very same entity that had haunted their dreams for more than a decade, they stood a decent chance of reclaiming their children from the man who held them.

Jack read these same thoughts in Espy's eyes, and he saw her come to the same conclusion. Principle couldn't stand against parenthood. He turned his attention to Rousseau.

"What would you have us do?" he asked.

Rousseau's eyes twinkled, whether from pleasure or too much scotch, Jack didn't know.

"We can discuss the terms of your employment later," Rousseau said. "But I can assure you that none of your duties will include anything you'd find morally objectionable."

Except for the prospect of working for an organization that was by its nature morally objectionable, Jack thought. He already had a sick feeling in his stomach at the thought of selling his soul to these people, but he tried to content himself with the belief that the job was temporary—that he and Espy would somehow find a way to extricate themselves once the boys were safe.

But even as he thought that, he couldn't ignore the feeling of pride that welled up in him. A long time ago he'd set off in search of biblical relics and had along the way uncovered clues to the existence of an ancient and powerful society. Now he was positioned to become a member of that society. He couldn't deny a certain sense of accomplishment.

And he found that that accomplishment, that invitation into the family, gave him the opportunity to ask one more question after all.

"Can I see them?"

Rousseau had the look of a man who'd been waiting for a gifted student to ask the right question. He gave his answer with a smug smile.

"Of course."

26

✝

AS ROUSSEAU ESCORTED THEM from his office, Jack had no preconceived notions regarding the area that would hold the bones. He was certain they would be close by, within the Rousseau estate. The man led them to the stairs, one of his bodyguards trailing. They descended to the first floor, where Rousseau preceded them down a long hallway.

"You have them here?" Jack said.

Rousseau nodded. "The business in Australia has caused us to rethink one of our last surviving customs."

"The subcontracting," Jack said. "To people like George Manheim."

"At the time, that arrangement was the best way to ensure the safety of the relics through political and social upheaval," Rousseau said. "But in an age when the entire world's information is available to everyone on the planet, and where explorers such as you and your wife can crisscross the globe sifting through clues, it may be time to find a more permanent resting place."

Arriving at the end of the hall, Rousseau opened a door into what looked like a library. Before entering, he told his associate to wait in the hall.

Two walls were lined with bookshelves, each crammed with antique volumes. A pair of plush chairs positioned on either side of a small fireplace provided places in which to peruse the books, with an assortment of lamps offering subdued but adequate lighting.

Rousseau walked across the room and stopped before one of the bookshelves, and Jack knew right away what the man was about to do. When the shelf slid out on concealed hinges, revealing a dark opening and a flight of narrow steps, Jack shook his head. Rousseau then turned and gestured for Jack and Espy to lead the way.

Jack stepped through first. The air took on a different quality, mustier, and had the smell of cedar. The steps were hard to make out, but there was a light at the bottom and Jack advanced toward it. When he reached the last step, he saw a large, open area dominated by stone walls and a tiled floor. The impression Jack had was of a mansion basement. He wouldn't have been surprised to see a water heater in the corner, or a washer and dryer. Instead there was a single wooden door, such as might have opened into a utility closet.

A moment later, Rousseau had joined Jack and Espy at the foot of the stairs. The man saw the question on Jack's face.

"Believe me," Rousseau said with a chuckle, "the bones have been held in places far more humble than this."

He walked over and put his hand on the doorknob. Jack and Espy reached Rousseau's side just as the man opened the door. It opened into a hallway that led to the right, the walls and floor made of the same material as the room to which it was connected. Rousseau went first, Jack and Espy following close behind.

Jack saw that it was a narrow passage, not very long, and at the end of it was another door. The door stood open.

Alain Rousseau froze.

Near the open doorway, two bodies lay sprawled on the floor. From a dozen feet away, Jack could see a small hole in one man's temple, a line of blood running to the tile floor.

Rousseau hadn't moved, and Jack thought he saw the same expression on the man's face that he'd witnessed on Olivia's only hours before—that of a great lord unable to comprehend that an enemy had breached his inner sanctum.

Jack took the lead, stepping around Rousseau and making his way to the open door. Beyond it, he saw a small, round room, brightly lit. In the center was a pedestal, a short column of black stone with intricate carvings on its surface. To Jack, the pedestal seemed a nod to the old priesthood charged with the care of the relics, a last tie to the religious affiliations of the Priests of Osiris. An iconic pedestal surrounded by white walls and track lighting.

But the pedestal was empty, the relics that should have topped it held under the arm of a man now turning toward the door. In his other hand, the man held a gun. Cold, dark eyes found Jack in the doorway, and the gun came up. Jack didn't have time to react; he could only watch as the thief raised the weapon.

But a flurry of movement behind Jack broke into his consciousness and he found himself being yanked from the doorway, wrenched backward even as the man pulled the trigger. Jack registered the sound of the shot before he felt the pain in his arm. Then he was on the tile, lying next to one of Rousseau's dead guards, Espy on the floor next to him. They'd taken shelter behind the open door, and as Jack raised himself up, he caught sight of something black in the shadows. He reached for it, feeling the cold metal of the fallen guard's gun.

Espy was struggling to a knee, pinned between Jack and the wall. Jack looked over his shoulder and saw Rousseau, the man's anger taking hold, reaching beneath his jacket. He never got the weapon out. With the door blocking his view, Jack didn't see the shooter, but he saw the bullets strike Rousseau's chest. The rest seemed to happen in slow motion. Rousseau flinched under the impacts, then looked down and saw blood, disbelief in his eyes. He crumpled to the floor, his hand still tucked under his jacket.

What tore Jack's eyes from the scene was movement at the door, the thief exiting. The man led with his weapon, bringing it around to get an angle on Jack and Espy. Jack threw his shoulder at the door with all the force he could muster. The door slammed into the thief, kept him from shooting. From his knees, Jack raised the guard's gun, leaning out from behind the door and touching the weapon to the other man's stomach. He squeezed off a shot.

At his precarious angle, the recoil sent Jack to the floor. He came down hard on his elbow. In front of him, the thief was bleeding out, the close-range shot fatal. As the man slid down the doorframe, the bundle in his arms fell to the floor.

Breathing heavily, Jack struggled to his feet. He looked to his left and found Espy, standing now. "Are you okay?" he asked.

Only after she nodded did he look at his arm. His jacket was stained with blood, but he didn't have to remove his clothes to know it was only a graze. That meant he could concentrate on what was truly important.

He recognized the bones from the wrappings, the same ones that secured the relics when he'd found them in Australia. They were tightly bound, not a hint of the aged bone showing. He went to the bundle and gathered it up, and the feel of them in his arms took him back a decade—to the first time he'd seen them, the moment that had validated all the trials he and Espy had walked through. He felt something of the same exultation now.

He took hold of a corner of the wrappings, but before he removed the fabric, he turned and motioned for Espy to join him. Years ago they'd found the bones together and had dealt with the ramifications of that event together as well. There was no way he could look upon Elisha's bones again without his wife at his side. When Espy reached him, he took her hand and brought it to the wrapping, and together they lifted the fabric.

When the cloth fell away and Jack saw the relics he'd once interred in the Australian desert, he found it curious how little they seemed to differ from the bones beneath Trubetskoy Bastion, or the ones in the Catacombs. They appeared as dead things that, long ago, gave up their claim to any life they once had. And yet he knew that within them coursed the power of God. It was a revelation that, surprisingly, left a bitter taste in his mouth.

Rousseau's words came back to him, the question of who got to decide how this power was used. It was something Jack couldn't help but ponder, even though he knew that much wiser people than he had wrestled with it throughout human history.

He knew about the goodness of God. His power had saved Espy, and it had saved him. It brought them two children he couldn't imagine not having met. It had given him friends far better and more loyal than he deserved. Yet it was that very goodness that made him angry at the apparent limits of God's kindness, that caused him to question why a God powerful enough that his leftover energy could bring people back to life thousands of years later would allow a boy to progressively weaken, to eventually die well before his parents.

It was the kind of puzzle Jack hated, because it was the kind he couldn't solve. But he supposed that one of the evidences of spiritual maturity was that he didn't always have to solve the puzzle.

Espy put her hand on his, and Jack looked up. She was smiling. It took a moment before Jack identified it as contentment. He let the cloth fall back down.

———

Bundle in hand, Jack stared down at the man he'd killed. As he studied the man's face, the dark military clothing, Jack knew he'd killed a member of the Mossad. The Israelis had followed him. Through all the twists and turns over the last week, he hadn't shaken them. After all, they had come for what they felt belonged to them.

With a sigh, Jack and Espy started back down the hallway. Jack paused when he came to Rousseau's body. He knelt next to him and placed the wrapped relics on the floor. He took hold of the man's shoulders and rolled him over. He checked for a pulse and found none. Jack leaned back, looking on the face of the leader of the Priests of Osiris, a man among the most powerful men in the world. He considered the irony that mere feet away were the relics he had protected for so long, relics that had the power to restore his life.

Espy placed a hand on Jack's shoulder. "We have to go," she said.

After a moment, Jack stood. He and Espy reentered the mansion basement, retracing their steps, heading back the way they'd come. At the top of the stairs, the door to the library was still open. Once they passed into the room, Jack didn't bother covering the secret entrance. He stopped at the door, remembering that Rousseau had left a guard in the hall. Jack had no way of knowing how many more awaited between this room and the exit. Worse, he didn't know if more Israelis were in the house or perhaps circling the grounds. Sometimes, he decided, there was little a person could do but take a leap of faith.

He pushed the door open and stepped quickly into the hall. The guard Rousseau had left behind was still there, his back to the library. As the man began to turn, Jack brought the gun down hard on the back of his head. The guard collapsed to the carpet with hardly a sound.

Jack led the way down the hallway, pausing when he reached the stairs leading back to the room in which they'd been held. To the right was a door, and since the only other choice was to return to the second floor, Jack chose the unknown.

When the door swung open, Jack and Espy stood in an enormous foyer of marble floors and white columns. It was nighttime, and there was no one in sight. With the ancient bundle in hand, Jack started for the front door. He waited for Espy to join him, and after securing the bundle at his side, they headed out.

27

✝

JACK THOUGHT IT WAS THE ONLY appropriate place. For more than two weeks, he and Espy had concerned themselves with flying under the radar, with passing from city to city as unobtrusively as possible. Now that the moment they'd worked toward had arrived, a public place—the most obvious public place—seemed to make the most sense.

The Eiffel Tower loomed over them, but Jack walked along the metal barricades and barely noticed it. He scanned the length of the avenue, looking for the man he'd come to meet. He and Espy were ten minutes early. Jack, who on any normal occasion would have watched the meeting place from afar until he'd determined he wasn't walking into a trap, had been unwilling to delay the meeting.

The line to ascend the Eiffel Tower filled the area beneath the Tower's base and stretched along Quai Branly, and while Avenue Gustave Eiffel was almost free of its usual bus traffic, a number of people were crossing over from the adjoining park. Jack studied the faces in the line, yet there were too many of them crammed into the small space for him to notice anything amiss, to pick out someone who didn't belong.

He turned to look out over the park, at the footpaths that bisected it. He saw nothing but families, young couples, and groups of tourists aimlessly wandering over the grounds.

As he took in the scene before him, Espy tapped him on the shoulder. When he turned, she pointed up the street.

At first, Jack didn't see him, the unassuming figure approaching, but when his eyes settled on the man, he knew right off it was McKeller. Jack adjusted his grip on the bag hanging from his shoulder, the bones secured within. He didn't move from his spot, allowing the rogue agent to come to him.

As McKeller drew closer, what struck Jack was how normal the man appeared. In his mind, McKeller had become a monster, a villain from an action movie. The man in front of him, though, was smaller than Jack. His clothes were rumpled, his face lined. It looked as if he hadn't slept in days. What hit him the most, though, was that McKeller was alone.

"Where are they?" Jack asked, his voice hard.

"Near," McKeller answered.

"That's not good enough."

Jack felt the tenseness of his wife next to him. He knew there was a thin line between her maintaining a measure of equanimity and her going for the man's throat.

McKeller's eyes moved to the bag at Jack's shoulder, then back to Jack's face. He slipped a hand in the pocket of his coat. Jack tensed, but McKeller pulled out a phone. He dialed a number and, after a moment, spoke a single word, "Wave."

The agent looked to his right, to the large expanse of green. Jack looked with him and found his attention attracted by a movement different from that of people traversing the space.

He saw the hand in the air at the other end of the green, the man attached to it—and the two smaller forms at that man's side. They were almost a hundred yards away and yet, to Jack, they seemed so close. He felt something in his throat. He heard a noise like a gasp coming from his wife. He took a step.

McKeller's voice stopped him. The man still held the phone open. "The bones first. If you even think of trying to reach your boys, my associate will have them in a car and gone before you're halfway across the park."

It took a great deal of effort, but Jack forced himself to turn away from his sons, to face this man who'd barged into his life and threatened everything that was dear to him.

Without a word, Jack took the bag from his shoulder and unzipped it. Reaching in, he moved the fabric aside, revealing the bones that once carried a great prophet of God through ancient Israel. McKeller looked at the relics, mesmerized. He reached out and touched the yellowed bone. He kept his hand there for several seconds, and Jack allowed the man his moment before speaking again.

"Now the boys," he said.

The sound of Jack's voice seemed to break some kind of spell. McKeller looked up and then withdrew his hand. He spoke into the phone. "Bring them."

Jack held the bag tight as he watched his sons draw near. It was all he could do to keep from rushing toward them. Espy stepped forward. Jack took her hand and held her in place.

When they were close enough for Jack to see them clearly, he was relieved to find they were unharmed. He paid special attention to Jim. The boy was walking well, and his color was good. Jack was watching his face at the moment Jim recognized him, and when the boy broke into a smile, Jack felt tears threatening to surface. Realization came to Alex an instant later, and he grabbed his brother's hand and began to run. Their escort didn't try to stop them.

Espy was the first to move. As soon as the boys stepped onto the walkway, she ran to meet them, going to a knee and embracing them both. The tears flowed freely down her cheeks. Going by the look on Jim's face, Jack knew she was squeezing too hard.

Jack wanted more than anything to join his family, so he completed the transaction, handing the bag to the rogue agent without a second thought. Suddenly the ancient relics had lost their meaning. The only treasure that mattered was wrapped up in the arms of his wife.

He was starting toward them when McKeller spoke. "So it's true, then? The bones will bring someone back from the dead? Will heal them?"

Jack paused, just long enough to give the man a tired smile. "I wouldn't be here if they didn't."

Then he went to his boys. It took some doing to release them from Espy's grasp, but once he did, he gathered them in his arms. Jim's tears touched Jack's neck, while Alex, his older brother, didn't cry.

At last, Jim pulled back from his father. "Mr. McKeller said the bones can heal people," he said. "Is that true?"

Jack nodded. "Yes, it's true."

Jim seemed to take that in, to process the meaning. "Then I'm glad you gave them to him so that he can help his wife."

Jack found himself unable to speak. He grabbed his son again and drew him close. He was still holding Jim when he heard the shot.

Instantly, Jack reached out and pulled Alex down. Espy also

got down, crouching before the echo from the gunshot had dissipated. Jack cast his eyes about, looking for the shooter. He saw the people in line for the Tower—people now gaping at each other, reacting in fear, many of them running for cover.

Then Jack heard the screams. People in the line were yelling, pointing. Jack followed the line of their fingers, causing him to turn.

McKeller, who'd begun to walk away with his prize, was down, unmoving. The bag had spilled its contents onto the avenue, some of the bones coming loose from their wrappings.

Jack continued to look around, searching frantically with his eyes, but still he couldn't locate the sniper. Which meant no one was safe. He shouted at Espy to stay down. Then he grasped the boys' hands and sprinted toward one of the food trucks parked along the walkway. When he reached it, he pulled both boys down, forcing them onto their stomachs, using the truck as cover. Just seconds later, Espy joined them.

The throng of tourists was scattering in all directions, a few of them joining Jack and his family behind the food truck. Jack heard shouts in a half dozen languages, the voices of the terrified caught out in the open.

Jack peered out from behind the truck and saw McKeller's associate. He'd moved back across the grass, separating himself from McKeller. He was crouched low, but the area was wide open and provided no cover. He had a gun out as he scanned the surrounding park. He was at least forty yards from McKeller, from the bones. Even with the distance between them, Jack could guess what was going through the man's mind. His boss was down, probably dead. And the bones, while valuable, weren't worth trying to collect when their ultimate purpose had been the preservation of the dead man's wife.

Jack told the boys and Espy to stay put, and then, staying low, he ran toward the nearest tree to get a better look.

Jack was watching McKeller's associate when he saw two men proceeding down Avenue Gustave Eiffel. They walked with purpose, covering the distance quickly.

Israelis.

Neither of the men held a weapon, which told Jack they had a third man hidden nearby. With his attention diverted, Jack didn't see Jim step out from behind the truck. He didn't notice until he heard his wife scream, and by then Jim had almost reached McKeller.

"Jim!" Jack shouted, but the boy didn't stop.

Jack hurried after his son, a sharp pain shooting through his knee. He'd closed half the distance by the time Jim reached the fallen agent. The boy went to his knees next to the man's body. For a second, Jim didn't do anything. Then Jack saw the boy reach for the bones spilled onto the avenue. Jim picked one up, freeing it from the wrappings that still clung to it. He studied it briefly before extending it to touch McKeller's hand. Jack arrived a moment later. He reached for his son.

A flash robbed him of sight. He felt his son in his arms as a bright light rose from the relic, as it moved to envelop McKeller, and then began to expand, creating a bubble of light around Jack and his son. With the light came warmth, an otherworldly sensation that settled over them. Jim looked up at Jack with a beatific smile on his face. The light grew brighter, the warmth turned hotter. Jack held his son tight as the bones did their work. And then both light and heat vanished, gone in an instant.

Slowly, Jack released Jim, and together they looked down, and together they witnessed McKeller's hand move. The bone

310

was gone, in its place a dust that, even as Jack watched, began to scatter in the breeze. He looked at the bag. He saw only rags and more dust. Their power spent, the bones of the prophet Elisha had returned to the stuff of which they were made.

A shadow fell across McKeller. Jack glanced up and saw the Israelis—witnesses to a scene from their own past. Their eyes went to the now-empty bag. They moved toward Jack.

His son back in his arms, Jack returned the Israelis' gaze. "Let the dead keep their own," he told them.

He didn't know if they'd accept that. In truth, he didn't care. He just held his son, and when Espy and Alex rejoined them, he gathered all of them up and started walking, leaving all the rest of it behind.

Epilogue

JACK SAT ON THE FRONT PORCH, his feet up on the rail. A cigar burned down in his hand, a half inch of ash hanging. The night air was cool, but it held the promise of warmer weather. He breathed deeply, smelling the Bradford pears.

Through the screen door he could hear the sounds of family, of Alex and Jim playing. They were kicking the soccer ball inside, and Jack wasn't about to make them stop. The fact that Jim could kick the ball—that he could run without losing his breath—was enough to make Jack bend the rules.

He still didn't know what had happened in Paris, whether Jim's healing was a result of the power of the bones or if it had been something else, perhaps a reward of sorts. In the end, it didn't matter.

There were only a few things that did. And all of them were in the house behind him.

Don Hoesel, author of *Elisha's Bones* and *Serpent of Moses*, lives in Spring Hill, Tennessee, with his wife and two children. Don holds a bachelor's degree in mass communication from Taylor University. To learn more, visit DonHoesel.com.

More Action and Adventure from Bethany House

BETHANYHOUSE